The Quarry Driven

He dodged left, then right, hurtling himself over a rising shadow that he hoped was a bush and not another of those seeking his life. The brambles snagged at his clothing and flesh, some of which were torn away in his flight. Snarls from behind told him his pursuer not only remained on the hunt, but was also closing fast. Barely keeping his balance he ran on, looking desperately through the gloom for the game trail he knew to be close.

Behind came death, sometimes on four feet and sometimes on but two. Either way it was faster than its prey and could bide its time until they reached open ground. Ignoring the wounds of the brambles, it tore through the brush at full speed, the scent of its quarry so close its mouth watered in anticipation of that first juicy bite.

The ground broke away somewhere ahead. The trail ran along the lip of the cliff. The woodsman in the boy knew that the open trail was not the place to avoid the beast pursuing him but that part of his mind was closed with fear. All of his thoughts, all of his instincts said that he had to flee, to get away. To outrun this beast that sought his life. Brambles and tree roots stole his speed here among the trees. Only the game trail offered a clear path for his flight. Only there could he reach his full speed.

He didn't make it.

Albrim's Curse

by Trevis Powell

A BlackWyrm Book
Louisville, Kentucky

A BlackWyrm Book
BlackWyrm Publishing
10307 Chimney Ridge Ct, Louisville, KY 40299

Printed in the United States of America.

ISBN: 978-0-9820067-4-0
LCCN: 2009927033
Cover by Jeff Easley
Edited by Dave Mattingly and Jason Walters

First Edition (as "No Hero"): September 2006
Second edition: May 2009

To Mom,
who always knew I could

Chapter One

It was just after noon that a band of armed men approached the edge of town, shouting warnings of beasts in the woods. Albrim dropped his hoe, thinking to run after the other lads to hear the news. He had forgotten about his Gran.

"You! Albrim! No haring off after foolishness for you! You have six more rows of cabbages to weed and six after that of rutabaga," the old woman dutifully screeched from her chair in the shade of the Alderberry tree. Even as she did her duty she craned her neck to see what the ruckus was about. The babe in her lap chose that moment to cry.

"There lass, there there," shushed the old woman as she rocked the child. Albrim's eyes returned to his work but his ears strained for some hint of what brought the men to his small town.

"Like as not it's a wolf has killed a sheep again," snorted Albrim's watcher. Expertly rocking the child back to sleep she cast a stern glare towards her grandson. "And like as not the men will use it as an excuse to go a-wolfing for a week and leave all the work to be done by the womenfolk."

Albrim smiled at her words. Laziness was something his Gran would never tolerate in anyone, but particularly not in a man. He struggled along towards the end of the row despairing at ever having any free time. The sun shone bright, the grass fairly glowed green and the scent of fresh baked bread from the common ovens was driving him mad with hunger. To top it all off men were shouting news of killer beasts in the forest and he was trapped here with a hoe in his hand.

Two long rows later and another shout was heard, indicating another visitor leaving the shadows of the forest and approaching the town. From where he stood, Albrim could just make out a figure on horseback coming along the southern road.

"Another troublemaker from Skallist, like as not," snorted the old woman. "Nothing but trouble ever comes out of those haunted woods."

Albrim didn't argue, just began hoeing faster. He'd heard far different tales of Skallist but wouldn't dream of arguing with Gran. The old woman could still handle a switch. But his mind was free to wander and it did. A man on horseback held a possibility for news, particularly from the wilder lands to the south. Perhaps he was a dispatch rider with news of the coming war. There were always wars, his father said. Wars and rumors of wars.

"Watch yourself boy, you're getting mightily close to them cabbages," shouted the old woman, bringing Albrim's attention back to his task. "Like as

not we'll all starve this winter because of you," she grumbled, patting the
infant despite the child's continued slumber.

"If we starve because of one cabbage, we probably deserve it," Albrim
said softly, knowing his Gran would never be able to hear him. He started the
next row with a little more care, heedful of the woman's words despite his
protests.

Distantly Albrim could hear the clops of the horseman as he crossed the
cobblestones of the main square. The town was small and new, the
cobblestones of the square were a mark of great civic pride. Even Albrim had
helped in their placement last spring when all the men were commandeered
by Lord Ferule for the task. Now the square remained clear no matter how
deep the mud grew in the fields. It was these very cobblestones that gave the
town its name of 'Cobble,' which to Albrim's mind was far better than 'The
New Village' as it had been called previously.

Albrim picked up the pace of his hoeing as much as he dared. He was
aided by the soil as it was dryer here and fewer weeds had managed to take
hold. The smell of the bread was making him so hungry that he was almost
willing to forgo the news for the time necessary to eat. With only two rows to
go the bell in the town center began to ring.

"Law," croaked his Gran, struggling up to her feet, the baby clutched in
her thin arms. "They are getting up a wolfing, like as not," she grumbled,
although this time she didn't bother to hide her concern. The ringing of the
bell meant trouble.

Tossing the hoe aside, Albrim set off at full sprint towards the square.
The sounding of the bell meant all able-bodied men and women of fighting
age were to report and Albrim, only recently turned fifteen, was now old
enough to be considered a man. He leaped over the narrow creek that ran
between his father's land and the town and ran full speed into the square,
happy to escape his chores even if only for a little while.

A crowd had already gathered around the new arrivals just outside the
Bucket of Ale and buckets of the brew were being passed around the excited
crowd. The grateful looks shot towards the young man who still sat astride
the dappled mare gave testimony to who had paid for the drink. Did this
mean good news or bad? Albrim didn't know, but was intent on sliding into
line to share in the bounty.

"Albrim, get to your Gran," came the deep voice of his father, followed by
a hearty slap to the back of Albrim's head. Knowing better than to argue, he
spun immediately about and raced back to the narrow plank bridge just in
time to help Gran across, the baby now riding contentedly on one bony hip.
The old woman's grip on his arm was firm as steel.

"Like as not... like as not," Gran puffed as she crossed the bridge.
Whatever she was trying to say was lost to the boy who was desperately
afraid he'd miss some important bit of news. Little enough came this far off
the main roads. They reached the rear of the crowd just as the young man
dropped off his mount and climbed onto a horse trough, raising his hands to
encourage silence. Yogarn, a blacksmith and the Lord's Reeve of Cobble,
scrambled up beside him. The other new arrivals, now double the number
Albrim had seen arrive, clustered around the trough with their backs to it,
proclaiming by their actions to all that they were a part of the coming
pronouncement.

"Law, that's the young Lord," cackled Gran. "He's the spitting image of his father."

Albrim studied the young man intently. He'd never seen the heir to Lord Ferule despite seeing the Lord himself a number of times during the building of the town. He was light of skin with dark hair and a charismatic smile that had the young ladies of the town tittering and the men feeling brave and bold. His clothing was similar to that of the peasants of the town but made of better material, and cut to fit him. The young man stood atop the trough for a long moment, allowing the crowd to have their look and the last of the whispers to quiet before speaking. When finally the mumbling died, it was Yogarn that spoke first.

"Alright now, everybody quiet," he yelled unnecessarily. Yogarn liked to feel important. "This here is Sir Garen, the son and heir of our Lord Ferule. Listen to him if you value your hides, you louts."

Some in the crowd laughed at Yogarn's theatrics. If the young man had been an ogre from the mountains, they would have listened if he had news to share.

"And a knight besides!" whispered a nearby girl of Albrim's age. Somehow, he felt offended by the words but had no idea why.

Albrim looked around the gathering. As near as he could tell the entire population had turned out. Not that surprising really. Very little happened in this remote backwater, other than the occasional wolfing. Albrim felt somewhat proud to see his father standing at the front of the crowd. As a member of the Reeve's advisors, appointed by Lord Ferule himself, he was there by right.

A tall thin man, Albrim's father was stronger than he looked. Borel was a master bowyer and able to pull any bow he'd ever made and Albrim was proud to follow in his footsteps in that regard. He was the best bowshot in Cobble; other than his father, and hoped to one day grow as tall. Borel stood a full head taller than anyone else in the crowd and commanded a level of respect that even Yogarn envied. Albrim wished that he could push through the crowd and join his father but didn't. He likely wouldn't have made it through the press as everyone would be loathe to give up their spot anyway but then Sir Garen finally began speaking, causing him to hold very still so he wouldn't miss a word.

"Good folk, I bring you my father's blessing as well as my own," he began, bringing sighs of appreciation from the young girls at the sound of his melodious voice.

"Some of you may already be aware of the problems at Spicer," he continued, nodding to the armed men from the village just south of Cobble. "Night before last they lost several sheep to wolves."

The men from Spicer growled their agreement. They weren't exactly friends to the folk of Cobble but they were certainly not strangers either. The men of the two villages had joined together three times in the last two years to thin the wolf population.

Sir Garen waved his arms for silence once more at the outbreak of mumbles and the clearly audible, "I told you so, fool men," that emerged directly from Gran. Everyone within reach studiously ignored her. She'd switched every one of them at one point or another in their lives.

"Hunters from Spicer have found a number of large wolf tracks in the vicinity of their flocks. They also found the body of one of their own."

"It was me that found him," yelled one of the Spicer men. "It was ole Jule and he'd been tore apart by them wolves!"

A fresh wave of mumbling washed through the crowd. Most of them had known Jule as he often came to Cobble to visit the local girls.

"Are we sure it was wolves?" demanded Albrim's father. "Wolves do not usually attack men, but there are other things in the mountains that do."

The men of Spicer immediately began arguing but quieted at the lifting of Sir Garen's hand.

"Each of these men saw the tracks, as did I. We are all satisfied that the tracks were those of wolves, though a decidedly large breed. My father believes, and I agree, that they may be a new species of wolf bred by the Quargs in the mountains and sent down to plague us."

The rumbling that arose from this pronouncement was beyond even the knight's ability to quell and he didn't even try. Albrim was busy ducking the swinging switch from his Gran.

"I told you, I told you! Like as not we'll all die," she said, letting her arm drop after only a few swings. Where had she come up with that switch? Albrim would have sworn she didn't have it a moment ago. He didn't bother asking why he'd been the target of her ire. It was likely she didn't know herself and questioning her would just earn him an earnest whipping. Her heart hadn't even been in that one.

"Instead of a wolfing, we should go roust out those Quargs!" came a shout from the crowd. Another agreed but added, "After the wolfing is through." Both of these proclamations gained increasing support from the crowd.

Finally, Sir Garen regained control of the group. "The Quargs will be dealt with in due time. My father has given me his word on that. Today, however, we must now deal with the wolves. Jule was a young man, strong and certainly not a cripple. He served with my father's hunters and was more than capable of handling himself in a fight, yet a handful of wolves pulled him down. That is where we must concentrate our efforts."

"If they can kill Jule, they could kill anyone here," moaned a woman with a cluster of young children gathered to her skirts.

"Like as not they will, too!" snarled Gran, her latest assault on Albrim diverted by the baby starting to cry.

"You can't take the men folk, the wolves might come here," argued another woman. "How will we protect ourselves if the wolves come here?"

Sir Garen hushed their fears with a mere half smile and one easy wave of his hand. "We do not intend to divest Cobble of all its mighty warriors, only a few to supplement those from Spicer, Hemlet and Torude."

"How many are we talking here?" asked Borel. "Half?"

"Yes, half should be sufficient. With the Reeve and his council choosing the half to remain. That way we shall be assured that enough remain behind to protect the town to the satisfaction of all."

A few mumbles were heard but no one felt like arguing. Albrim's heart fell to his knees. He knew he would be one of those 'chosen' to remain behind.

"Like as not they'll leave us nothing but beardless boys and not a hard day's work among 'em all!" stated Gran, this time loud enough to ensure everyone heard her.

Sir Garen gave his full smile towards the old woman. "I'm certain we can arrange for a few hard workers to remain behind, dear lady," he said, bringing guffaws from everyone.

"Like as not we'll..." sputtered Gran. Like as not..." unable to finish her thoughts she began crooning to the baby as if she had cried out. Not even Gran could find the words to argue with the handsome young knight.

His smile still at full bore, Sir Garen turned to the fawning Yogarn. "Good Reeve, how many fine warriors does the town of Cobble boast at this time?"

Yogarn rose up to his full height, hooking one thumb in a greasy suspender as he proclaimed, "Twenty-eight, M'Lord, with three new ones coming of age in the past couple of months."

The look on Sir Garen's face was somewhat surprised. "Only twenty-eight? I had thought a town of this size would have more," he said, quickly covering his surprise. "Then we shall need no more than fourteen of your citizens, good Reeve."

Having finished his proclamation he leapt to the ground. "Come, good Reeve, and bring your council to a meeting here within the tavern. We shall determine who shall be accompanying me and what supplies they will need."

Most of the crowd surged forward as if to follow, only those with young children turning away but Yogarn moved quickly to head this off. He didn't want people fawning all over the young Lord when it was his own time to be important. Catching Borel's eye, he gave a toss of his head, and somehow the bowyer understood the meaning of the gesture. As Yogarn followed Sir Garen and the council into the Bucket, Borel stopped the remainder of the crowd with upheld hands.

"K'jord!" he yelled, looking about for the burly farmer he had just named.

"Here, Borel," shouted the bald man. K'jord was something of a local legend, as he was the only person in Cobble not born within the kingdom. He was an outlander from somewhere far away, a place that Albrim would love to visit, just because it wasn't here. Unfortunately for Albrim and his generation, K'jord didn't like to speak of his old homeland, and had never chosen to share it with his new neighbors.

Borel snapped to attention. As an officer in the militia he was now acting in an official capacity. "Sergeant K'jord, assemble the militia," he ordered before following the others inside.

All the men groaned at the command. Now they wouldn't be able to hear what was going on inside the tavern. With much grumbling and complaining they slowly allowed K'jord to bully them into ranks. The men of Spicer laughed at the hangdog expressions of those from Cobble as they filed into the tavern.

With the Reeve and his advisors inside only twenty-four militia were left for K'jord to yell at, but he did a fine job at it all the same, Albrim thought. Four ranks of six was the order, archers in the front and pikemen in the rear. It seemed simple enough, but there was some confusion when they came up one man short in the last rank until K'jord realized that he was the one not in the formation. He quickly took a roll call to cover up his embarrassment at the blunder. As an archer, Albrim was in the first rank. In the distance he could hear his Gran complaining loudly to someone about the laziness of men-folk and the sham that wolfing really was.

"They just go off and drink, that's all," she was saying. "They'll need more jugs along than arrows, like as not."

The sun was warm but there was an occasional cool breeze from the mountains. It wasn't late enough in the summer for the really hot days that would come. Albrim stared at the doorway of the tavern, waiting expectantly for some sign of what was happening. His heart beat in his throat at the thought of being left behind to 'guard' the town when the others were off wolfing. 'Guarding' in this case meaning weeding not only Gran's cabbages but also performing twice as much menial labor as normal.

Fifteen was old enough to be a member of the militia, but Albrim knew that the younger members had rarely been allowed to participate in previous wolfings, the elders claiming something about having to prove yourself capable, first. It was all just a part of the plan he had sniffed out years ago, the plan by which those in charge of him ensured that he himself was never allowed to do anything he wanted to do. If it was something like digging a root cellar or retrieving a dead varmint from someone's loft, he would be the first one chosen. The excitement of chasing after man-killing wolves would undoubtedly be given to someone else. Someday, Albrim knew, he would just die of boredom or overwork. Could you hoe yourself to death?

"We ain't gonna get to go," moaned Vert from his position just behind Albrim. Only a year older than Albrim, the redhead had been left out of the last wolfing as well. "They never let us younger ones go."

Albrim didn't need to turn around to see who was talking. Vert was the son of Corad the Tanner and always stank of his father's trade. K'jord was also nearby and was taking his job as sergeant seriously at that moment. Albrim didn't have anything to add anyway. He knew Vert was right.

"How long we gotta stand out here, K'jord?" asked someone from the last rank.

"Yeah, you know we're all here. Let us go inside and get a drink," added another.

"Or at least let us go sit in the shade," demanded a third.

"You're in ranks, so just shut up," snarled K'jord. "You been training with the militia as long as I have, Abe, you know you ain't supposed to talk in the ranks."

The grumbling quieted but failed to disappear entirely. K'jord walked up and down, staring hard at whoever was talking the loudest but he was mostly ignored. Albrim passed the time counting his own heartbeats and watching a far away hawk circle lazily in the sky. He wished he had brought along a hat. A pregnant dog wandered past, ignoring Vert's whistles of invitation. Apparently she didn't want to be petted.

Timed dragged by until Albrim began to think that hoeing the garden might be better than standing still in the square all day, just waiting to hear that he'd be left behind for the next few weeks to do not only his work but that of someone who had gone on the wolfing. At least the hoeing would eventually be over. How many rows had he needed before he would have been finished? Two more? Or was it four? Gran had probably finished them by now, cursing his laziness with every chop. At least that brought a smile to his face. She was a strict taskmistress but Albrim loved her and knew that she loved him, switchings aside.

He looked over the small town, nothing more than a village really. The buildings were mostly logs with a very few of actual cut timbers. Only the tavern was built differently, with walls of fieldstone pulled up by the plows during the first year of the town's existence. The people themselves were as plain as their homes; most were peasant serfs of Lord Ferule. A scattered few were freemen, or goodmen, including his father, Yogarn, and a few others. Even they were Ferule men, all having lived their lives under the rule of the family. That was why they were here, so far from any sizeable town, because they were Ferule men.

Serfs had little say-so in their own lives although no one here had anything but good to say of Lord Ferule. When the lands here had been given over to the Ferule family to administer on behalf of the crown, peasants had been needed to till the land and harvest the natural resources such as the Krim spices of Spicer and lumber from the forests. So peasants had been chosen by the Lord and towns had been built. In twenty years they would have a pleasant community built here. Right now, though, they just had one of hard work and monotony. Forests were supposed to be filled with dangers and excitement but Albrim had yet to see anything.

Just as Albrim knew he was about to fall down from boredom, the men of Spicer came stomping from the tavern walking a little less gracefully then when they went in. Apparently the stout ale of the Bucket had accomplished its task well. Behind them emerged the others with Sir Garen coming out last. The knight fairly leapt into the saddle, struggling briefly to keep the horse from bolting, and then turned back expectantly to the waiting militia.

Borel didn't even look towards his son, just stepped down onto the cobbles and started walking for home. Confused, Albrim was torn between looking after his father and back at Yogarn, who had regained his precarious footing on the horse trough while only getting one foot wet. Around the square doors opened and the citizens who had left earlier hurried back to hear what Yogarn had to say.

This naturally caused Yogarn's head to swell up even more than usual. "Ok everybody, listen up. We made a fair deal with Sir Garen and we don't want to hear no griping out of nobody. He's taking fourteen of us so not everybody can go and that's that! Anybody has a problem with not going this time will not get to go the next time either. Everybody hear?"

Some in the crowd mumbled that they did but most remained silent. Albrim's heart was hammering away in his ears in anticipation. Was his father not going? Wouldn't they need his sharp eye with the bow on a wolfing? Particularly this wolfing?

"If I call out your name, step out of the formation and wait over there," Yogarn said in his most authoritative voice. Albrim cringed. These would be the people staying home. He knew that his name would be the first one called.

He was wrong. It was the second, after Vert. Shoulders slumped, he dragged himself to the appointed place and stared sullenly back at those not called out of formation. One by one the names were called and eleven other dejected men and women stood clustered around Albrim and Vert. So intent was Albrim on staring back at Yogarn that he didn't notice Sir Garen's horse stepping daintily across the cobblestones to stand nearby. It looked as if the only archers going were the oldest among them. The same people who went on all the wolfings.

"Well I hope you're not too disappointed in our choice," the knight on the horse offered. "But we felt that we needed the archers more than the pikemen on this wolfing."

Albrim didn't understand the knight's words at first because he was listening to Yogarn, trying to hear what the Reeve was telling the other group. He finally caught on after Vert's whoop of joy.

Sir Garen laughed at the enthusiasm. "You see, we felt that archers would be a necessity on this hunt as we certainly don't want to get too close to the wolves and, since we may be out for an extended period of time, we decided we needed to take the younger men. In this case we decided that youthful strength was more important than experience. Besides, the other villages have provided us an adequate number of veteran trackers."

Vert laughed. "M'Lord we don't care why, we just want to go on a wolfing!"

Yogarn joined the group, a piece of parchment clutched in one hand. "Listen up, men of Cobble. I have a list of supplies and equipment each militiaman is expected to bring with him. You'll have time to run home and get what you need. If you don't have it, you'll be supplied with whatever you need from the town's stores."

"I'll need a new bowstring, Yogarn," shouted one man. "But I ain't got the copper to pay for it right now."

"All supplies are courtesy of Sir Garen," answered Yogarn. "Be sure you don't take more than you need." They all laughed.

"Yes, I'm not prepared to provide new cooking pots for everyone in the village," added Sir Garen, bringing even louder laughs than the jest called for. "My dear Reeve, please read the list of needed equipment to the fine fighting men of Cobble so we can be about our wolfing."

Yogarn read from a lengthy list that included bows and extra strings, a full score of arrows and extra flints to make more besides. Also water skins, cooking pots, blankets and enough food for a week were announced- far more supplies than were normally taken for a wolfing.

"That's a lot of food and arrows, Yogarn," noted one woman.

"And it may not be enough to the do the job. Sir Garen here has vowed to resupply us in the field as necessary."

A good deal of grumbling broke out among the older men. "I have a new field of wheat," argued one. "I can't be gone for weeks at a time."

"Your neighbors will look after your wheat. They've already been told," snapped Yogarn.

"One of my neighbors is more than seventy years old and the other is Fat Happ," came the incredulous reply. "You telling me those two are going to clear the weeds from my garden and watch over my wheat?" These words were followed by a nervous laugh.

Sir Garen returned to the conversation with a placating gesture. "The men left behind will be rotated around to cover the duties of everyone here."

More grumbling sounded, again from the older people. Albrim didn't care who had to weed the gardens, just so long as it wasn't him.

"I know that typically wolfings are only a few days long, perhaps a week. This one may go longer and I want us to be prepared for the necessity."

"Is there something you ain't telling us?" demanded the wheat farmer, who Albrim could now identify as Porter, a grumpy man but the best farmer in the town. "Something like a Quarg raid? Or is it goblins?"

This shocked the crowd. It had been years since the Quargs had dared leave the mountains and longer still since goblins had entered the area.

Sir Garen laughed at the words. "I am in awe of the men of Cobble! Here you are, as brave as any Lord could wish for his army! You are so brave that man-killing wolves are nothing to you! We shall sally forth and destroy such wolves so easily that you require a Quarg infestation simply to justify leaving your village for a week!"

The crowd laughed heartily at the joke, not the least bit forced this time.

"The wolves are our only quarry, but we deem their destruction so critical that we must be prepared to track them however long it is necessary to finish them off. So critical is the task that the men of Cobble were called to service," he finished to a rousing cheer from the warriors.

"Alright, you all get home and get what you need. Be back here under this tree in one hour," ordered Yogarn.

Albrim pushed his way through the others, dodging around older or slower men in his haste to get his gear. He couldn't believe he was going on the wolfing and felt that he had to hurry before someone noticed and decided that his inclusion had been a mistake. Ducking his head to avoid one elbow, he almost collided with someone else. Only a glimpse of a pair of waiting boots helped him avoid the collision. He didn't even glance up or bother to wonder why someone was going the other direction, just made to move around the fellow. A strong arm caught him around the chest and prevented his maneuver.

His hopes sank. A single glance at the face above the blocking arm sank them even lower. It was his father. Albrim straightened up, staring hard at his own feet as he waited for the words he dreaded to hear.

"You don't need to go home and pack, Albrim," said Borel.

What could he say? Albrim just nodded, hoping that he wouldn't cry.

"I've already been home," his father continued, pretending not to notice his son's distress. "And I've packed for both of us."

"You're going too, Father?"

"Someone has to command the men of Cobble."

Albrim's smile made his cheeks ache.

Chapter Two

"How long we been out here?" demanded Vert, throwing down the last bit of his travel bread in disgust.

"Sixteen days," groaned Albrim. He wasn't groaning from boredom, but from hunger pangs. The supplies provided them were simple and only barely enough to keep them going.

"I've been out twenty days and don't really know where we are," snorted Tomo, a tracker from the village of Hemlet. He spit a strong line of brown juice into the brush from his squatting position, working the chaw more firmly into place within his bulging cheek.

"We're close to Cobble," answered Albrim. "Six, seven miles by straight line north and east."

"Think maybe we're heading there?" Vert asked, looking between his two companions.

"Naw," replied Tomo. "The tracks don't lead that way; they're turning back to the mountains again. I would guess they're about to give up and run for home."

Albrim didn't argue with the man. Tomo was a veteran at this wolfing business, despite their lack of success on this particular wolfing, and by the stories he told knew both Borel and Gran quite well. Rumors abounded of other groups killing a number of wolves, but they had yet to even sight one.

Vert sulked, his shoulders slumping as he sat upon a log. "Can't believe we ain't seen a single wolf in sixteen days."

Tomo pulled out his pipe. Vert had complained loudly and often that it was the stink from that very pipe that scared all of the wolves away from their group but this time he only mumbled under his breath. Tomo had been out of weed for the pipe for three days now and only sought the comfort of holding it between his teeth. Albrim wondered why the weed Tomo chewed wouldn't also work in the pipe.

Studying the tracks himself Albrim had to agree with Tomo's pronouncement, which wasn't that surprising since most of what he knew about tracking he had learned from Tomo in the previous weeks. They had followed this pack of wolves for days without ever getting close and now it looked like they were indeed turning westward towards the mountains.

"It ain't no matter anyway, Vert. These wolves here ain't those man-eaters they had over to Spicer."

"How can you tell?" asked Albrim. Vert was studiously ignoring them both as he stripped the leaves from a stick.

"Size, that's all," was the answer. Tomo was likely too lazy to be a good farmer, but he knew his business when it came to tracking. "I was there when they found Jule, and those tracks were huge for a wolf. These are about regular size."

"And we did our job nudging them away from the towns. Wolves ain't stupid like deer, they knew we were back here all along," added Tomo. "They'll look for something easier to eat. Now that people are more alert, the flocks will be better guarded and these wolves are too small to take on a man, much less a bunch of us with dogs to boot."

Albrim looked at the tracks a little closer. They looked big to him, much bigger than the dogs back home but he had no reason to doubt Tomo. He placed a thumb alongside one of the tracks, roughly measuring it against future sightings. When he looked up, Tomo winked at him.

"Good thinking, Albrim."

Proud of the praise despite himself, Albrim pretended to study the tracks a little closer. He too was disappointed in not having taken a wolf but he was still happy to have avoided the seemingly endless labor of his normal life, even if he was starting to feel a little guilty about leaving his Gran without both he and his father. Surely one of their neighbors was seeing to the heavy work.

"We'll all die of the sunstroke, like as not!" grumbled Gran as she stalked down the rows of vegetables. A dozen people worked under her command, hoeing as if a demon was on their heels. Despite Yogarn's efforts at organizing the workers in the absence of half the militia, it had been Gran who had taken command, going from farm to farm and garden to garden with her crews, completing all the needed work and then moving on to the next one. Not only were the work crews keeping up with the necessary chores, they were actually ahead under the watchful eye and spiteful tongue of Gran.

"It's getting dark, Gran," offered one old codger named Nord, in appearance only a decade or so short of her age but not sharing her clearness of eye.

"Aye, darkness is coming and we have two more gardens to hoe before supper," came the expected reply to the chuckles of those far enough away that Gran wouldn't hear. They'd had two more gardens to hoe since sunup. Tomorrow they were supposed to clean out a well before moving to the larger grain fields outside of town. By anyone's count, this had to be the last in-town garden left to feel the caress of the hoe this week.

"How long have they been gone?" groaned a woman, straightening out the kinks in her lower back.

"A year, it seems like," grumped her husband. Neither was known for having hard working natures.

"It's been more than two weeks," replied another woman. "Two weeks my boy Vert has been away from me."

The hoeing continued at an ever-slowing pace for another hour. Even the grumbling subsided as the sun closed with the horizon. Everyone was looking forward to a quick meal and an early bedtime. The only sounds were the striking of the hoes and the grumbling of Gran.

"Like as not we'll be here until midnight," she grumbled, even though they all could see that they were but minutes from finishing.

Sheep bleating in a nearby pen alerted them that something was approaching. One by one the workers stopped their tasks and looked around.

"Someone's coming," shouted a farmer named Jud. "There by the woods."

A man was indeed coming towards the town. Clearly he was a stranger, judging by his bright red hair. He was moving slowly, staggering across the grass as if unsure of where he was going. He noticed the workers about that time, and changed course towards them. After only a few steps, he staggered once more and collapsed.

• ———————————————————————————————— •

"Rider coming," stated Tomo, standing up and then stepping behind a tree before peeking around it to watch the game trail to the east. Vert claimed that moves like that marked Tomo as a thief, or at least a veteran poacher. Albrim noticed that Vert never said that sort of thing where Tomo could hear them.

The tracker had explained to them that taking care in the wilderness was always smart, as you never knew what might be stalking you even while you were stalking something else. Quargs were good trackers, Tomo said, and you should never assume that they weren't looking for you.

Albrim followed Tomo's lead and kept his body mostly hidden as he looked for the rider as well. Vert had simply stood up, leaving himself clearly visible to anyone on the trail. Albrim couldn't miss the look of disgust on Tomo's face.

"It's Sir Garen," announced Tomo, a full minute before the others were able to pick the moving horsemen from the vibrant foliage. Then again, he had heard the horse long before anyone else had either. Albrim was very intrigued with the grizzled tracker.

Gathering up their gear, the three made their way down the hillside towards the trail. They had time to get there ahead of Sir Garen, who was undoubtedly looking for them to coordinate further sweeps for the wolves. When they reached the narrow trail they dropped their gear and waited as the hoof beats came closer. The man was riding entirely too fast for this rough trail.

"Something ain't right," announced Tomo, who gathered up his gear and stepped back off the trail. Albrim and even Vert followed him, unsure but uneasy all the same. In moments the horse came into view. Again it was the tracker that picked out the details first.

"That's Sir Garen's horse, but that ain't Sir Garen!" he stated, expertly stringing his bow as Vert stepped back out into the trail and raised his hand to hail the rider. Albrim was unsure why the Tomo was readying his bow but followed suit, even going so far as to pull an arrow from his quiver.

Whatever danger Tomo had expected proved groundless as the man atop the horse pulled up on sight of Vert and walked the horse the last few feet. The animal was covered in lather and appeared to have been ridden to the point of collapse. Neither Vert nor Albrim recognized the man on its back, but Tomo apparently did.

"What's going on, Jon?" he demanded. His bow was not only ready but he also had an arrow notched and ready to be drawn. Albrim nervously noticed that Tomo wasn't looking at the man on the horse but was instead scanning the trail behind him. "Somebody chasing you?"

Jon whirled about as if expecting to see someone on his trail. "Sir Garen is calling in the patrols," he shouted, panting as hard as the exhausted horse he rode. "We meet at the crofter's shack by dawn."

"By dawn?" demanded Vert. "That's ten miles from here on the Cobble road! There's no way we can get there by dawn." The rider either didn't hear or ignored him, turning his full attention on Tomo.

"Where is Borel's patrol?"

"Over west somewhere," Tomo replied. "We were trying to drive some wolves into his bunch, set up a little ambush for them."

"Can I follow the trail or should I go overland?" Jon demanded, draining the last water from a skin.

"It doesn't really matter, that horse isn't going to make it either way," Tomo said, clucking his tongue at the condition of the poor animal. "You're going to kill it."

"Don't matter, Sir Garen said to ride it into the ground if I had to."

"What's going on?" demanded Vert, grabbing the horse's reins. "Why isn't Sir Garen riding his own horse?"

"He's hurt, like as not," stated Albrim, not even realizing how much like his Gran he sounded. The look on Tomo's face told Albrim that they were in agreement.

"Sir Garen's patrol found them big wolves. It was a trap, an ambush. Three men died. It was awful. Sir Garen broke his leg when his horse fell."

"An ambush? Wolves?" asked Vert.

Jon slide from the saddle, tossing the reins to Tomo. "I'm going on foot; you take the horse back with you."

"Wait, who was it that died?" queried Vert.

"Labrin and two fellows from Spicer. I didn't know 'em." He panted, accepting the water skin offered to him by Albrim as he tried to move past and into the trees. "Do I just go due west or should I be looking for some sort of landmark?"

"You can't go on, man, you're dead tired too!" added Tomo, grabbing Jon by the arm. "You come back with me and I'll send one of the lads here for Borel."

"I'll go," offered Albrim. Right at that moment he really wanted to find and warn his father.

Jon hesitated, looking hard at Albrim as he made his decision.

"Borel is my father, after all," Albrim added.

That settled the matter for Jon. "Ok son, you look like a steady lad. Find your father. If you do it by nightfall, you all get to the crofter's hut. If you find him after dusk, make your way home to Cobble and rouse the rest of the militia."

"Over some wolves?" Vert asked incredulously.

"Not wolves," Jon said, his words reaching Albrim as he sped on his way. "Weres."

Chapter Three

"Pick him up and bring him along," ordered Gran, gripping her walking stick and using it to prod two of the younger men forward. "He'll die out here, like as not."

"He's bleeding awfully bad Gran," said Jud.

"Yeah, Gran," added Ina. "He might die if we try to move him."

Gran stepped forward, peering intently down at the wounded stranger. She saw a great deal more than the others. Gran's wisdom covered a lot more areas of experience than anyone knew.

The stranger was middle aged and dressed no differently than the farmers kneeling around him. If anything his clothing was less dirty, but made up for this with the encrusted sweat stains. His beard was long but trimmed, with no visible parasites. A few twigs were of recent addition; as if the fellow had picked them up that very day and just didn't stop to remove them.

If Gran had to guess, and she certainly didn't mind doing that, the man was from a nearby village. That she didn't know him didn't surprise her, the villages from this area were only built in the last ten years and they had all been imported from their Lord's various estates. When you combined those facts with a lack of travel among simple peasants, people could live within ten miles of one another for many years and never meet. His wounds were obvious. One leg of his simple cloth trousers was soaked with blood but the bleeding appeared to have stopped. A great deal of other information was obtained in her quick viewing, but she had seen enough to know what to do.

"He's already stopped the bleeding, you durn fools, lift him up and let's get him into a bed somewhere so I can look at him."

Accustomed as they all were to obeying Gran, as she was by far the oldest person any of them had ever known. She also had, without exception, been the midwife to each of them, even Nord, who mistakenly claimed to remember Gran before she married. No one even hesitated before they moved to obey. Some lifted the stranger and carried him off towards the nearest home as others scurried ahead to prepare a bed or gathered the fallen hoes. Two men scurried to finish the hoeing after a tongue-lashing delivered by Gran.

"He'll die or he'll live, but those who live have to eat this winter," she spat, swatting one and then the other of those chosen to continue the labor. "I don't need the likes of you in my way."

The injured man was taken into the small home and placed gently on the only bed. Gran quickly drove those she didn't need out of the shack, sending some on legitimate errands and inventing tasks for others where the firm planting of her boot did not work. Then she and her two chosen helpers undressed the redheaded stranger and searched him for wounds.

"Law, Gran, what caused a hole like that?" asked Mertie, indicating the jagged wound in the man's thigh.

"Looks like a bite," added Ina. "But what kind of animal has a mouth that big?"

"It's a wolf, like as not," snorted Gran, studying the knotted rope the man had tied tightly around this upper thigh to stop the bleeding.

"Wolves don't have teeth that big," argued Ina.

"Well that one did," Gran snapped, ripping apart the blankets from the bed for bandages.

Her initial inspection completed, Gran washed the grime from the man by dumping pails of water on him, soaking the bed and floor with the muddy runoff. Then her two helpers scrubbed the man down, looking for hidden injuries. By the time they had completed that task, those sent to fetch Gran's medicine bag returned only to be shooed back out of the shack immediately, without even a thank you for their efforts.

With the door firmly closed, Gran began mixing a variety of ingredients into a wooden bowl. Both of her helpers watched closely every move that she made, as always hoping to learn a little of Gran's hard-won wisdom. The paste she produced was smeared liberally over the bite mark, the only wound they had found, and then plastered down with fresh clay mud and covered with the blanket-bandages before being left to dry. Once the mixture had hardened, Gran would release the knotted rope. If the man didn't lose his leg from the loss of blood flow or have the black rot set in, he might live. She had done all that she could for now.

Gran left the final details of the man's care to her helpers and eased her tired body into a chair near the fire. It was all but dark now and she was far more exhausted than she wanted anyone to know. No sooner had she begun to relax than a shout was heard from outside. Before she could struggle back to her feet the shout was followed by a scream.

Albrim's feet settled into a steady rhythm as he jogged through the forest, his stamina enhanced by the fear in his heart. Small beasts and birds watched his passage with alarm but he failed to notice most of them, so intent was he on completing his mission. Even when he startled a pair of deer he didn't pause in his efforts; to fail now could be to see his father die.

Weres! In Aldragal? Even here on the borderlands where occasional Quarg raids were not unheard of and vicious monsters sometimes came down from the mountains to rampage, Weres were something you only heard about in legends. Not since the Were War, at least, had any been known to exist in these parts.

Ducking under a low-hanging branch, Albrim continued to wind his way along the ridgeline. The trees down slope grew more thickly than along the top and the ground was more likely to be level. When the ridge ran out he would have to run down the slope and up the next one, but all in all this was the best route through the forest unless he found a game trail.

He didn't know exactly where his father's band was, other than the general direction. They had circled to the west so that Albrim's group could drive the wolves to them if they couldn't catch up to the pack, a plan that may have actually worked. In fact, Weres weren't the only dangers Albrim might be facing. There was every chance that he could stumble upon the very wolves they had been pursuing, or accidentally blunder into his father's ambush. Borel might have even ordered traps to be laid for the wolves. As if all those dangers were not enough, there were far worse things living this deep into the forest than simple wolves. He ran on, not even trying to be silent. Weres were worse than anything else, he decided, and the safest place for him now was with his father.

Albrim picked up speed down one side of a saddle then felt it bleed away as he climbed the other side. He weaved in and out of the trees as the legs of his muscles burned and a deep ache began in his side. How far would he have to run? How would he know if he had gone too far? The only landmark he had been given was to look for a big 'bowl'. He would know it when he saw it, Tomo had told him. Borel would be somewhere near there.

Albrim knew that he would have to stop soon, but he was reluctant to do so because of the increased pain that would immediately set in when he did. Not to mention the difficulty of regaining his pace after cooling down. It would better if he could stop near a stream or spring so that he could at least drink. Albrim knew that water would be no problem as many creeks ran along the bases of the knobby hills. All he would need to do was stop next time he had to descend from a ridge, assuming he could maintain his run until then.

It seemed like hours since he had left the others. Darkness was not far away. The sun was already dropping behind the mountains. He tried to maintain his pace but began to stumble. He'd better find a stream soon or he'd have to stop without one. That meant a second stop when he did find water and without it he might cramp up in between.

Ahead of him the ridge suddenly fell away, causing Albrim to work his feet quickly to avoid falling. Last year's leaves rustled loudly as he ran down the slope, leaping once to clear a fallen tree and then tearing his arm on an unseen briar. It was getting dark fast. Albrim ignored the scratch and the painful stitch in his side because he could see that a stream awaited him at the bottom of the hill.

Dropping gratefully to his knees, Albrim carefully leaned his bow against a convenient Alder before plunging his head into the cold water. Alternating gulps of air with others of water, he allowed his body the needed rest while he studied the area.

It was a beautiful place. The trees were tall and strong and the land was filled with game. Squirrels were visible in the trees and a mink hissed at him from the far bank before disappearing into its den. He wished that he could live here, away from the town and its endless chores. Albrim even allowed himself a brief fantasy; pretending for a moment that he could return here someday and live the life of a recluse, like the old hermit that was rumored to live in the forest, one of the many tales told concerning these dark woods.

Stories said that the recluse was a giant, centuries old, hideously self-mutilated, or some combination of the three, depending on who you listened to. Others said that he wasn't human at all and killed anyone passing through his forest or that he was a forester who protected the settlements from Quarg attacks. Albrim didn't believe any of those things or even necessarily in the existence of the hermit, but he could not avoid a young man's fantasy about being such a figure; dashing and heroic, strange and mysterious. Protecting the settlements from the rampages of evil and rescuing beautiful women from Quargs and worse.

But with full darkness almost upon him, his fantasy suddenly seemed less attractive than before. The sky through the branches above was a deep purple and the boles of the trees themselves were disappearing into the deeper blackness of the night. Only along the creek did enough light slip through from the just rising Jacet, which was going to be full tonight, to allow him to see anything more than indistinct blobs where he knew boulders and stumps had stood but moments before.

His chest had slowed its heaving but the pain in his side was barely diminished. Still Albrim knew that it was time to move on. He had to find his father. Lives depended on him.

Splashing through the water, Albrim looked nowhere besides at his own feet to avoid the tangle of roots that protruded from each side of the creek. Using them as a sort of ladder he made his slow way to the top of the western bank and was grateful to find a game trail there. The packed earth shined brightly in the filtered light of Jacet and would be easy to distinguish from the surrounding blackness. It even seemed to be heading in the right direction.

Albrim had taken but two or three steps along the path, starting slowly and saving his strength for the coming climb up the far ridge, when a flash of movement caught the corner of his eye. He stopped immediately and quickly slid behind a tree, peering out over the joint of a thick branch praying that he had found his father rather than something from the forest had found him. No more than one hundred paces upstream he saw the movement again. Something was crossing the same stream he had just left. Something moving slowly, as if stalking something, or someone. Stalking him, perhaps.

There it was again. A slow glide of movement only a few inches above the level of the water. Another pace and it would leave the shadow of the bank and enter the dim light of the moon. Albrim didn't realize that he was holding his breath until it exploded from his chest at the sight of the stalker.

It was a wolf. A very big wolf. His expulsion of air had been heard, as the beast froze, standing on three legs in the stream as it listened for another sound, something to explain the presence of danger or prey. Slowly, silently, the wolf lowered its fourth paw and turned its head slightly.

Heart pounding so hard his head was hurting; Albrim followed the wolf's lead and froze in place, gripping the rough bark of the tree as if clinging to life itself. Was it a mere beast or a Were? Was it searching for him? Tracking him? Or stalking his father or another from his band? The moment passed, as did the moon's glow behind a cloud. Albrim knew that there was now little chance that the wolf would see him, but since when did wolves rely only on sight?

Fear forced him to move. The wolf was likely moving towards him under cover of the deepening darkness. He couldn't just wait here until it came for him. Reaching out cautiously, Albrim found the trail and placed one foot lightly upon it. Finding no sticks to snap, he eased his other foot onto the packed dirt and took a few halting steps forward. At that moment, the cloud passed away and the moon's glow again lit the landscape, leaving him standing in the open without even the shelter of the tree.

Heart hammering all the more, Albrim cast a fearful glance back to where the wolf had been. He wasn't sure which would be a more terrible sight; seeing the wolf still in position, looking towards him in recognition, or finding the beast gone and so not knowing exactly where it might be. Stalking him, certainly, but where? How close? Within pouncing distance? Perhaps he hadn't known which would frighten him more, but the truth nearly unmanned him. The wolf was gone.

Albrim fled along the trail, now thankful for the light of the moon to guide his steps. The path was narrow and branches of both trees and brush hung over it, indicating that the regular users of the path were smaller creatures. These grasping branches hindered his progress and forced him to make much more noise than he would have liked. His thin footwear was little protection from the thorns and briars. He knew that the wolf was nearby; likely a whole pack was on his scent even now. They were all around him and every distant sound produced by the woodlands was heard by Albrim as the stealthy pad of a wolf's paw.

For the first few hundred steps, Albrim made some attempts at running quietly but fear finally erased that idea from his mind. Putting his head down and positioning one arm to protect his face, he ran. Another hundred paces and there was no longer any doubt; he was being pursued.

Off to his left came the snap of a dried stick. Behind him came the slither of a thorny branch through matted fur. To his right came the whisper of a panted breath. Albrim wished that his bow was strung but didn't dare stop to do it, nor could he have seen enough to use the weapon, though he would have felt the better for it.

Two shadowy figures were pacing him on his right. He could see them occasionally passing through patches of moonlight between the trees. His trail was opening up, becoming wider, so he thankfully increased his pace to his full capability. No longer did he think to conserve his strength, but ran full out.

The ground suddenly fell away before him and he only narrowly kept his balance as he turned to follow the path downward along the side of a steep bluff. Below him to the left was a round valley clearly outlined beneath the moon by the steep cliffs. Perhaps it was the steep incline of the path that gave him a single burst of even greater speed, but to Albrim's mind his newfound fleetness of foot had a different source. It came from the howl of a wolf on the cliff wall above him. Albrim was enough of a woodsman to know what the howl mean. It was a signal to its pack-mates. The quarry was in position.

Chapter Four

Somewhere a horn was blowing. Gran figured it was likely that fool Yogarn trying to summon the militia. Or what was left of the militia.

Gran's two helpers were staggering along under their shared burden, the red-haired stranger now even heavier due to the drying mud cast on his leg. He moaned in pain but the two women ignored him. It was a choice of pain or death at this point and neither wanted to see him die. Besides, Gran had told them to carry him and it would never have entered either of their minds not to obey an order from the older woman.

"Like as not we're goners," Gran huffed, moving more quickly along than anyone in the village would have believed possible. She had good reason to hurry. Behind her three people were dead. She had seen them die.

The shout Gran had heard while resting had been one of surprise while the first scream had been one of pure fear, such as Gran had heard as a young woman when Quargs had attacked her village. The second scream had been one of pain- a mortal wound had been dealt and the one suffering it had recognized the fact. Death had come to Cobble and Gran had seen it.

She had looked out the door and seen the beasts in the very field they had just been hoeing. Two wolves of tremendous size were there and one was feeding from the still moaning Nord. The other was standing upright on two legs, laughing at the man's struggles.

Standing on two legs! Gran knew what that meant. Wolves they may be but at least one was also a man, and these had a taste for human flesh. She remembered the Were War, the great purge of the hideous half-men/half-beasts that had once plagued the kingdom known as Aldragal. The Weres had come forth to rampage during the double solar eclipse that came every seventeen years. Since the Were War had occurred, four more such eclipses had passed with no sign of werewolves in the kingdom.

"Gran, you got to get out of here," screamed Jud, pushing the door open so fast he nearly knocked the old woman from her feet. "We gotta run!"

Gran had moved quickly, seeing to her patient and her assistants first of all. She saw Jud pick up a rusty old pike from its place in the corner but said nothing. The man had some sense and Gran could respect that. He wasn't panicking despite the fear in his eyes. He was also the first person back out the door, gaping at the approaching wolves even as Ina and Mertie darted out the door with their patient carried on a blanket between them. Gran came last, clutching her bag of medicines in one hand and her walking stick in the other. The wolves were moving their way.

Jud tried to help her along but she slapped his hand away. She didn't need anyone's help and told him so. The wolves were closing fast. They would be caught just after they reached the next nearest house. Screeching her orders, Gran diverted the women ahead of her into the narrow alley between the nearest house and her son Borel's Bowyer shop, where the long shafts of unused yew piled up waiting his attention were easy to make out within the gloom of the rear overhang. She cursed her charges, using her walking stick to urge Ina along by repeatedly jabbing her in the rear.

A figure stood gaping beneath the rear overhang of the shop, it was a man wearing his nightclothes and clutching a pike in his hands. Gran recognized him as Hod, the dull young man that Borel allowed to sleep in his shop.

"Hod, get over here," she ordered, risking a look back. The wolves were close and Jud had already stopped to face them. She quickly changed her order. "Kill the wolves, Hod, kill them now."

Hod, never bright but ever faithful, shuffled forward to take up position next to Jud. The two men shared one glance and then set themselves, one dressed in drab homespun and the other in nothing more than his small clothes facing a pair of wolves that likely massed more than they.

The wolves quickly closed the gap, one holding back as the other leaped for Hod's throat. The big man made a thrust with his pike but had no chance of striking the speeding wolf. His thrust passed high and the wolf's massive jaws clamped down on its target. Blood sprayed from between its jaws.

Jud hesitated when the larger wolf held up its charge, then turned, too late to help his comrade avoid the attack. When the first wolf clamped down on Hod's throat it began shaking the dying man, whose knees immediately buckled from the additional weight. With the wolf occupied with its prey, Jud had no problem driving the head of his pike deeply into its side.

Snarling its rage even as blood of its own burst from its nostrils to mix with that of Hod, the wolf spun in a circle, snapping at the wound. Jud nearly lost his grip on his pike but managed to withdraw it as the second wolf slowly stalked him.

He studied the beast, seeing that it was even bigger than the one that had killed Hod. Its fur was darker too, black with a thin band of white around the neck. Its eyes were a deep red, reflecting the light of the lantern that shown from a nearby window. Eyes that were unsettling to look upon, not only for the death Jud could see there, but something else as well. Something Jud couldn't quite place his finger on. Something that was almost... intelligent.

The wolf circled to Jud's right, pausing only once to sniff the still trembling body of its fellow and again to lap at some of Hod's spilled blood. When it reached the alley where Gran had fled with the others, Jud made as if to attack and the wolf turned and circled back to its original position. There it sat, just out of the reach of Jud's long pike, and delicately licked the blood from its paws.

Jud began to back into the alley, figuring to leave the wolf alone if it didn't want a fight. He kept his eyes firmly planted on the beast even as his mind screamed that he was backing unknowingly into a trap in the alley. Feeling that he had no choice but to keep his attention focused on the danger he knew rather than on the one he imagined; Jud kept his eyes on the wolf.

Growling loudly, the wolf dropped to the ground, a snapping sound from its hindquarters causing Jud to start. The forelegs began to stretch, to extend, and clawed fingers grew from the paws. With a moan that mixed unimaginable pain with unmatchable ecstasy, the wolf suddenly snapped upright to stand only on its rear legs.

Jud's eyes threatened to pop from his head. It was the same wolf, yet drastically different. This wolf was no beast of the forest like the one he had killed. His pike fell to the ground at his feet; he knew it was of no use against a Were, and turned as if to run but barely made two steps before the weight of the werewolf drove him to the ground.

Gran only looked back once before they turned the corner with their patient. It was enough to see that Jud and Hod were bravely doing their duty holding off the wolves but she knew that they would be quickly pulled down. She hoped the wolves would stop to feed; otherwise the sacrifice of the two men would be in vane.

Now Gran was leading her helpers and the unconscious stranger across the very cobbles of the town square itself. Other people were running about on mindless errands, some shrieking in fear while others barked orders. Yogarn was trying to get the militia lined up. No one was accomplishing anything until Gran arrived on the scene. Between her outraged shrieks and the well-placed blows of her walking stick, she soon had the remaining militia in place and the others taking shelter in the tavern.

"What'll we do, Gran?" whimpered Yogarn as a howl was lifted up to linger upon the air. The sound could have come from any direction but Gran suspected a certain alley as the source.

"We'll line the militia up here on the porch of the tavern and we'll fight," she grumped, slapping him across the stomach with her staff. "That's what a militia is for, ain't it?"

Yogarn seemed to take courage from the woman's gruffness. He looked over his command ruefully and shook his head.

"Gran, only six men answered the horn and not a bowman among them."

"They're already dead, like as not and besides, you make seven."

"Already dead? Wolves have killed seven men and women right in the town?"

"If you think these are just common wolves, Yogarn, you're not even as smart as I hoped. Now get up on the porch. If the wolves show up before we get the windows boarded up, you have to hold them off."

"You, Ina," Gran ordered, pointing the woman out with one bony finger to ensure she was paying attention. "Take charge inside the tavern and get the windows covered over. There's only three, it shouldn't be hard. Send someone out here to ring the alarm bell, someone strong enough to make it heard."

"Yes, Gran."

"If they're not wolves, what are they?" persisted Yogarn after Ina had left.

"Never you mind, Yogarn. If they show up here you kill 'em or I'll find a switch and make sure you wished that you had, like as not."

Yogarn was frightened, that was clear to Gran, but he obeyed her out of habit. She wished that she could tell him exactly what he was facing but she didn't dare. If word got out that the attackers were Weres the people would panic even worse than they already had.

Night had fully fallen and the nearly full moon had yet to rise. Gran ran through her significant store of knowledge. She knew what they faced and she knew what was needed for them to survive. That it was likely that none of them would survive, she also knew quite well. She had to take some risks, but they had to be smart risks.

"Mertie!" she screeched, while urging a woman with several children up the steps and into the tavern.

"Here, Gran," came the response as the middle-aged woman hurried to her side.

"Fetch me a youngster, not too young. Find one who will do what I say and can run fast."

Mertie was obviously shocked at the woman's words, but again, long custom at obeying the old woman's commands won over and she fled to obey. For the first time in her life, Gran felt a moment of hesitation. She had felt badly when she had left Hod and Jud to die but that had been necessary. Both had been in the militia and had sworn to defend the people of Cobble. Both had been fully grown adults. This was something quite different.

A girl of thirteen, the daughter of Fat Happ, by the name of Aquina, Gran recalled, came out of the tavern and scurried to her side, dropping a curtsy despite the oversized leather pants she wore.

"You wanted me, Gran?"

"Aye child, I need you," Gran replied, feeling a tear building in one eye over the beauty before her. A child whose life she was about to risk. "Nay, we all need you... are you a brave lass?"

"I'm as brave as my father," she stated, lifting her head and staring Gran in the eye.

Gran smiled. People spoke disparagingly over the slothfulness of Fat Happ but Gran knew more about her people than anyone else. She knew that Fat Happ was lazy and disdained work but the man was no coward, as a run in with an angry she-bear the year before had proven. The man had saved his children by facing the beast down with a broom.

"Child, do you understand that we're all in danger and the only safe place in the town is here in the tavern?"

"I do, Gran. That's what my father told me."

"Good, child. Now, I'll need you to run to my house and get something for me. You'll be in danger every step of the way, do you understand? If the wolves come after you, all you'll be able to do is run."

"Yes Gran, I'll go for you."

Gran allowed the tear to fall unimpeded.

"Thank you, child."

Albrim raced down the trail, unaware that the wolf on his trail was jumping from one switchback to the next and gaining on him with every leap. The great beast moved silently while its brother above continued its mournful howling, alerting all within hearing that the pack was close to a kill.

The path down the side of the cliff was relatively bare of vegetation but the floor of the valley below was a different story. Even with the moon the valley floor was completely in shadow and the thickness of the trees would likely have prevented the light from penetrating anyway.

Albrim's breathing was ragged and despite his fear and the steepness of the trail his legs were slowing. When he reached the bottom of the valley, he was barely able to remain upright and finally he stumbled. His legs felt like lead and it was becoming impossible to retain his footing. He stopped at the foot of the cliff and leaned against the first tree he came to, staring fearfully back the way he had come, blissfully unaware that the wolf was closing in.

He knew that he couldn't go on. He was completely exhausted and blind until the moon arose high enough to point down into the sheltered valley. Did the trail continue on from here or did it end? Where were the wolves? Still on the rim above where the lone lobo still howled? Or here below, maybe behind him among the trees? Albrim could hear nothing, could see nothing.

The trees of this valley were tall and straight, probably necessary to get adequate sunlight. The brush was thicker near the base of the cliffs and the air was thickly scented with pine and whipsnatch, a particularly pungent fern that apparently grew here in abundance. Normally he would have tried to avoid the smell but he desperately needed air and so was forced to suck in the stench by the mouthful.

His breathing finally slowed enough to at least consider walking. Feeling around with his hands he found the trail and moved along it, trying again for stealth, as he knew that speed was now beyond his ability. If they came for him now, he'd never be able to run.

Albrim staggered on a few steps more, deeper and deeper into the grove. Somewhere ahead was a deep sinkhole or gully, he could tell that by the shape of the terrain and his brief glimpse from above. The cliffs on all sides formed a round bowl and assuming he had not gotten lost on the way here, this should be the place where his father had set the trap. Somewhere near here in any event.

Yet another howl sounded from above, giving Albrim a start of renewed fear. Then another howl, this time somewhere not far ahead of him. He paused, debating what to do. If the wolves were on the game trail, he should leave it and try to make his way around it. If they caught wind of him, they would easily run him down off the path and he would be constantly stumbling over roots and brush in the absolute darkness. To stay on the path would leave him trapped between at least two of them. His choice was made for him when he heard the growl.

Deep, dark and terrible, the snarl spurred Albrim into action. The wolf couldn't have been more than a few feet away, a dozen at most. Why it had not already pounced, he couldn't understand, but he knew he had to move. The growl was likely intentional, meant to startle the beast's quarry and frighten it into motion. He was the quarry, but he knew that to remain on the trail was to be found almost immediately. He had to move.

Easing off the trail Albrim was gratified to find the ground somewhat clear, the ground clutter wet and soft and no grasping brush to scratch noisily across his clothing. He moved steadily and silently away from the trail, and, noticing a slight rise in elevation to his right, he chose that direction. He heard a soft whine from somewhere to his right. He could only imagine that the wolf had found his scent on the trail and then lost it when he had left the path. It wouldn't be long before it found it again.

Cautiously Albrim worked his way uphill, paralleling the path, he hoped, in case he needed to regain it. His ears strained as he groped his way along, feeling the ground before each step. He wasn't making fast progress but at least the wolves hadn't found him yet. A thought struck him; perhaps the abundance of whipsnatch in the valley had worked to his advantage? The odor of the weed was strong. It just might be strong enough to mask his scent, and so the wolves were having trouble finding him.

At this point, Albrim felt that he had little to lose. The next patch of whipsnatch he came to, easily found just by following his nose, he used his belt knife to cut away several handfuls of the fronds which he then rubbed over his body and clothing. Finally he stuffed the ferns into his belt and made sure to rub his footwear through the patch as well before moving on. Had he made any noise? He didn't think so.

Continuing his stealthy movements, Albrim climbed the gradual slope for several long minutes. Terror threatened to cheat him of his efforts, as every small sound or movement urged him to blind panic. Even his breathing failed to slow completely and the stitch in his side refused to ease despite several minutes of walking. He would have to stop soon for a serious rest or pass out from exhaustion. He was already light headed but didn't know if it was caused by fear, exhaustion, or the unholy stink that arose from the severed whipsnatch fronds.

The ground finally leveled out again and Albrim began to make a little more progress. His back had begun to ache from moving in a stooped-over position and he was about to fall to his knees from exhaustion. Still he stumbled onward, hoping to find his father or a place where he could defend himself. Finally he realized that he simply could not continue and collapsed at the base of a massive fireoak tree.

Albrim placed his back to the rough bark and drew his belt knife before stringing his bow and placing it beside him. By feel he chose an arrow from his quiver and laid it upon his knees before allowing himself to relax. He pinched himself to remain awake and alert, but it was getting difficult to hold his eyes open. Not being able to see anything didn't help, but his exhaustion made it almost impossible. In the end it was only fear, an emotion it seemed that he had been carrying in his heart for a lifetime, that gave him the strength to fight off sleep.

He told himself to count to a slow one hundred and then he would move on. Then he gave himself a second hundred. His legs were like dull weights and he didn't feel like he could even stand up, so he added another two hundred. Somewhere around the halfway point he stopped counting and simply sat, too numb with fatigue to even care, all his willpower was tied up in staying awake. However, he soon found out that awake did not mean alert.

Albrim had seen many a sunrise in his few years. Gran would often make everyone in the house rise well before sunrise, to get a good start on the day, she would say. No stranger to the gradual lightening as the sun approached the horizon; Albrim expected the same thing here as the light of Jacet caught up to him here in the valley. It didn't work that way; instead the darkness went from absolute to barely dim in one swift moment, leaving the groggy Albrim looking into the eyes of a wolf not a dozen feet away.

Startled, the youngster let out a strangled bleat of surprise and snatched up his bow, his fingers feeling thick and clumsy even as sheer terror burned away the sleep from his eyes. No less surprised than Albrim, the wolf leaped backward before recovering its wits and darting forward. Here was the prey! Here was its meal! Now it would feed. Teeth barred and saliva dripping, the beast took two running steps forward before leaping for its victim's throat.

Albrim held up his bow horizontally; sitting upon the ground as he was, it was his only option. He grabbed his prepared arrow and lifted it to the string but the attack of the wolf was too quick. The beast was simply too close for him to take the time to find the notch, to set the arrow properly, to aim, to even pull the bowstring all the way back. In desperation he placed the arrow and pulled the string in one motion, yelling in fear as he released the string almost immediately.

The half-powered arrow had little momentum and could not have caused the wolf any lasting harm wherever it had struck. Fortunately for Albrim the range was point-blank so he couldn't have missed. The shaft struck the beast in the right nostril, passing into the opening without causing real harm but surprising the wolf nonetheless. With a startled whine the wolf landed just before Albrim, who scrambled back against the tree, regaining his feet and grasping at another arrow as the wolf pawed desperately at the arrow in its nose.

Staggering and growling, the wolf turned away from Albrim as it struggled to pull the arrow out, attempting to step on the shaft with a forepaw in order to pin it down. The awkwardness of the situation caused it to miss twice and it lost valuable time on a third attempt as it tried in vain to bite it. Finally it successfully trapped the shaft beneath a paw and pulled its head back amidst a spray of blood. Turning towards the youth, the wolf barred its teeth, ready to take a measure of blood in return for its pain.

Albrim's shaking hands pulled a second arrow free, spraying several others onto the ground at his feet. He slapped it onto the bowstring as the wolf turned towards him, again too close to miss, but again Albrim didn't have time to aim. However, this time he did have the luxury of pulling the string all the way back to his ear before letting it fly.

The wolf's snarl of rage turned to one of pain as the arrowhead punched through its skull, dropping it instantly to the ground, although Albrim could see that the beast was still alive. It yelped at the impact, trying desperately to claw the shaft free.

Grabbing at his quiver, Albrim's immediate thought was to finish off the beast but a howl alerted him to the approach of another wolf, so he spun about and moved into a shambling trot, the best pace he could manage even with the rest.

The light of Jacet lit his way in disparate patches of dimness between the larger pools of pitch black beneath the trees. To his right, brush crackled as something large forced its way through and behind him both wolves were now howling. Despite himself, Albrim found his steps quickening until his gait finally achieved enough speed to be considered a run. There was little doubt that he was being pursued now.

Running was a losing proposition, even if he could keep it up, and Albrim knew that he couldn't. Where he was finding the energy to keep his feet moving even now, he had no idea, but the wolves were closing in. He felt that he had to regain the path and so began angling slightly to his left, looking to intercept it. A whisper of noise alerted him and he dared a look behind him. There, coming at a full run, he saw the biggest wolf he'd ever seen. It was closing the distance between them at an unbelievable speed and would be on him in seconds.

Albrim dodged left, then right, hurtling himself over a rising shadow that he hoped was a bush and not another of those seeking his life. The brambles snagged at his clothing and flesh, both of which were torn away in his flight. Snarls from behind told him his pursuer not only remained on the hunt, but was still closing fast. Barely keeping his balance, he ran on, looking desperately through the gloom for the game trail he knew to be close.

Behind came death, sometimes on four feet and sometimes on but two, or so Albrim's fearful imagination believed. Either way, it was faster than its prey. Ignoring the wounds of the brambles, the beast tore through the brush at full speed, the scent of its quarry so close its mouth watered in anticipation of that first juicy bite.

The ground broke away somewhere ahead. The trail ran along the lip of the gully. The woodsman in the boy told him that the open trail was not the place to avoid the beast pursuing him, but that part of his mind was closed with fear. All of his thoughts, all of his instincts said that he had to flee, to get away. To outrun this beast that sought his life. Brambles and tree roots stole his speed here among the trees. Only the game trail offered a clear path for his flight. Only there could he reach his full speed.

He didn't make it.

Albrim tripped over a log he never saw, then tucked his shoulder and managed to roll over so as to land on his back rather than face first. The rotted leaves beneath him cushioned the blow but he was too frightened to care. No sooner had his gaze cleared from the fall then his vision was filled with the features of the wolf. Its snarling visage had appeared mere inches away, drops of its spittle falling liberally onto Albrim's upturned face. Unable to move his legs or arms from exhaustion and fear, he knew he was looking at his death.

Chapter Five

Aquina turned onto the main street at a full sprint, a pair of massive wolves well behind but gaining on her. Beneath one arm she clutched a leather satchel Gran recognized from her own home. The girl had been successful in her task, but could she make it back to the tavern alive? If she didn't, none of them would survive.

"Yogarn, you must save that girl," Gran screeched, thrusting a bony digit towards Aquina.

Yogarn swallowed, visibly frightened of leaving the relative security of the tavern's porch. However, he did as commanded, lifting his grandfather's ancient sword and speaking to the gathered militia.

"Cobble Militia!" he shouted, his voice noticeably shaking, "Forward pikes... charge!"

To their credit, the militiamen didn't hesitate but responded with a yell of 'Cobble' as they lowered their pikes and went off the porch in a rush to meet the wolves. These were not true fighting men, merely peasant farmers with little real training, but that did not stop their charge.

Trotting down the steps, the militia moved forward in a relatively disciplined line. Gran watched them go even as she ordered a late arriving family into the tavern. Her real attention never left the six men and one woman that was all that remained of the Cobble militia. None of them were young which, to Gran's mind made them steadier, more reliable. However, not a one of them had ever had to fight for his life.

Closer and closer came the wolves to their prey and slower came Aquina's steps. Would she make it to the militia? Would it matter, thought Gran? If Aquina did not make it, everyone in the tavern would die. If she did make it, but the last of the able bodied warriors of the town died protecting her, then everyone in the tavern would die. Gran needed both to have a chance of saving anyone.

The first wolf snapped at Aquina's heels, narrowly missing the worn leather of her boots. The girl screamed at the near miss, watching over her shoulder as she fled across the level cobblestones. Her mother began to scream as well from her vantage point at the lone window of the second floor of the tavern. The flickering light of the torches mounted on tall poles outside the tavern gave the scene a dreamlike quality, as if everyone was moving in slow motion.

Yogarn sped forward as fast as his aching legs would drive him. He was an old man; far too old for this sort of nonsense but found himself outstripping his 'command' as he moved. He knew himself to be a coward and had always known that, but now he found himself face to face with a pair of wolves as big as ponies and he was charging them! An old sea chantey learned from his grandfather passed through his mind and he began to sing it aloud to keep his real thoughts from his mind, lest he run screaming into the night. Somehow, despite his age and avowed cowardice, it was he who reached the sobbing girl first.

His initial thrust with the sword was wide left and the wolf deftly sidestepped it as Aquina darted by him. Now Yogarn realized that he was defenseless; having made so broad a thrust that he no longer had any means of defending himself, a mistake he had cautioned young militia members against for more than twenty years. The wolf was a blur as it suddenly changed directions after avoiding the thrust and dived for his unprotected arm. In desperation he tried to swing his sword with enough force to deflect the beast's jaws but he knew he was going to be too late.

Yogarn's scream of fear and pain caused three of the militiamen to stop in their tracks and begin backing up. The others continued forward but now were little more than individuals and resembled nothing of the unified force they should have.

Kareyta, the lone woman and youngest of the group at thirty, was the closest to Yogarn. Realizing that the wolf biting the Reeve was distracted with its attack, she drove forward with the intention of killing the beast before it even saw her coming. In her haste she stumbled over Aquina's foot as they passed each other and rather than delivering a killing thrust, her pike barely scratched the wolf along its flank.

Growling and snapping at the blade, the wolf leaped backwards and then was joined by its brother in a straightforward rush on the off-balance woman. Yogarn collapsed beside her, the meat of his right forearm hanging loosely from the bone even as he clutched his left hand to his chest. The wolves darted left and right around the wavering point of the pike and rushed Kareyta, one snapping for her legs while the other bunched in preparation of leaping for her throat.

"Cobble!" screamed Tonk, Kareyta's husband, as he drove his pike into the leaping wolf, carrying through its throat and pinning it to the ground. The beast gurgled mournfully as its companion finished its attack, avoiding Kareyta's pike and biting deeply into her ankle. Hearing its packmate's distress, the wolf pulled away, barely avoiding the thrust of another pike. Seeing that the odds were now in favor of the prey, the wolf backed away, its hackles rising. Pausing only to take a single sniff of its dying companion, the wolf turned and darted into the safety of the night.

For once moving as if they were acting together, the remaining militia picked up Yogarn and Kareyta and made a hasty retreat to the porch. The night around them erupted into a dozen mournful howls.

"Law, Gran, they're all around us," whimpered Tonk as he struggled beneath the weight of his wife.

"Inside with the wounded, hurry now," whispered Gran, ignoring Tonk and waving the men past. She was too busy digging through the satchel brought to her by Aquina to note the wounds but knew that Ina or Mertie would have to take care of them. Finding everything she needed she patted the sobbing girl on the head and sent her inside.

"Gran?" someone called.

Gran looked up and saw Ina standing in the doorway. Her eyes were worried but Gran could see that the woman was still under control.

"What is it, child?"

"The windows are boarded up; the flue is blocked by a grill. We have everything filled with water that will hold it, just like you said."

"Fine," Gran cackled, hurrying as best she could to the doorway as she ordered the youngster ringing the bell to leave off and get inside. At the doorway she met two of the militiamen coming out.

"Get back inside, you fools," she snarled, fetching the first one a sharp rap on the shin with her walking staff. She barreled ahead as if they weren't there, which by some amazing footwork they weren't by the time it mattered, and pushed her way past the knot of concerned people waiting there.

"Bar the door, the back one, too, if you haven't already," she ordered, tossing her staff into a corner and grabbing Mertie by one ear, urging her towards the cold fireplace.

"Get me a fire going; I need it as hot as you can make it. Ask Yogarn how if he isn't dead. You, Ina, make sure that he's not and check on Kareyta too. I don't have time to deal with scratches."

She grabbed onto another ear, this one of a young man of ten. She pushed him into position with a woman more than twice his age. "Get yourselves up onto the roof and keep watch for the wolves. Take two of the children to run messages to me of anything you see."

"But Gran, what of the wolves?" squeaked the woman, which earned her a slap on the backside.

"They're wolves, you dolt, not eagles," Gran huffed. "Like as not we'll starve to death before they get in through the roof."

Next Gran spoke to all of those gathered together, somehow determined to remain in her way and under her feet at every step. She pointed out several and commanded, "All of you get up the ladder to the upper floor. Now get!"

Gran ignored the stampede of people up the ladder and fished around in her satchel, pulling out various bags of herbs and liniments, all of which she tossed aside. She was looking for one specific salve. Finally finding her prize, she pulled the small bone jar out of the bag along with two tarnished candlesticks and set them on the nearest table.

Grabbing another woman by the ear Gran explained what she wanted done next, supervising the filling of five tin pails with hot water and then measuring an equal amount of a pale green dust from the small bone jar into each.

"Carry one pail to each window and door, don't worry about the front door, and don't forget the trap door into the cellar just in case the wolves figure a way to get down there," she ordered, tapping a different person or child with her switch in indicate which bucket was their responsibility. "Wrap a rag on a stick for each bucket. Use the rag to smear the water around each doorframe, each window jamb. Every time it looks like they might be drying out, wash them again. All the way around, mind you," she shrieked after the scurrying townsfolk.

"Like as not someone will fall asleep and let the wolves come right in," she thought.

Taking stock of what remained of the citizens of Cobble; Gran was saddened to see how few had made it to the dubious shelter of the tavern. How many were already dead? How many were hiding out among the outlying buildings, praying for salvation? Unless help came from outside the town, nothing awaited them but death. Of those here, some were prostrate with fear, having seen friends or loved ones ripped to shreds by the massive wolves. They would be of little use.

Once all her preparations were under way, Gran took stock of the villagers, trying to determine who she could most trust with what she needed to share. Yogarn, the Lord's Reeve and the official leader of the village, was certainly out of the question with his injuries, if he still even lived. All of the Reeve's council were either away on the wolfing or missing and most of those remaining were fools or worse. She was beginning to feel very alone. Ina and Mertie, so valuable to her in healing or birthing, were of no use in the defense of the tavern against those with the Curse. Gran knew what they faced in the werewolves, but it was likely that she was the only one here that had a clue exactly what threat they faced.

Her choice made, she plied her switch to clear her way into the taproom, finding the person she wanted right where she had expected to find him; drinking ale as around him wounded people lay on tables and stretchers.

"Happ, come with me," she ordered, moving into the larder and waiting for the man. It didn't occur to her that he wouldn't obey.

Sheepishly, the man did come, turning sideways to work his massive frame through the door. Gran studied him as she did everyone, with a sharp piercing gaze that saw everything the man wanted to hide. She saw the hanging belly, the fierce crop of black chest hair protruding out over his collar. She saw the unwashed thinning hair and the soft hands. Fat Happ was what he seemed to be; a lazy man. Not that she needed to study him to know these things; like all the others in town save a very few exceptions, she had been there at his birth and every day of his life since.

"Yes, Gran," he said meekly, wiping the froth of beer from his unkempt beard. "You wanted me?"

"Hmph, what is there to want? You're a lazy slob, Happ, and like as not you'll die a lazy slob. I don't want you, but I need you. We all need you."

Happ's face was always flushed but now Gran had the pleasure of watching the color drain away, leaving him as pale as the skin of his belly.

"I can't go out there, Gran, them wolves would catch me quick!"

Gran snorted. "I know that better than you do, like as not, and don't think me an imbecile that would send a man like you on a mission that requires fleetness."

The man looked embarrassed, but not unduly so. He really didn't mind that others saw him as fat or lazy.

"Sorry, Gran."

"And keep your apologies to yourself, too! I'm going to do the talking and you'll do the listening or feel my switch! And you'll keep your mouth shut about what I tell you, too!"

Beyond arguing, Happ simply nodded and kept quiet, wondering what in the world the old woman could need to tell him that demanded such secrecy.

"Happ I want you to take charge of the militia."

"Me, Gran? I'm not in the militia..."

She interrupted him with a pinch on the underside of his upper arm.

"I know that, you dolt, but you are in the militia as of right this minute."

"Gran, I'm too fat to fight, everyone knows that," Happ began weakly.

"And who else is there to be in charge?" demanded Gran. "Tonk? He can't even lace his own breeches. "Crag? He's sixty if he's a day and a coward besides. There is no one else, Happ, and so it's you and I'll hear no more lip!"

Happ started kicking at something but kept his mouth shut beyond a mumbled curse. Working his weight up onto a nearby barrel, he sat waiting for Gran to continue.

Seeing that the fight was out of him, Gran did continue.

"What do you know about our attackers?"

Happ shrugged. "Wolves, big ones. Likely the same ones that killed ole Jule."

Gran nodded. "True enough, as far as it goes, but not the whole story. There's more."

Intrigued in spite of himself, Happ leaned closer.

"You'll keep your mouth shut," Gran reminded, brandishing her switch for emphasis. "We're not just facing big wolves, although they're certainly bad enough. There's more to it than that. The wolves are being led by something, something worse than a whole pack of wolves."

Happ blanched again. "Quargs?"

"No, you fool, worse than Quargs too! I'm talking something that can command wolves; speak to them in their own language. Something unnatural."

His eyes moved rapidly back and forth, searching his mind for an answer.

"What can speak to wolves? Do they even have a language..." his voice trailed away and his eyes suddenly widened. "You don't mean a Were?" he breathed.

"That is exactly what I mean," whispered Gran, pulling the door to the pantry back open to check for eavesdroppers.

"But Gran, what are we going to do?"

"We're already doing it, Happ. Get a hold of yourself!"

Abashed, Happ eased back onto his barrel.

Pausing to pick an imaginary bit of lint from her shawl, Gran continued. "We have everyone we can in the tavern, which is the only building in town with stone walls. Wolves can't chew through stone. We have watchers on the roof and five healthy militia members, six counting you as their new leader, armed and ready to fight if they don't wet themselves and run off first."

Happ smiled weakly at the jibe.

"But none of that is going to be on any use against a Were."

His smiled died.

"So what can we do Gran?"

"You'll keep the militia strong, that's what."

"How?"

"Urge them, shame them, threaten them, sit on them if you have to, but you'll make sure that they'll stand and that they'll fight!"

"Gran I'm no leader. I can't even take care of my own farm."

"You can do this, Happ. I know you can. You're brave, for all your slothfulness. You have to do it or your family will die."

"What can I do to a Were? Provide him with so much food that he dies from overeating?"

Gran chuckled despite herself.

"You don't worry about the werewolves; I'll give you what you'll need to deal with them."

"What of the Curse? What of our friends and neighbors out there that the wolves have already gotten? Won't they all be Weres now, too? Will I have to kill my own?"

"That may be the first intelligent question you've ever asked me, Happ."

Happ grinned despite himself.

"Wolves are wolves; we can kill them, like as not, and already have. If you look out on the square you'll see one lying dead. The Were that's leading them, and I pray there's only one, is not here to make new minions. Besides, it takes a while, weeks - maybe months, for the Curse to kick in after you're infected."

Gran could see the question that was coming. "If they kill you, you don't get the Curse. Only if they bite you and you live."

Happ looked thoughtful. "So how are we going to kill them? I always heard that they can't be harmed by anyone but a church knight."

"More foolishness!" she spat. "Weres are protected against a regular blade or plow handle but they're not immortal!"

"What's immortal mean, Gran?"

"Don't you worry about it, Happ, neither you nor me will ever have to worry about that. Werewolves can be killed by weapons if the proper preparations are made. I'm seeing to them right now."

"What if the Were comes around before we're ready?"

"The Were won't come until he's absolutely sure that nothing in here can hurt him, like as not. He'll let the wolves do his dirty work until he's convinced that there's nothing in here but a bunch of ignorant farmers. Then he'll come."

"So how do we stop him? How do we stop the wolves until he does come?" Happ asked nervously.

"Like I said, the wolves are just wolves; if they get in we'll stick them with a blade, or pike, or bash them over the head with a chair. You and the militia will have to take care of that."

"And when the Were comes?"

"Why, we'll have a surprise or two ready for him when he comes in the front door," she cackled, her single tooth glinting dully in the dimness of the larder.

"How do you know the Were will come in the front door? Why not the back door, or the window? Or maybe he'll climb to the roof."

Gran waved her hand dismissively. "I've already taken care of all that. I mixed wolfbane in buckets of water and had some of the young ones paint the door jambs and windows, all except the front door."

Happ smiled. "Right, they can't pass wolfbane, it'll kill them."

Gran kicked him in the shin. "Fool, it'll do no such a thing. However it will make them uneasy, even nauseous, so they'll avoid it if possible and so the front door will be 'bane free. If the Were doesn't ignore it as a trap."

"So what surprises will you have for it when it does come?"

Gran cackled again. "Well..." her words were interrupted by someone excitedly screaming her name.

Pushing her way past Happ's belly flab, Gran flung the door open and looked out into the kitchen. There, in the ceiling she saw the face of a little girl looking out of the hole just above the ladder that led to the second floor.

"Gran! Gran!" she shrieked.

"What is it, child?"

"Wolves, Gran. Mama says there's a dozen of them gathering just outside the front door!"

A snarl of victory from the wolf turned into a yelp of pain as the beast suddenly turned to its left, the claws from one paw inadvertently leaving a line of blood across Albrim's forehead. From his upside-down view he couldn't see what had distracted the wolf until he heard a dull thud that he recognized from a lifetime of target practice: an arrow had struck true. Three more thumps and a last whimper and the wolf collapsed atop Albrim, his face buried in the dank fur of the animal's chest.

His arms still weak; Albrim struggled to get out from under the wolf, the smell of its fur redolent of old blood and canine sweat. It clogged his mouth and cut off his breath, leaving him powerless to move and unable to get away. He tried anyway, doing his best to pull himself from under the crushing weight. How could a wolf be so heavy?

With a rush, the weight disappeared as the wolf was pulled away, leaving Albrim to gasp at the mossy air. As he did so, relief at his salvation brought back the forgotten pain of his run, combined with that of his numerous cuts and bruises., leaving him gasping at the sting as much as he did for air. He couldn't see any faces but he knew that his father had found him.

Muted voices came as someone examined the wolf, ensuring that it was dead even though it carried five arrows in its sides and flanks. Someone else hurried to Albrim's side, kneeling down as if to check his health but the darkness was too deep for a thorough examination. A soft curse from the man sounded suspiciously like his father but Albrim couldn't be sure.

Gentle hands lifted him as voices cautioned him to relax. He wasn't carried far, only a few steps, before being gently lowered to lie upon a blanket. Next the blanket itself was lifted and he was carried a longer distance. He was placed gently atop a pile of soft leaves, or was it a bed of thick moss? No matter, it felt like his Gran's feather mattress to Albrim. Then his father was indeed there, his strong hand gripping Albrim's shoulder.

"Father," he gasped, "I have a message..."

"Quiet for now, Albrim. Just drink this," came Borel's calm voice. A cup was held to Albrim's mouth and a few drops of cool liquid was splashed onto his lips. That was all it took to divert his attention as he quickly drained three cups in quick succession. A fire sprung up somewhere close by.

"Father," he tried again, pushing away a fourth cup. "I was sent to warn you about the wolves... they're not just wolves."

Borel sat back, his face lost to shadow but Albrim could easily tell his concern by the outline of his form against the moon's indirect glow. Borel's face, what little Albrim could see by the light of the small fire, had been haggard with worry. Something he wasn't used to seeing in his father.

"Not just wolves, you say? More than just wolves the size of ponies, you mean?"

"No father, Weres!" Albrim blurted, only after realizing that he might have been better to have told his father in private.

Someone nearby began cursing. Borel's fingers gripped Albrim a little more tightly.

"Weres! Are you sure, Albrim?"

"Yes father, Sir Garen was attacked in the forest, and some men died. I didn't know any of them. Sir Garen is calling all the wolfing patrols back in."

"Where to? Spicer? Sir Garen was near there last we heard," asked an unknown voice. Albrim found it to be familiar but couldn't quite place it.

"No, I was told to find you and tell you to go home, back to Cobble."

"That's all you were told, son?" asked Borel.

"Yes father, if I found you after the sun went down, to tell you to go back to Cobble."

"Cobble is not my home, am I supposed to go back to Spicer?" asked the voice.

"No, we're all supposed to go to Cobble."

"It is the closest settlement," stated Borel thoughtfully.

"Where are the others going?" demanded the voice, sounding a little shrill in the darkness.

"Calm yourself Lonn, we can't lose our heads now," cautioned Borel.

"They were meeting at the crofter's hut, the one there along the main road. Where we all stopped that night?" Albrim answered, assuming this Lonn had been with them.

"Where were they going from there?" Lonn asked.

"I'm not sure, I wasn't told. If I couldn't find you before nightfall, we're supposed to go to Cobble, that's all I know."

"That's ridiculous, we need to join everybody back up, there's strength in numbers," argued Lonn.

"Or we need to go back home, to see after our own," came a deeper voice. Albrim recognized the voice and knew the man slightly. He was a huntsman from Torude and somehow a friend of Borel's.

"Yeah, that's right. My family is going to need me if there are Weres in the forest!" agreed Lonn.

Borel ignored both men for the moment, pushing his son back on the blanket. "Rest for now, Albrim," he said, loud enough that the other men would certainly hear. "We're not going anywhere tonight, that's for certain, so you sleep a while."

The three older men spoke for some time, arguing as to the best course of action, but Albrim heard none of it. As if his father's voice carried some type of divine magic, he was asleep in moments.

Sunshine in his eyes awoke Albrim. His eyes opened slowly and an attempt at lifting his arm to block the sun's rays left him groaning in pain from the knotted muscles in his forearm. Suddenly the rigors of the night returned and he tried to sit up, only to find that he hurt too badly to do even that. Rolling to one side was possible but only barely. By doing so, he at least removed the sun from his eyes.

Looking about the camp brought back memories of his youth: his father squatting over the small campfire turning over a brace of roasting rabbits. The wetness of the morning dew had yet to burn away from the rotted leaves and the smell of wood smoke lay over everything. Beyond his father a thin man with oversized forearms stalked about, peering alertly into the forest with an arrow ready on the string. He was Treed, the huntsman from Torude known for his mok-hunting dogs.

Albrim wished they had the dogs with them now, even though they would be little use against the wolves, or Weres either for that matter. They were trained for the mok, a large rodent that would rather climb trees than fight.

"Good morning, Albrim," spoke up his father, somehow sounding cheerful even though his son could see that he was worried.

"Good morning, father," Albrim said, struggling up to a sitting position. His back and legs were in bad shape.

Borel grimaced at his son's discomfort.

"Sorry we don't have any of your Gran's porridge this morning, we'll have to make do with rabbit," Borel said, only the slightest hint of humor in his voice.

Albrim smiled at the jest. His Gran's porridge was legendary for its bland perfection. She always claimed that eating her porridge made one healthy and long-lived but no one that ever tasted it exclaimed over its wonderful taste.

"I'll try to make do, father."

Using a pair of knives Borel cut away a sizeable portion of one rabbit. He dropped it onto a linen napkin and brought the food to his son.

"Here, first portion goes to the hero. Even if the hero stinks like whipsnatch."

Two bites of the meat were cooled and eaten before Albrim realized what his father had said.

"Hero? I'm no hero!"

Treed came back into camp long enough to spear the rest of one of the rabbits on a long knife.

"Reckon you are, boy," he said, carefully nibbling off a bit of flesh. "You risked your life in a Were-filled forest and ran for hours with wolves chasing you just to warn us. Sounds as heroic as any of them tales the bards sing about. And you do stink like whipsnatch."

Albrim grimaced at the thought. Being a hero was something he'd always dreamed of, always thought that he could be in his own mind. However, the deeds he pictured himself doing had nothing to do with him running away.

"I'm no hero, Treed. I just wanted to warn my father. The whipsnatch was just desperation. I didn't think that the wolves could smell me so easy."

"Whatever," grunted Treed, carrying his meal back out of camp. He continued his slow patrols in a circle, his bow still at the ready but the arrow had been returned to the quiver so he could eat.

Biting off another mouthful, Albrim looked about the small camp. He could see four small shelters made of branches but saw only his father and Treed. He remembered another voice from the darkness the night before, hadn't his father called the man's name? Yes, it was Lonn.

"Father, where are the others?"

Borel sat down next to his son, his own meal spitted on the end of his long knife. He looked as his son for a long moment before smiling.

"They left, son. Early this morning. Making their way back to their homes."

"They left in the middle of the night, when Lonn was supposed to be on guard duty," stated Treed around a mouthful of rabbit. Apparently he was just within hearing range of the camp. "Could've killed us all."

Borel's features tightened at the man's words, but he said nothing. He chewed his rabbit deliberately.

"They deserted?" Albrim asked his father.

"Sure did, boy," answered Treed. "They decided to abandon us and run for home, leave us sleeping and unaware with wolves and worse stalking us." Treed shook his head. "I sure look forward to meeting up with him again."

"The Lord will handle it, Treed," interrupted Borel. "It's the Lord's justice for him but first we have to do our duty, and that's returning to Cobble."

"Why would they just leave, father?"

Borel grimaced at the question. "Son, they were scared. Scared for themselves and scared for their families."

"So they ran away? What if the wolves got them?"

"They probably did get them, like as not," Borel grimaced again. He hated sounding like Gran.

"But why didn't they stay here? Didn't they know we were ordered back to Cobble?"

Borel tossed a bone into the fire. "We talked long into the night after you went to sleep and they wanted us to go after Sir Garen. I said no, that I was in authority and our duty is to return to Cobble as commanded."

Albrim ate silently for a while, finishing his meal and disposing of the remains as his father had. Once finished he dragged himself to his feet and took a few turns about the camp, trying to loosen his muscles. He drank a great deal of water as well. Thanks to the resiliency of youth, within an hour he was ready to travel.

They broke camp quickly, dousing the fire and burying their waste quickly. The supplies were divided among them, as were the four wolf skins the group had taken. Once their water skins were refilled from an almost invisible spring, they went back in the direction from which Albrim had come the night before, pausing only to inspect the carcass of the wolf that had attacked Albrim. Treed skinned it as Albrim looked on.

"I wanted you to see what they look like up close," his father had explained, "and we need the skins for Sir Garen."

"I think I've been close enough," laughed Albrim, pretending to pick wolf hair from his teeth.

The three shared a laugh, but it was forced.

"How many of the big wolves did you kill?" Albrim asked, then told of the one he had killed.

"Only this one. Up to now we'd only seen the usual kind," Treed replied.

Climbing the cliff face along the switchback trail was hard climbing with the heavy pack on his back, but Albrim endured. His legs were shaky with fatigue by the time they reached the summit, as were those of his companions. Borel called a brief halt before they continued.

"Father, how far is it to Cobble?"

Borel looked towards Treed.

Seeing that he was being called upon, Treed answered. "I make it 'bout two days if we push it. Bring us there about nightfall tomorrow evening."

"That's too long, father!" protested Albrim. "We have to be there to protect Gran from the Weres!"

"Unless you got some wizard in you, boy, that's as quick as we can make," stated Treed.

Borel couldn't resist adding, "I think we need to get there to protect the Weres from Gran! She'll have them hoeing out the cabbages!"

Albrim laughed. "Or hitch them up and make them pull her around in a wagon!"

Again they all laughed; even Treed knew Gran. This time it didn't sound quite so forced.

Borel then turned serious. "From here on we need to be as quiet as possible. The wolves are out here and even if Weres need the night, and I don't believe the tales that say that they do, the wolves certainly do not."

The others nodded their agreement and they moved on.

Treed set a stiff pace but seemed always able to find a game trail running somewhat in the direction that they needed. The easier going saw them making good time and Albrim started to enjoy himself despite the situation. Treed often pointed out wolf tracks along with those of mok and other creatures. Once he even found the scat of a big forest cat. Unfortunately for Albrim who had never before seen any tracks of the reclusive cats, there had been nothing to see this time, as the beast had left its sign while perched in a tree. Twice they found tracks of wolves so large Treed's hand couldn't cover them. Only the presence of his father kept Albrim from being afraid. Unlike the earlier part of his trip, the wolf tracks were now easy to see and plentiful.

Pausing at noon only to drink from a stream and refill their water skins, Borel passed out some dried rations for the three to eat as they walked. This consisted of an oat cake so hard Albrim wouldn't feed it to Fat Happ's mule and a square of dried venison Borel had harvested on a hunt the previous summer. Ever a dutiful son, he followed his father's command and tried to eat, eventually dropping the oat cake along the trail and contenting himself with sucking the salt out of the venison.

An hour after their noon 'meal' Treed held up a hand, halting the others. Albrim quickly strung his bow and placed an arrow on the string as Borel moved up to Treed. The two men conferred for only a moment before moving on.

"What was it father?"

"He smells smoke."

"Campfire?"

"No, too strong. Not just wood smoke either."

Any thoughts of enjoying the trek vanished from Albrim's thoughts. A few minutes later he smelled the smoke himself and knew exactly what Treed had detected. He recognized it from once dropping a piece of pork into the fireplace at home. The smell had been just as sickly-sweet as this. His stomach growled at the thought. He said nothing and kept walking, mimicking the actions of the older men as they moved silently down the trail. Everyone had their bow ready and an arrow notched.

Following their noses the three switched back and forth a few times before finding a sheltered hollow. From there the smell came and it was much stronger. Albrim no longer found the scent appetizing; it was now so thick he thought he might be sick. When they turned the last outcropping of tree and stone they found nothing but a blackened place in the earth that had once been a dwelling.

"Stay here," Borel ordered. "Keep watch along our trail."

Albrim turned about and readied his bow, his hands shaking even as his stomach made ready to empty itself. He knew now that he hadn't been smelling pork.

Treed and his father were only gone a few minutes.

"One man, maybe two. The Weres must have burned them out," explained Treed. "Wolf tracks everywhere, and one set were made by a wolf walking on two legs."

"That smell, is that the men?" Albrim asked.

"Sure enough boy, that's what a man smells like when he's burning. Of course, the Weres didn't let him burn all the way. Once he was dead, they put him out long enough to feed and then tossed him back into the shack when they were finished."

"We need to hurry, Treed," said Borel, ignoring Albrim as the boy emptied his stomach.

They ran for a while then, covering the next few miles in a ground-eating trot. Borel believed that speed away from the area was more important at that time than stealth. The wolves might still be around.

Alternating long walks with short periods of running when the way seemed safe, the three men traveled the rest of the day and on into the night, stopping at midnight to catch a couple hours of slumber. Each man stood guard by turn and they moved out before the sun came up, having seen neither sign nor sound of wolves during the night. Albrim was relieved to be moving again. He had slept little and when he did his rest had been filled with nightmares of wolves seeking to suffocate him with their bodies or set him one fire. When the sun arose, they were again running down a forest trail.

At noon they stopped for a good rest by a stream. Albrim sat down against a tree and immediately fell asleep. The night's horrors were for now forgotten in his exhaustion.

Borel and Treed shared a cup of strong spirits as they rested.

"Will we get there by nightfall?" Borel asked.

"No, that little side trip to the burned cabin slowed us down some. Plus, we've spent a lot of time being careful, which I don't mind at all, if you want to know. We'll get there around midnight or so. Maybe an hour after at the latest.

Borel nodded, and then coughed as finished off his drink. "I think your homebrew is going rancid."

Treed smiled and drank his own portion down. "Yep, I make it rancid on purpose. People don't try to share too much that way."

All too soon, in Albrim's mind, they moved on. They ran for a mile or so and then started walking again. Treed was certain that something was wrong and demanded that they move stealthily again. Soon after that they found another body.

"Wolves, no doubt about it," announced Treed. The man had been ripped into two major pieces and a dozen smaller ones. Much of the flesh was gone. "The tracks show a dozen or more."

"Any Weres?" asked Borel as Albrim stared in sick fascination at the body. It was impossible to know for sure, but this could have been someone that he knew.

"Not sure. If I remember my night stories right, Weres can be wolves when they want to be, so one could have been here. There are no two-legged tracks here."

An hour later they found another body. Then three more in a shack the Weres hadn't bothered to burn.

"They likely didn't want to alert Cobble with the smoke," explained Treed.

By the time darkness fell, the land they traveled through was very familiar to the two men from Cobble. Borel and his son had hunted these hills many times. They stopped again to drink from the well of a small temple just off the main road. The temple itself was deserted but that was no surprise. The last monk had died at his post the previous winter and no replacement had ever been sent.

It was while there that Albrim noticed the red glow above the trees in the direction of Cobble.

"What is that, father?"

Treed cursed as Borel readied an arrow. It was obvious that Borel didn't want to answer but keeping it from his son made no sense.

"Cobble is on fire."

Chapter Six

Again and again the wolves threw themselves at the boarded up window, Gran's wolfbane concoction doing nothing to discourage them. Gran was disappointed with the lack of results but wasn't completely discouraged as the wolfbane had mostly been meant for the Were. The planks cracked and groaned with each impact; they couldn't last much longer. Fat Happ had his militia clustered together just inside the window, intending to rush the first wolf through with overwhelming force. If one made it through, more would quickly follow.

"Stand ready!" He yelled, for at least the tenth time. Happ had no idea he'd said it even once but in truth the militiamen didn't hear any of them. All were concentrating on the window and the death that lurked beyond.

"What news on the roof?" demanded Gran from the foot of the ladder. It took a moment for someone to relay the message up to the watchers and return with the answer.

"Momma says there are at least a score of wolves outside and that a house on the north end of town is on fire!"

Gran cursed, frightening a nearby child with her vehemence. She snatched a small pot of soup from the fireplace and hurried it back to the foot of the ladder. "Get this up to the roof," she snarled at Ina. "Pour it on the wolves by the window; see if we can't get them to leave."

Ina went up the ladder with the soup and her aim was true. The wolves outside the window yelped as the boiling liquid struck them. The cheer of the militiamen ended quickly as fresh attackers instantly replaced the scalded wolves.

"One wolf ran off, Gran," came the report from Ina.

"Well that's one less," she retorted, hurrying to the fire to check the progress of her other project. In a larger pot her two silver candlesticks, possibly the only silver in the entire town, still sat solid and unmelted. Their sides were soft but as of yet no silver had become liquid enough to coat the head of a pike.

"This fire isn't hot enough!" Gran yelled over the thump of another wolf. "Didn't someone ask Yogarn how to make it hotter?"

"I did, Gran," replied Ina, climbing down the ladder. "He said to 'use the bellows,' but we don't have one."

"Well go back and tell him that, and tell him to think of something else," Gran ordered, pushing Ina towards the back room where the wounded were.

"But Gran, I did. He said we needed a 'blue' flame and then he passed out," Ina protested as the old woman quick stepped her from the room.

"Then wake him up and find out how we do it."

Gran waited for Ina's return by jabbing the soft candlesticks with a poker. The flame seemed plenty hot enough to her; she knew that she was sweating profusely just standing this close.

With a crash the window boards gave in. Gran wasn't surprised, as the boards were simply the best of those left after the roof was rebuilt last fall. The first wolf, apparently surprised when the wood gave way, fell awkwardly across the window frame and was trapped, scrabbling its hind claws at the stone of the walls trying to find purchase enough to push itself through and into the building.

Happ was ready, and he and his command quickly pounced on the helpless beast and plunged their pikes repeatedly into its head and shoulders. One of its pack mates tried to climb over its yelping brother but was kept back by a pike thrust into its chest. Both wolves had taken enough damage and dropped back out of sight. Before the militia could breathe even a small sigh of relief, another wolf came through the window in full leap and was among them.

Happ drove his pike straight down into the beast's back, trying to cut its spine as the gathered militia dove upon the wolf. One man went down, the wolf's jaws clamped onto his thigh even as another beast missed its leap and landed astride the window rather than jumping through it, then slipped and fell back out of sight. Releasing his pike Happ pulled a butcher knife from his belt and brought it down onto the first beast's neck.

"The window, the window," Happ screamed as he drove the knife down again.

One man finally reacted, leaping in to drive his pike into the next incoming wolf's throat. The man on the floor grabbed a piece of a broken chair, which he had crushed when he fell, and pounded the wolf between the eyes. Despite the bludgeoning by its victim and the thrusts of Happ's knife, the beast refused to release its hold on the thigh and continued to hold tight until the life faded from its eyes.

Gran picked up a thick iron frying pan and stood ready if needed. The surviving militiamen were back at the window and had apparently driven the wolves back for the moment. Happ finished his wolf and struggled back to his feet, panting hard at the unaccustomed labor.

"The table! Put it against the window," he finally managed to gasp. Two of the men grabbed the nearest one and slapped it over the opening, finding it a perfect fit. Just as it fell into place another wolf struck it, the massive beast driving the men back two steps before they could recover and slam it home again.

"Find a hammer," yelled Happ.

"And nails," gasped Tonk as he leaned into the table.

One of the men scooped up a long bench and tried to use it as a wedge, but it was too short to hold the table. Someone threw a hammer down the ladder from the second floor and a moment later a handful of nails followed. Gran scooped them up and brought them to Tonk who began driving them home as quickly as he could.

"Will it hold?" someone asked.

"The table is too heavy for these nails," gasped Tonk. "But they'll hold until we can get some more planks."

Ina returned to the room just as a yelp and a crash sounded from outside and a cheer came up from the women on the roof.

"What's going on up there?" demanded Gran, scurrying back to the ladder.

A child of six answered. "Aunt Meg threw a shoe at one of the wolves and hit it. It knocked over a stack of buckets when it ran off."

"Gran, I need you," stated Mertie from where she knelt next to the recently bitten militiaman.

Gran hurried over to see. Mertie was struggling with a tourniquet on the man's upper thigh but didn't have the strength to hold it tight enough. Gran knelt on the man's other side and helped her tie it off. Then she lifted an eyelid to check on him.

"Mertie, let it go," Gran said, stopping the other woman from spending further time working on the man's wounds. "He's gone already."

Mertie looked at her in disbelief. "But Gran it's Rory! You have to do something."

Gran patted the woman's hand in a rare show of affection. Rory was Mertie's younger brother.

"Mertie if I could, I would. I hope you know that. But he's already dead."

More slams against the window's barricade began, this time with a steadier rhythm. In just a few such strikes, the head of an ax appeared through the wood.

"Quargs!" shouted Crag, his old voice quavering. "The wolves got Quargs with 'em, I knew it."

Gran said nothing, but she didn't believe that it was a Quarg handling that ax. It was the Were trying to help his pack get in for the kill.

Another commotion outside, this one nearer the front door, caused the ax blows to briefly stop. A man's scream followed by that of a woman upstairs saw the end of the problem and the ax blows began again.

What's happening up there?" Gran demanded, watching Ina and another woman working frantically at the fireplace. They had pushed aside the woodpile and chose out specific pieces to push into the fire. They had chosen only well-cured hard woods such as oak and a large piece of fireoak. Gran had seen Yogarn use fireoak many times and cursed herself for a fool. It was called fireoak because of the long-burning and very hot flames it produced. She should have thought of that herself.

A woman's wails came from the roof. "It was uncle K'Jord," said the young girl. "He came out of a house and attacked the wolves from behind. They killed him," she added matter-of-factly. The girl was much too young to understand what she was saying.

The table across the door shuddered with another impact. It was nearly split in two now. The remaining militiamen had stopped trying to hold it in place and had regained their weapons. Crag slipped in the blood on the floor despite the sand put down by someone after the bodies of Rory and the wolves had been dragged away.

Gran hurried back to the fireplace to check on the progress of her candlesticks, noticing with disdain that she still carried the frying pan. What good was a frying pan against a Were? They needed silvered weapons and they couldn't even make a couple of candlesticks melt!

Ina had concentrated all the burning wood into a central pile that was now blazing strongly. The hard woods had been slow to catch but after being doused with lamp oil they were putting forth a strong blue flame. Two women had joined Ina in blowing through hollow reeds, directing their breath directly into the flames just beneath the pot that held the candlesticks. They were using the reeds as small bellows to stoke the fire. Gran peeked into the pot, squinting against the smoke from the oil. The candlesticks were beginning to melt!

Turning about, Gran grabbed Happ's nearest ear and dragged him to the pot. To his credit he understood at once and dipped his pike into the pot, stirring it around frantically as he tried to get as much silver onto his pike head as he could. He opened his mouth, presumably to order his remaining militiamen to join him in silvering their blades as well, but the Were chose that moment to finish the destruction of the barricade.

The broken table exploded into the room with half striking another table and the rest bouncing harmlessly off the wall nearest the door as the wolves outside howled their victory. Beyond the window stood a nightmare.

The Were was massive, standing much taller than the tallest man in Cobble. Its form was stout, powerful, with thick muscles showing beneath the fur on its chest and arms. It stood like a man but its face was definitely wolf-like as long canine teeth dripped drool from its snout. Its eyes reflected the light of the fire but Gran suspected that they glowed red naturally. Its fur was black, and there was again that thin line of light colored fur around its bestial neck. She recognized it as the Were from the field.

Crag froze, his mouth opened to scream but nothing came forth. Tonk and another man made as if to charge but stopped after a single step, the expected sight of more wolves or Quargs replaced by something they had no reason to expect. Only Happ had the presence of mind to act.

"Cobble!" he screamed, pointing his still steaming pike at the Were and rushing forward.

Moving with a grace Gran couldn't believe, the Were slid over the windowsill effortlessly, entering the building before the charging man could even reach him. There it crouched, ready for battle even as its wolf brethren crowded against the window looking to join their master. The spittle continued to drip from its mouth, a thick whitish foam forming there that told Gran the bestial man was not only a Were, but mayhap diseased as well. Little did that bit of information matter; they were not going to live long enough to die from a lingering disease. Gran had a moment to wonder why her carefully placed wolfbane had had no obvious effect on the creature but then she remembered the blood of the wolves wounded and slain in that very window. The blood had washed the wolfbane away and they had never replaced it.

Disdainfully the Were slapped aside the point of Happ's pike, reaching with the other clawed hand for the fat man's throat. The silvered tip, deflected from its target in the Were's chest, instead cut a thin line up the monster's arm from wrist to elbow. Something changed in its eyes as it realized that it could have been killed by this clumsy weapon.

Roaring its anger the Were snapped the pike off near the head with one hand as it slapped Happ with the other. The big man's bulk kept him from falling but he was still stunned. The Were's next blow was a full-bodied punch of its fist to Happ's chest, lifting the massive man into the air to crash against the nearest wall.

Tonk finally found his courage and jumped forward with a yell, only to see his pike snap harmlessly off against the Were's stomach. His blade was not silvered. He didn't understand why it hadn't worked and never had the opportunity to learn as the werewolf ripped out his throat with a simple backhand maneuver. The monster then stalked deliberately towards Crag.

Gran looked around for a weapon, anything with an edge to dip into the silver. All she could find was her discarded frying pan where she had placed it on the mantle. Knowing it would do her no good she grabbed it anyway but never saw the flying body of Crag as it slammed into her, driving her head into the mantle and bringing blackness to cover the screams of the dying town.

●——●

A horn was sounding somewhere to the north as Albrim raced with his father down the single street of Cobble. Houses were burning on the other side of town and the bodies of some of their neighbors lay strewn about, many having been fed upon. Women and children mostly, as many of the fathers had been away on the wolfing. Above, Jacet stood high and proud while Nyret sat fat and full just cresting the horizon. Twice, wolves came for them only to be routed by the flight of arrows from their three bows. The sounds of battle could be heard nearby but the echoes were distorted by the buildings. Albrim gagged from the stench of the smoke, but he kept pace with the others; intent on taking some measure of revenge on the wolves for those killed this night.

The sounds of their boots were drowned out by the blaring horn and the mad howling of the wolves. They reached the carefully laid cobblestones of the square only to see two dozen wolves running away at full speed, rushing towards the north and the blaring horn. Another half dozen remained by the tavern, whining as they circled nervously, as if unsure whether they were to join with their pack or continue with their battle here. From inside the tavern came the screams of women and children as the slaughter of the innocent continued.

Borel slid to one knee; unmindful of the damage the cobblestones were doing to his flesh. He took careful aim by the light of the two full moons and placed an arrow into the side of the nearest wolf. Albrim followed suit, aiming at another wolf. As he took aim Albrim saw Treed's first shot miss high and disappear into the darkness.

At this range it would be difficult to kill a moving wolf with a single arrow but Albrim chose a different target from his Father intentionally. Their purpose now wasn't to kill the wolves but to drive them away, and wolves were unlikely to stay once they had felt the bite of a wound. Within seconds each man had fired three arrows and the wolves were gone, one panting its last near the mangled body of K'Jord while the others fled.

Again came the call of a horn followed by the shrill scream of someone taking a dying blow. Wolves howled and growled in the distance, but for now none were in sight, save those dead or dying around the tavern. Within the tavern, however, the screams were still sounding.

"Inside," ordered Borel, motioning Albrim for the door as he and Treed rushed towards the first floor's only window. Light streamed from the open portal and for the first time Albrim noticed three women and twice that many children on the roof, alternately screaming and jumping up and down or lying prostrate in fear. The flames were close now; he could see their orange tongues licking up above the nearest homes.

Albrim made a quick count of his arrows. He had but three left and nothing larger than a belt knife to protect himself with after that. He knew that he had nothing to fight a Were with at all, but he would do what he had to do. The front door of the tavern was closed so he lowered his shoulder and charged into it, intending to break it down and be upon whatever enemy awaited within before even his father had a chance to fire through the window.

Bouncing hard from the stout door, Albrim very nearly fell down. He did drop his arrow and went to one knee to retrieve it before leaping back to his feet intending to run around the corner to join his father at the window. The screams of the women on the roof alerted him of the approach of another wolf. Leaping back down the porch stairs he turned away from the tavern just in time to see a large wolf bearing down on him. At nearly point blank range he fired, striking the beast directly in the right eye.

Moaning and snarling the beast slowed, turning as if looking for Albrim with his remaining eye. It took another step towards him only to be struck on the snout by a well-aimed shoe.

"A shoe?" Albrim thought, even as he brought the fletching of his latest arrow to his cheek. Just as the wolf recovered from the surprise of the shoe assault, Albrim released his missile, driving it into the wolf's chest until only the feathers were visible. The wolf's legs immediately collapsed and the beast lay there, groaning in pain. It was not dead, but unlikely to last much longer.

Albrim pulled his last arrow from his sheath and turned back towards the tavern. The shouts inside had subsided but not stopped completely. Albrim thought he recognized his father's voice shouting something incomprehensible. Breaking into a run he turned the corner of the building, scanning the street for wolves and seeing none. He did see a few dead ones piled up at the base of the tavern, their blood staining the wooden porch and the rocks of the wall. He was only a step from the window when something came flying out.

Rather, someone was thrown out, Albrim realized as the body landed on the cobblestones. The light of the distant fires were just bright enough to reveal the sightless eyes of Treed staring upward at the night sky.

Notching his last arrow Albrim ran to the window, screaming something even he did not recognize. The bow was at full draw when he arrived, leaving him to scan briefly about for a target. The scene in the room was like something out of a nightmare.

Bodies lay everywhere about the common room of the Bucket of Ale. Most were unrecognizable in the instant Albrim had to take it all in, but he did see Fat Happ moving feebly in one corner, and the crumpled form of his Gran lay near the fireplace. A pair of wolves were worrying something near the foot of the ladder that led to the upper floor, and the color of the dress made Albrim think that it might be that of Ina, one of his Gran's assistants. Three other wolves were among the dead, one with a pair of his father's arrows jutting up from its flank. However the two figures in the middle of the carnage caught and held his attention.

A massive hairy beast of midnight black stood there on the ruins of a table, its fur soaked in blood and chest heaving with exertion. In one hand it casually held Borel by the throat, causing the bowyer's face to turn a deeper and deeper red as he slowly suffocated. The other hand was empty but soaked to the elbow in fresh blood; its claws barred and ready to gut his father. His wordless cry alerted the beast and the werewolf's eyes swung to meet those of Albrim, its canine snout jerking upwards in an approximation of a smile.

To Albrim it seemed that time stopped. An hour must have passed, a year perhaps, as he and the Were stared into one another's eyes. The red-glowing eyes, the white lather of disease frothing at its lips, the feeble struggles of his father whose eyes were bulging from lack of air. Albrim was very much aware of every movement, every sound as if he himself was the room, or as if he himself was each and every person in the room. The snap of his father's neck was not loud, but to Albrim's ears it sounded like a thunderclap.

Still in mid-howl of rage and fear, Albrim was surprised to find himself shifting his aim from the Were that had just murdered his father towards the nearest of the wolves feeding on Ina. Perhaps somewhere in the back of his mind he knew that his single feeble arrow could not hurt the Were and that only by using it on one of the great wolves would it do any good. Perhaps he only thought that killing one of the wolves might cause the werewolf some type of personal pain such as he knew was awaiting him when he had the time to think of his father's death. Perhaps it was simple spite. Whatever the reason Albrim found himself looking down his arrow's shaft at the point just behind the wolf's front shoulder. The exact spot where his father had taught him to place an arrow when shooting at a deer.

The arrow sped away, still in slow motion to Albrim's eyes. It was a perfect shot, punching easily through the wolf's hide and into its powerful heart, dropping the beast as if it had never been alive. Albrim dropped his bow then, intending to draw his knife. The Were gave him no opportunity, closing the distance to the window quickly and grabbing Albrim's left wrist in his massive paw.

Albrim screamed in pain as the wolf clamped down on his arm. With a single move, the boy was snatched through the window and held up for the Were's inspection. The beast looked him over, still smiling its evil smile as the foam gathered to drip from its snout. The only sound now was the steady pounding of Albrim's heart, which was so loud in his ears that it drowned out the distant blares of the horn and the steady plop of the Were's dripping drool.

Albrim knew that he was dead but thought perhaps he could scar the beast, perhaps put out an eye. Finding the haft of his belt knife, Albrim pulled it free and swung wildly at the thing's face only to have the point deflect from the monster's magical hide as if a fly was head-butting a bear. Smiling even more broadly, the Were caught Albrim's other wrist in his free hand, crushing it without effort.

Screaming as he never had before, Albrim passed out from the pain. Almost casually the Were sniffed the limp young man's arm before delicately and deliberately biting it off below the elbow. So engrossed in its meal had it become that the werewolf failed to hear the movement of its next attacker.

Gran staggered to her feet to find herself covered in blood, just as much of the room was. Some of it was hers from her collision with the fireplace; most was not. She staggered to her feet just in time to witness the death of Borel and the subsequent capture of Albrim. She noticed a wolf feeding upon Ina's corpse but the beast ignored her, so she did the same. Gran wanted desperately to strike at this beast that had killed her town, her children, but she still had nothing to use as a weapon save for the frying pan she still found gripped in her hand. With nothing to lose she shoved the pan into the pot of melted silver, finding enough there to coat the bottom of her makeshift weapon. Turning again to the Were, she witnessed the powerful jaws biting into Albrim's arm, and she attacked.

Sir Garen's horse was long dead, as was the plow horse he had commandeered to replace it. One leg broken, he limped on a makeshift crutch down the single street of Cobble, his crutch making a dull thudding sound each time it struck a cobblestone. Behind him came a dozen men, all that were left of his once proud wolfing squad, and beyond them the rising flames of several outlying homes. In his right hand he bore his sword, a minor magical artifact but hopefully enough to drive off any Weres they encountered. The bows of those with him had proven more than a match for wolves, even when they were the size of ponies.

Atop the stone building ahead, which Garen believed was the tavern he had visited a few weeks back, several figures sat dejectedly on the roof. Hopefully the bulk of the local population was hiding within as well. A lot of good people had already died this night and even more in the past days. When he and his men came into their view the roof-sitters leapt to their feet, screaming for joy and urging them to hurry.

"They're still fighting downstairs," one screamed.

"Come on lads," ordered Garen, wishing once again for a horse to speed his movement to the tavern. "This wolfing isn't over just yet."

Growling and roaring the men rushed forward, weapons ready to reap the harvest. A few were Cobble men and they invariably surged to the front, all of them quickly outpacing Sir Garen who cursed at the injury that slowed him. The men closed the distance quickly, urged on by the frightened voices from above.

If the men noticed the change in the shouts from those on the rooftop, they did not slow their charge. Sir Garen did, and looked up to see a plump woman in a red-splattered apron on the roof trying to tell him something while pointing to the far side of the tavern. Seeing a new movement from the corner of his eye, Sir Garen looked back down in time to see another of the massive wolves bound from the tavern window, its muzzle dripping with blood and the fur of its neck and chest stained crimson from its feeding. Its hackles arose, and then it lifted its muzzle and released a long mournful howl at the twin full moons.

The howl was answered immediately. Sir Garen had just enough time to realize what the woman on the roof had been trying to tell him before battle was again joined. Another ten or so massive wolves came around the corner of the tavern in a pack, backed by three times their number of normal wolves.

"Cobble!" screamed a man, who dropped to one knee to release an arrow. Six more flew in quick succession, four striking and two missing completely, those hitting true dropping the lead wolves of the pack. Then the pack was upon them and the bows were dropped. Melee weapons were needed now.

Sir Garen hobbled around the mob of darting wolves and fighting men. He had trailed the others far enough not to be pulled into the initial fighting and wanted to get his back to the stone wall of the tavern and rally the men to him. That was the only way they could keep so many wolves at bay, with the stone behind them and the wolves forced to attack them straight on. Also, something in his guts told him that he needed to see what was happening inside the tavern itself.

Throwing down his crutch, Sir Garen hopped three steps on his good leg and took a wild swing at a passing wolf. Catching it from behind, he dealt it a solid blow across its back with his sword, sending it howling off into the darkness. Nearly losing his balance from the impact, Garen hurriedly hopped up the two steps to the wooden porch that surrounded the tavern on all sides and threw his shoulder into the stones of the wall to keep from falling. Looking back on the battle he saw that his men were holding their own for the moment so he slid down a few feet to the lone window. Leaning to his right he tried to look inside without showing himself any more than necessary, and looked upon a room literally bathed in blood. The battle was finished in there and a massive black Were stood supreme.

Looking back just in time to see that a large wolf was running towards him, Sir Garen swung his sword desperately at the beast's muzzle and caused it to pull up just short of the porch, then a child's shoe followed by a chamber pot filled with night waste struck it in quick succession. Growling, the beast sidestepped, its ears lying back as it tried to find its new attackers. Garen hopped forward, swinging and missing as the beast ducked back. With that the wolves broke as if on command, the survivors turning and fleeing towards the south.

Sir Garen rallied the men, calling for them to gather around him. Only he had a weapon that could harm the Were as it carried a slight enchantment but he knew that he would need the other men to keep the beast busy while he delivered the killing blow. Only six responded to his command, the others lying dead or wounded on the cobblestones.

Garen gathered the able men to his left along the stone wall, whispering instructions of how he wanted to handle the battle. A steady rhythm of thumps began inside the building, piquing Sir Garen's interest. What could the Were be doing? The thumps sounded hollow, as if someone were plying a hammer. Three thumps, pause. Three thumps, pause. As steady as if someone was beating upon a drum. Above the thumps came a long heart-shuddering howl that weakened the knees and perhaps the bladder as well. Perhaps this was a werewolf song of victory? A song of bloodlust temporarily sated? Nothing made sense to him but Garen decided that whatever the Were was up to, it did not matter to him. Only its death did.

His plans ready, Sir Garen motioned the men into movement and then led the way, hopping to the window with his family's battle cry on his lips. And there he paused, his battle cry drifting away to silence in disbelief.

Gran gripped her frying pan firmly in one hand and, almost as an afterthought, turned and dipped it into the melted silver. On another impulse, she scooped up a potholder and took the pot of silver with her as well. She staggered a little as she hurried to the Were's back, as she was still a little dizzy from her head wound, but the sight of young Albrim hanging helplessly as the Were chewed on the boy's arm was plenty of inspiration for her to remain upright. With a silent curse she lifted her frying pan and brought it firmly down upon the back of the beast's head.

To her utter disbelief the Were staggered from the blow, dropping Albrim to the bloody floor. The beast turned towards its attacker but then felt the pain as hot melted silver dripped down the back of its head. The howl it let at that point was enough to freeze a mortal's bones. Any mortal besides the outraged Gran.

She flew into the monster with a will, pounding it over and over with her silvered frying pan. When the beast covered its head, Gran switched to another area, occasionally dipping her pan in the still molten silver. As she beat the creature, she told it why, naming each blow with that of one of her friends and neighbors killed this night. She shrieked, she cursed, she beat the Were for every sin she could think of including things it could not have been guilty of. She hammered it until its howls of pain and disbelief were heart-rending to anyone not aware of the thing's evil nature. It staggered and fell more than once as it tried to flee the enraged old woman, but it could not escape her in the common room of the Bucket of Ale. Teeth rained from the Were's muzzle and anywhere the molten silver touched the beast, a faint eldritch flame arose, visible only to those with some magical training. When the silver seemed to be beginning to harden, Gran dumped the bucket onto the Were's back before returning to her beating.

Finally the incredible pain forced the Were to give in to its wolfish nature and it lost all ability to reason. Taking a last series of blows the creature launched itself at the window, its only thought to escape. The faces of seven stunned men stood waiting for it there but it cared not. Only fleeing the woman with the frying pan mattered.

Sir Garen was not a warrior experienced in actual combat, but he had had years of martial training that allowed him to react quickly now that he was faced with a real battle. While the other men instinctively leaped back from the Were, the young knight braced himself on his good leg and drove the point of his sword into the beast's chest. In retrospect it had been easy, too easy, as the Were had basically driven the blade home on its own. Snarling in pain the Were fell across the window sill, allowing the screaming woman a few more blows to its head before Sir Garen found the presence of mind to chop into the thing's neck.

The Were found one more burst of energy and pulled itself out of the window, tumbling to the porch where it lay on its back among the dead bodies of the wolves that had fallen earlier. Gran leaned from the window, still swinging her frying pan and screeching but her arms were too short to do further damage to the Were. Sir Garen had to dodge the occasional backswing as he drove his sword repeatedly into the Were's chest. He could have sworn that the beast looked grateful to him as it died.

Sir Garen dispatched the remaining militia to care for the wounded and to stand guard. He slumped back against the wall and sat down near the Were with only the blood-covered old woman leaning out the window for company. They watched in near silence, the gasps of Gran the only sounds between them, as the Were slowly changed. From its bestial humanoid form, it gradually faded into that of a normal human. A man unremarkable save for the length of his long black hair. The thin line of lighter fur about the Were's neck became a medallion on a golden chain. He was a stranger to both, though neither bothered to say it.

Chapter Seven

Over the next two weeks more of the wounded died than survived their injuries, which was likely a blessing considering the number of sick wolves found among the slain. The population of Cobble was devastated by the wolf attacks, leaving it better off only than Hemlet which had been destroyed completely. Gran worked each day over the wounded until she collapsed from her exertions but still the old woman was up early the next morning, giving commands and expecting them to be obeyed as always. Fat Happ was on his feet within days and was appointed the acting Reeve until Yogarn regained his health. Many of the wounded were up rather quickly, all things considered.

Albrim was the exception. He lapsed into a deep fever and suffered dreadfully, not regaining consciousness for several days. Despite her heavy workload, Gran was always within sight when he did awake, there to sooth him with cool water and soft threats over letting the cabbages go so long without weeding. Even through his fever he would smile at the jest before again fading away.

Gran made it known that her grandson had the 'phobee, a nasty disease that caused those bitten by a carrier to foam at the mouth and die screaming with convulsions. Few, if any, were said to survive. No one ever had, to anyone in Cobble's knowledge. Albrim's right arm was missing just below the elbow and Gran did her best to keep the stub clean despite the 'phobee, causing many in the town to smile sadly at her efforts. Keeping the arm free from infection was useless when it was clear the boy would die of the disease.

Sir Garen, nominally in charge from the cot he had placed on the porch of the Bucket of Ale, allowed Gran to set his broken leg. This she did cleanly and efficiently, leaving the knight unconscious for several hours afterward. Someone asked her if she could have accomplished the same thing without causing the man such pain.

"Yes," was her only reply. Gran faithfully believed that pain was a good way to build character and that the nobility needed all the character they could get.

The morning of the third day Gran was summoned to Sir Garen's cot. There she was graciously thanked by the knight for her efforts in the battle against the Were and her tireless work with the wounded since. For his thanks the knight received a sound tongue-lashing and learned at least one new curse word. Gran didn't need his thanks for doing what was right.

The abashed knight asked her about the wounded.

"The ones that have lived up to now will survive, for the most part," she grumped, helping herself to a seat on the edge of the man's cot, bumping the man's broken leg accidentally as she did so.

Sir Garen didn't make a sound but his face turned ashen from the pain. "And what of your grandson?" he managed through gritted teeth.

"He's going to be fine," Gran stated, the light in her eyes rigid and unyielding as she glared at the knight, daring him to say different. "The arm will heal and the fever will pass!"

Garen dropped the subject. Others who had been to see the boy had told him differently.

"And of our good Reeve, Master Yogarn?"

Gran snorted. "He's old and suffering from a bad heart more than the bite. He'll live, like as not."

"That is wonderful news."

Another snort. "His house has been burned to the ground, his wife killed. He'll be naught but a burden to me for at least a year along with everyone else in this town."

Sir Garen eased his injured leg from the old woman's vicinity. Just in case.

"And we are certain that no one was bitten by the Were?" he asked softly, unconsciously sliding a hand down to his injured thigh.

"No one that didn't die. The closest to him was myself and Fat Happ, and he didn't do anything but fall down after a punch. The Curse died with him, young knight. Of that you can be certain."

Gran's voice was straight and true. She would never be caught in a lie, not by any indications in her voice or mannerisms at least. And certainly not by any young pup of a knight!

Nodding acceptingly Garen asked, "What of the Were? I know that the body was burned. Did anyone recognize him?"

"No, he was a stranger to all and I'm not surprised. There's been no Weres around Aldragal for fifty years or more."

"And what of this?" Garen asked, pulling the medallion from his pocket. "You are very wise and experienced; do these markings mean anything to you?"

Gran snatched the medallion from his hand, pretending to study the markings even though she had made sure to memorize them the night the Were was killed.

"They mean nothing to me, other than this thing that looks like a tree. I don't read 'squiggle' so whatever these words are remain a mystery to me," she declared.

"I thank you for the report. Now I have some information to share with you," he said, rising to one elbow. "The rider I sent to my father has returned. He is sending a company of horsemen here to protect the villages until the militia can be rearmed."

Gran looked away in disgust. Rearmed meant bringing in more settlers. Even if you counted Fat Happ among the militia along with Yogarn and Albrim, they only had five surviving members. That meant only two healthy men and one of them, Vert, only a boy.

"Isn't it clear to your father that this area isn't ready for settlement yet? One village completely destroyed, Cobble all but wiped out. Hunters and woodsmen missing for miles around? I told your father when he sent us here that we weren't ready and just look!"

Sir Garen ignored the outburst. His father had said that the 'crazy old coot, Gran' had actually been supportive of the relocation of the peasants. His father had described her perfectly.

"I have also heard from the scouts; the wolves have left the area. If there were other Weres about, they have lost control of their packs. Likely the one we killed was the only one involved."

Gran sniffed. "Not sure what you had to do with it, but fine."

Garen smiled in spite of himself. "What of the red-haired stranger you found. Did he survive?"

"No, he did not. The wolves ate him as he lay on his sickbed in the back room of the tavern," Gran replied. "One of the fellows from Hemlet said he was from there. Like as not he came here to escape the destruction of his village."

Garen waited a long moment out of respect for the dead.

"I'll be leaving here as soon as the horsemen arrive. I know that I can count on your helping Reeve Happ with the reconstruction of the town."

"You'll be counting on me to keep us all from starving to death this winter, too, like as not! That man hasn't done a hard day's work in his life and you aren't fit to travel, not for another week," Gran said, spitting into the street for emphasis. Her sudden movements shook the cot, sending another bolt of agony up the young knight's leg.

"I must go, Gran. Duty demands it," he breathed.

Gran stood up to go, her walking stick accidentally bumping the cot as she did, bringing a grunt from Garen.

"I'm sorry for your grandson," Sir Garen said to the woman's retreating back.

Gran spun about, her eyes wild and her walking stick pointed at the knight. "He's going to be fine, you young pup, and you mark my words! My Albrim will be up and about and hoeing my cabbages within a week, like as not!" she shouted before stalking away on her rounds.

Three days passed and Sir Garen left, riding in the back of a wagon to return to his father's estates, convinced that he would have died under the care of that crazy old woman.

Which was exactly what Gran wanted. Her plans depended on removing the sharp eyes of Sir Garen from Cobble. It was Albrim's only chance for survival. Three weeks to the day after the great battle, the wailing of a soul in torment woke the townsfolk.

"Law, what could it be?" asked one widow of another. The two carefully peeked through the log walls of Borel's home where the harsh spring rains had worried holes in the chinks of mud. There they saw Gran lying across Albrim's still form, wailing as if her last hope had gone.

"The poor old dear," one woman said. "That's her last living blood, gone forever!"

"At least we still have our young ones," whispered the other. "Who'll care for old Gran when the snow flies?"

"Who'll care for us when we ail?" replied the first. "Mertie and Ina have both gone to their reward as well."

"And me due with child in the fall."

What remained of the town brought food and spirits to share with the grieving old woman but she would have none of it, throwing things after them once she had ran them off with her switch.

"Me and mine don't need the likes of you!" she would shriek. The next morning she ordered Vert and Tomo, who had yet to return to his own home, to come to her home. They carried out Albrim's body in plain view of everyone as Gran wailed over the necessity of burning the boy's body rather than burying it properly in the cemetery of the town he had defended with his life.

"When you die of the 'phobee, that's the way it has to be done," the widows all agreed, repeating information given them by Gran herself only the week before. No one had reason to believe differently.

The funeral procession faded into the forest with an old pony pulling the litter bearing the body of Albrim. Tomo led the beast while Vert and Gran walked at his feet to honor him. Gran wailed anew at every step. An hour into the woods Gran stopped and sat upon a convenient stump.

"Vert, get that ax and find me some dry wood," she said, pulling a water skin from beneath her shawl and taking a long pull.

"Yes Gran," he said, gently lifting the blanket aside and removing the ax from its place next to Albrim. It was then he noticed the two leather sacks nestled near his friend's feet.

"Gran, what's in these bags?"

"Never you mind, boy, just cut me that wood!"

Tomo came back to Gran and eased into a squat beside her. He knew Gran well from his boyhood.

"Gran are we doing the right thing?" he asked.

Gran offered Tomo the water skin. "We are. The boy would have no chance at life in Cobble. We couldn't control him for long and when folks found out they would kill him, like as not. His only chance is to get help."

Tomo grimaced. "But who can help him? He's got the Curse, Gran."

Gran stood back up. "There are those who can, Tomo. Trust me on that. Now come over here and grab onto this for an old woman."

Tomo obediently removed the larger of the two packs from the litter, setting it down with a dull clunk against a tree.

"What's in that, Gran?"

"Bones, Tomo. Pig bones. People will expect me to bring back the boy's ashes, won't they? There are always a few bits of bone left over. No one will know the difference, like as not."

Tomo smiled. "You're a wonder, Gran," he said.

After seeing that Albrim was covered again and made comfortable, Tomo spoke again.

"Well Gran, I suppose I should get moving. I have a long way to go, at least three days, dragging this litter."

"Like as not," Gran agreed, patting Tomo on the cheek.

"Gran? Can you trust young Vert not to speak of this?"

Gran allowed a brief look of concern to pass her weathered features. "I believe so. He'll be under my eye, worry yourself not about that. I'll see to him, you just keep out of your cups or it'll be you that lets it slip! And if you do, I'll see to you!"

Tomo laughed outright. "I believe you, Gran. I really do."

He started to leave but hesitated, looking back at the old woman.

"Gran, are you sure we're taking him to the right place?"

"You just take him to where I said and leave him. Keep the pony and go home to your family and get them ready to move back here. He'll be fine. Someone will see to him."

Tomo nodded and led the pony away. Gran returned to her stump and watched her grandson disappear into the forest. This time the tears she shed were real.

Chapter Eight

When water was held to his lips, Albrim drank. When broth was spooned into his mouth, he ate. Occasionally the befouled leaves beneath him were changed but he didn't notice, wandering as he was in a land of fevered dreams.

Weres were there in his dreams. Weres in abundance and each thirsty for a taste of his blood. Fits of terrible rage frequently overcame him and unbelievable pain often coursed through his right arm. He never knew what it was he angered about but the pain had always to do with an attack by his dream phantoms. Above all in his dreams, both moons shown full and forever overhead. He discovered that he was drawn to the moons and found himself singing to them. Sometimes they were not moons, but beautiful women who came and sat by him. Softly glowing and alluring, hinting at promises kept and dreams fulfilled. Time passed, but Albrim was unaware of it, moving from one dream to the next without noticing their similarities.

And then they stopped.

Albrim knew that time had passed now. He did not awake expecting to see the black Were holding him by the arms like a child, nor did he expect to see Gran sitting peacefully by his bedside. Gran had sent him away. He was unsure how he knew, but he did. He even knew why.

He was Cursed.

Where was he? Gran had sent him away, but to where? Had she told him or had the fever wiped that memory away? He recognized nothing. Above him was a tangle of roots and beneath him was a pile of leaves. Had he been buried alive? No, he could see daylight between his feet. A clearing of some sort amid tall timber, he thought. The sound of running water seemed close. The ceiling of roots was too low for him to sit up, not that he had the strength anyway.

With a start he remembered his arm and the Were's powerful bite. Looking down he saw what he fully expected to see. What he had feared to see. His arm was gone.

Albrim cried then, great heaves of self-pity and loathing. He remembered that fateful night one scene at a time; his Gran lying motionless on the floor, his father dying. Other things he hadn't even consciously noticed at the time, such as Fat Happ lying against one wall and the vacant stare of Mertie's lifeless corpse, flooded back to him. He cried for hours, days perhaps. Sometimes he faded into unconsciousness only to regain his senses and find himself still crying. A long time passed this way, but then things changed again.

His self-pity was interrupted by a stiff kick to the bottom of his feet. The message had been clear; shut up. Albrim tried to sit up again, did the ceiling look higher now than it had? Either way he didn't make it, falling back weakly causing the stump of his arm to ache. Slightly dizzy from his exertions, he fell asleep again.

When next he awoke a simple wooden plate rested near his head, a small pile of brown mush heaped upon it. It smelled good but the first handful he managed to slide into his mouth was cold. It might have been a tuber of some kind. He'd seen boiled tubers served to Lord Ferule when the nobleman had visited Cobble. The flavor was bland but apparently that was a good thing as his stomach threatened to revolt and failed. He ate all of the mush and drank from a water skin that hung from a root above his head before sleeping again.

Three times Albrim slept and each time food and water was waiting for him when he regained consciousness. When he awoke the fourth time it was night outside and the sounds of insects were loud in his ears. A rumbling sound as of distant thunder made him think that rain might be on the way. He decided that he felt good enough to climb from his burrow of roots and see what he could see, but another plate of food, more tubers and a few small strips of some type of meat, diverted his attention. The tubers were seasoned with salt and the food was still warm from the fire, so Albrim made short work of it. He was certain that it was the best food he'd ever eaten. After another long pull from the water skin he found himself too sleepy to continue his explorations and so he lay back against the rolled fur under his head and slept again.

The next time he awoke, it was at the insistence of someone's boot. Again he was being kicked, this time not so gently as before. Someone wanted his attention. Albrim tried to speak; to ask that he not be kicked perhaps, or to demand to be left alone to die, but nothing came from his mouth but a dry crackle. He grabbed at the water skin; again forgetting and reaching with his missing right arm first. Once he had it, he drained it, clearing his throat sufficiently for speech.

"I'm awake," he said, amazed at how weak he sounded. How long had he been unconscious?

The boots kicked him again. This time Albrim noticed that they were very big boots. Much bigger than his bare feet.

He tried to pull his feet back to avoid the next kick so his visitor knelt down and a pair of powerful hands grabbed him by the ankles and easily pulled him out of his shelter. The loose cotton nightshirt he wore bunched up at the base of his back leaving him naked and exposed. However that became the least of his worries when he saw who had been kicking him.

Unsure what to expect of his benefactor, Albrim couldn't help but be surprised. The man was human, perhaps, but unlike anyone he could remember ever seeing. To say he was large was an understatement, for the man was much taller even than Borel had been. His head looked to be as large as a pumpkin and had the weathered, leathery appearance that farmers acquire after years in the sun. Despite the obvious differences from what Albrim thought of as 'normal people,' the man also looked somewhat familiar.

The man was dressed in buckskins with full-length sleeves and wore a hat and scarf of matching mok fur despite the warmth of the morning. His hair was almost completely hidden beneath the hat but a few stray locks indicated that the color might be close to Albrim's own brown. Knuckles and thick wrists boasted a covering of black hair and the man's feet were shod in coarse leather boots that looked to be made from untreated hides. He even smelled odd; with a thick earthy odor that brought to Albrim's mind the smell of a freshly opened carcass combined with loam and the scent of a forest breeze. A series of scars across the man's right cheek led downward to the scarf, which concealed the man's neck up to the chin. Another, thicker scar ran from the center of his forehead along the bridge of his nose. Albrim decided that this was easily the ugliest man he had ever seen.

Still in his crouch the man pulled Albrim a few more inches and then waved for him to stand. Albrim felt like a child next to this person and, remembering the ease with which he had been pulled from the shelter, he tried to obey; putting out one hand to lever himself to a sitting position. In doing so he promptly struck his severed arm against the ground, having forgotten once again that the hand was no longer there.

Cursing at the pain Albrim rocked, clutching his stub with his remaining hand as the tears once again flowed. The big man looked on impassively, never once showing even a hint of compassion on his disfigured face. When Albrim had wept long enough, the man slapped the boy lightly on the leg. When Albrim refused to look up from his pity, the man slapped him again, much harder.

His attention won by the tingle in his thigh, Albrim looked up at the man who again waved him to his feet. Rolling to his left this time, he managed to get up onto his elbow. From there he had to pause and think about how to accomplish such an ordinary task as getting up from the ground without the use of one hand. He finally chose to roll onto his face and push up with his good arm, holding his stub out protectively from any possible contact with the earth. This time he made it as far as his knees but there he stopped, his legs and arm shaking with the effort.

With a grunt from deep in his chest the man slapped Albrim lightly on one hip, indicating that he should lie back down. Albrim complied gratefully, collapsing again to his face and then rolling over. His breath was ragged and his chest heaved from the effort. He was so weak! How long had he been sick?

"My name is Albrim," he gasped, desperately realizing how long it had been since he had last heard someone's voice. His own voice, for that matter.

The man did not answer, simply resting in his crouching position, practically sitting on his own heels. He seemed to look on Albrim approvingly; as if he had completed a difficult task to exacting specifications.

"What is your name?" Albrim asked.

Albrim was ignored as the man turned away from him and picked up something from the ground behind him. When he came about again, Albrim saw the familiar wooden plate from previous meals with another water skin. Drops of water condensing on the sides indicated that it was full of fresh water. The plate was again filled with a pile of the cooked tubers. This time they were nearly whole rather than crushed and steam arose along with a wonderful aroma. His stomach growled at his delay at eating so he left his questioning and ate, cleaning the plate and draining most of the water before he felt sated. Throughout his meal the big man simply squatted at his feet, watching him from beneath his bushy brows.

"Thank you," Albrim said when he had finished. Again he was ignored.

"My name is Albrim," he tried once again. All he received in return was another flat stare.

Albrim felt himself growing unbearably sleepy once again. Had the food been drugged? Or was it simply that he remained weak from his injuries. He knew not, but his eyelids grew too heavy to hold open. So he slept.

He awoke inside his shelter. Once again he was awakened by the large man kicking him in the feet. This time he managed to crawl out on his own, but the effort cost him dearly. The food was different this time; some type of gruel in a wooden bowl with a fist-sized chunk of gritty bread. He ate it all and drank another skin of water. It was then that he noticed another bodily need. The man helped him to his feet for a brief few moments. Albrim's head swam from the effort but he managed to make his water without aid. Then he slept again.

A week went by in this manner, with each instance of his awakening finding Albrim managing to stay awake a little longer, do a little more. By the seventh day he was able to walk around the camp twice without aid. He even began waking at times between meals and would lay awake for a few minutes thinking about his situation and what he had seen around his shelter.

That they were in the deep forest was apparent. In no direction could he see anything but trees. Thick boles with layers of dark green moss and long vines draped from one to another filled his sight beyond his tiny clearing. No paths led in or out but one end sloped steeply down to a tiny stream of startlingly cold water. His shelter was made from the base of a fallen tree, the knot of roots at the base pulled slightly from the ground leaving an opening just large enough for him. His host, for that was how Albrim had begun to think of the big man, would never be able to fit inside. He would have to hang out from the knees down at least.

By the end of the second week, Albrim found himself able to move about completely without aid. His host no longer waited on him at all and stopped preparing his meals for him. Albrim was expected to cook whatever the big man brought to the clearing for both of them and then clean up afterwards. Albrim didn't necessarily mind but he would have like to have been asked. The man had never spoken a single word to him other than an occasional grunt, but still managed to make himself understood. Albrim cooked for them both or he didn't eat.

At times the food brought was tubers and other plant material from the forest, most of which Albrim couldn't even identify, much less know how to cook properly, and some days it was the carcass of a deer or smaller animal. Most of the meat would be smoked or salted for storage in an underground cellar there in the clearing. Albrim would never have found it if his host had not showed it to him.

When his chores were completed he was forced to exercise, running about the clearing when he felt good and lifting a large stone when he was able. His strength returned a little more each day and soon he began to feel more like his old self again. His silent benefactor must have noticed.

A morning dawned when Albrim almost felt like himself, except for the lingering pain from his arm and the perpetual depression he carried in his heart. He was alert immediately upon opening his eyelids and knew without looking that he was about to be kicked in the feet. Today Albrim would begin to run around the camp and in a few days he would leave the clearing and find his way home. Whatever purpose the big man had for keeping him here, Albrim didn't know. He also had no interest in the matter. He was grateful to the man for keeping him alive, but he was better now, and able to move on. However, he wasn't entirely sure that he would be allowed to go. Was he a slave now? Had he been bought and paid for? Had Gran sold him to keep him alive? What of the Curse? Had he avoided it? Whatever the answers to his many questions, Albrim decided that he would have to run away from the clearing, just in case. When he had his answers, maybe he would return to find the big man and thank him properly.

Right on schedule, the boot made contact with one heel and he obediently crawled from his shelter. His host stood waiting expectantly and so Albrim stood and made to go around the man, heading to the fire pit to fix the morning meal. No more than three steps into his short journey he felt the tap of a finger on his shoulder. He turned to face the big man just in time to see the fist coming in.

Blackness.

Albrim awoke lying in the middle of the clearing. The sun stood tall above him in the little bit of sky visible through the closely growing trees. His jaw ached as did the back of his head. What had happened? Why had the big man struck him? Had he done something wrong?

It took Albrim several long moments to clear his head, but he used them wisely to consider his every recent action. He had done nothing to deserve a beating; having cooked the meals and fetched water when needed. He had exercised when told to and slept in his shelter. There was nothing that he did that could have caused the big man to become enraged at him.

With a groan, Albrim sat up. A dull 'clank' followed his movements as he rolled over and pushed himself up. Something felt odd, different. Where had the sound come from? Albrim answered his own question as he sat, for neatly fitted to each of his ankles was a band of metal attached to one other by a length of chain.

He was a slave! The big man knew that he was getting stronger and suspected that he would run away, so he had been shackled to prevent it!

Livid with anger Albrim looked around the clearing, at first seeing nothing, but then catching sight of his 'master' standing motionless among the brush along the edge.

"Let me go," Albrim screamed at the man, adding several choice curses that would have made even Gran proud.

The man said nothing; Albrim was beginning to suspect that he couldn't speak. The man turned away and in moments returned with the carcass of a turkey, which he dropped at Albrim's feet.

"I'm not cooking for you, you monster," Albrim stated through gritted teeth. Again his words were ignored as the big man left the clearing, making no sound whatsoever as he passed through the brush. Albrim screamed after him, picking up the turkey and flinging it towards the brush before crawling back into his shelter. There he lay, crying at the injustices of life.

His father was dead, his arm was gone, he was likely Cursed, his home and everyone he knew was perhaps lost to him forever and above all other things, he was now a slave, shackled like an animal and forced to live like one, too. Somewhere during his pity he fell asleep, dreaming again of being in a horrible, killing rage.

Had he slept for an hour? Probably not, but he was certainly awake now. The big man had returned and pulled him from his shelter by the ankles, this time pulling him completely out and holding him off the ground by the chain that connected his shackles. The big man carried him only a short distance and then Albrim was dumped to the ground next to the turkey's carcass. Another clear signal.

"I won't cook for you," Albrim snarled.

The man picked up the turkey and dropped it in Albrim's lap.

Albrim threw the turkey away. "I said I won't cook for you! I'm not a slave!"

The big man shrugged and went after the turkey. Quickly and efficiently he removed the feathers, the head, and the feet. Next he gutted and expertly spitted it. When his fire was going he roasted the bird, all the while Albrim sat watching him suspiciously. Why had the man given up so easily to his slave?

Once the turkey was finished the big man took a small pouch, one of many, from his pack and sprinkled something from it onto the bird. The smell that arose only enhanced the delicate aroma of the roasting turkey and left Albrim's stomach complaining loudly as his mouth watered. However, when he made as if to approach the fire, the big man raised a hand as if to strike him. Even a casual blow from those massive hands could damage him, Albrim knew. Getting the message loud and clear, he returned to his seat and watched as the turkey was largely devoured. The remains were buried as he sat there.

Apparently he wasn't going to be eating this day. Albrim decided that he may as well sleep. At least the hunger pangs would be more easily ignored. Getting slowly to his feet, he didn't want to move too quickly and startle the big man into thinking that he was being attacked; Albrim shuffled the few steps to his shelter and dropped to his knees. No sooner had his head entered the shelter than a thick hand closed onto the back of his neck and he was jerked back out.

It was amazing how easily the big man could make himself understood without uttering a single word. If Albrim would not cook, he would not eat. Furthermore he would not be allowed to sleep in the shelter. In fact he was not allowed to move out of a small area once his master drove a wooden stake through a length of his chain. There he lay the rest of that day and then shivered through the night, including an early morning dew. Albrim wouldn't have thought it would be so cool; it was almost summer! He must be higher in the foothills of the mountains than he thought.

Albrim made the morning meal without even being asked. That night he was allowed back in his shelter.

Life wearing the shackles became a serious bore for the youthful Albrim. Now fully recovered from his injuries, although his arm continued to ache more often than not, he found himself with nothing to do between meals save for exercise. The act of repeatedly shuffling around the campsite quickly grew tiresome. He tried to explain his thoughts to his master but the big man just ignored him.

One night Albrim awoke well after the mid point, shivering from the cool breeze that blew directly into his shelter. He glanced outside, half-expecting to see snow in his half-asleep state. There in the clearing stood his master, staring up into the sky.

Albrim struggled to turn around in the tiny shelter, afraid to make any small sounds that might give him away. His master was a very mysterious person who wasn't helped at all by the fact that he either couldn't or wouldn't speak. Anything the man was doing in the dark of night might be something he didn't want Albrim to see, so naturally Albrim needed to see it. Once in position, he peeked out of the shelter to see the big man standing with hands on hips, looking up at a nearly full moon.

Was he a moon worshiper? Albrim had heard of such people but didn't know any. His own religious beliefs were almost non-existent. Naturally he had attended the once monthly services conducted by the priest who traveled about seeing to the religious needs of the widespread villages of the forest, but he hadn't bothered to really listen. His interest had been solely in the various young ladies that always came to town on those days. Gran's religious beliefs were closely held secrets. She always said that the priest "meant well, like as not, but was a durn fool anyway."

Albrim missed his Gran. He wondered who she was switching without him around. Looking back at the moon, Nyret, he saw, he found himself staring at it in fascination. What a wonder it was! It was like he had never really looked at it before.

His slumber that night was filled with dreams of the moons. They would rise into the sky and he would sing to them. They were beautiful, thrilling. They made him feel wonderful just to look upon them! When morning came he was only half-in his shelter and the cotton nightshirt that still remained his only clothing was muddy from the brief rain that had fallen. All through the morning meal, Albrim felt that his master was looking at him differently.

That night things changed again. Albrim was not allowed to retire to his shelter. Wary of the change in routine he did as his master wished and lay upon a smooth flat rock that sat at the end of the clearing furthest from the stream. Once the man had stared at him for a moment or two he gave a nod and allowed Albrim to get up. Then the younger man watched as his master drove five metal spikes into the rock and attached five thick rings of shiny steel to them. Was his master a blacksmith? He certainly was handy with tools.

When the task was complete darkness had almost fallen. With a grunt the big man indicated that Albrim was to lie down atop the rock. Was he to be a sacrifice? Tonight may be the time of the full moon, a time when moon worshipers might be required to sacrifice something. Or someone. Albrim was frightened. Had he been nursed back to health just so he could be killed in some ritual?

Running was impossible, but Albrim tried, tripping over his leg shackles within a dozen steps. He was dragged to his feet and pulled towards the rock, kicking and screaming at every step. Finally the big man grew annoyed and struck Albrim, dropping him back into the depths of unconsciousness.

Albrim's dreams that night were nothing but nightmares. His anger was unbelievable, he hated everything. His father, his Gran, himself, all felt the burning hate that welled up from his soul. In his dreams he killed everyone who had ever done anything against him, even dredging up the memories of children he had played with as a small child. People he hadn't seen in years. All of them died at his hands until only his master, his captor, remained above his wrath. In his dreams he pursued the man, attacking him again and again but always the man slipped away, somehow keeping Albrim at bay no matter how hard he tried.

When morning finally came Albrim awoke exhausted, as if he hadn't slept at all. He realized that could have been the case because he had apparently spent the night strapped down to the flat rock. Thick leather belts bound his legs, his good arm, and one across his waste. Everywhere the straps had been the skin was red and raw, as was his throat. He could not move until his master finally released him. Albrim took solace in the fact that the man looked as if he had not slept well either.

For two weeks the pattern held. Each night Albrim was strapped to the rock to sleep. Each morning he was allowed to continue his normal duties. After two weeks he was allowed to return to his shelter. He still had no idea why he had been punished.

Chapter Nine

The hottest months of summer came and Albrim no longer had to worry about being chilled at night. Now he perspired constantly and relished the chance to sit in the icy stream. His duties had expanded. Not only was he expected to cook the food, he was also expected to wash his master's clothes and even mend them on occasion. He found that he had little skill with a needle.

Part of every day was spent running. His shackles were removed and Albrim was even allowed to run along nearby game trails with the big man trotting wordlessly along at his heels. These brief expeditions helped him regain his stamina and built the strength of his legs. They also convinced him that he had no idea where he was.

His boredom remained but he ceased to care. His days were spent sullenly doing exactly what he must in order to be fed; never doing one thing more. His depression seemed to deepen with each passing day as he continued to contemplate living without his arm, without his father. Why had his Gran turned him away when he needed her? It was obvious to him by now that he had the Curse. He himself was a Were. That was why he had to be chained down every full moon.

Albrim knew now that he was not a slave. He was a prisoner here, a prisoner to the big man and a prisoner to the Curse. Never would he be allowed to leave here. Not alive at least. That was beginning to sound like an acceptable alternative.

The desire to speak was eating away at Albrim, along with all his other troubles, but each time he tried to start a conversation he was either ignored or the big man simply left. He tried talking to himself but felt like a fool. He wanted to know what was going on. He needed to know and only the big man was around for him to ask. A man that couldn't or wouldn't talk. Perhaps he simply didn't speak Albrim's language? The relationship between Albrim and the mysterious man had changed little until one evening as they sat up late around the cook fire.

"I can't just not talk," Albrim exclaimed, receiving another flat stare in return.

"Can you understand what I say? Do we speak the same language?" again the stare.

Albrim was frustrated. "Can you talk at all? Can you speak?" he demanded.

For a long moment the two men simply stared at one another. Just as Albrim was about to drop the subject, the man suddenly reached for his scarf. Never before had he removed it in Albrim's presence, but now he did;

carefully unwrapping it for the briefest of moments before quickly replacing it.

Albrim's nightmares that night were of what he saw beneath the scarf. At least now he knew that the big man could understand him. He also knew that the man would never be able to talk.

What could have caused such unbelievable scars? How could anyone survive such a wound? The skin was raw and red, appearing nearly devoid of flesh yet the man was undeniably alive. He ate, he slept, though apparently very little. Occasionally he bathed on a truly hot day. He lived, after a fashion, here in the deep forest, perhaps by choice and perhaps not. Either way, he was the only company Albrim had. The following day he tried speaking to the big man again.

"Look, I know you can't talk but you can understand me. I know you've lived out here in the forest a long time and maybe you don't need to hear me talk, but I do! I need to be able to talk once in a while or I'll go crazy!"

Albrim paused, watching to see if he had earned himself another beating. Seeing something that might have been resigned acceptance in the big woodsman's eyes, he went a little further.

"Also I need to know your name. I know you can't talk, but can you write?"

The big man looked down at his feet and chose a stick from the edge of the fire, tossing it back into the blaze. Albrim took that as a 'no'.

"I need to call you something. What do you want me to call you?"

This time the woodsmen met Albrim's gaze squarely and then shrugged with one shoulder. He didn't care? He didn't know? Perhaps he didn't have a name. Albrim laughed at himself. Of course he had a name, even if he couldn't share it with him.

"Well I guess I can give you a name until I find out your real one."

Another shrug. Albrim again took that as acceptance. He also decided that this must be their longest conversation ever and he had not been kicked in the feet even once.

"Well, you are big. I guess you're what they call a 'mute'... the big man's head snapped up. Did that please him?"

"You want me to call you Mute?"

A single nod. What an impressive conversation.

"Fine, from now on, until I find out something else, your name is Mute."

Summer's heat made way for the vibrant colors of autumn with little in the way of change within the tiny clearing. The water of the creek remained ice cold and Albrim's simple cotton shirt was exchanged for a new one twice but they all looked the same. Albrim's sparse beard had grown in as much as it seemed able to and his routine remained the same. Only their diet varied and that but slightly, as the tubers apparently passed out of season to be replaced by berries and then hardier fruit such as apples and pears. Two weeks out of each month Albrim slept strapped to his rock only now he didn't fight with Mute over the necessity. He now recognized the need.

Boredom fought with depression to rule Albrim's days. He often sulked over his missing arm and cursed soundly when he found himself unable to do even the simplest tasks. There were occasional small victories, such as learning to tie the laces of his shoes with one hand, once he was allowed to wear shoes again. Then one day a new twist was added, one that Albrim was not the least bit enthusiastic about.

Mute stalked into the camp one noon with something obviously on his mind. Albrim had spent but one night sleeping in his shelter since the last full moon and was tired enough to need a nap, but Mute's arrival snapped him awake. He felt that something was about to happen.

A new chain was produced from the hidden underground storage, this one much longer than the one that shackled his legs together. Then a metal collar was brought out and bolted around Albrim's neck and the chain was then attached. Albrim didn't even bother to fight about it; he knew he'd just wake up with another sore jaw. At least the leg shackles were removed, as it was obvious that he couldn't run away while wearing the collar.

Once Albrim was safely chained down, he had enough chain to reach the creek, the fire pit and his shelter but not the underground storage. Food enough was left inside his shelter to last him several days. Albrim demanded to know what was going on but Mute just ignored him. Holding up seven fingers the big man left the clearing and Albrim was alone for the next week.

Albrim had worked diligently during his seven days, using various stones and sticks in an effort to free himself from the collar or break the chain. None of his efforts bore fruit and that bothered him; he was concerned that Mute would notice what he had been up to and punish him.

For seven days he ate, he slept and he exercised between attempts at winning his freedom. On the morning of the eighth day he watched expectantly at the west side of the clearing, for that was the direction that Mute had taken when he left, and around noon his massive body finally came into view, bringing a surge of excitement to Albrim's dull world. This time when Mute came back, he did not come alone. Stalking along in Mute's wake was a Dwarf.

Albrim met Mute at the end of his chain, excited by the appearance of yet another person. He was somewhat surprised to see that the Dwarf was blindfolded, but even more so when he noticed that he was unfettered in any other way. Was the Dwarf a prisoner? A slave? Another one of those who, like Albrim, carried the Curse? He hoped that he wouldn't have to share his shelter with him.

Mute brought the Dwarf to Albrim and then tapped him once on the forehead. The Dwarf grunted and began untying his blindfold. The grunt frightened Albrim for a moment; perhaps the Dwarf couldn't speak either. Once the blindfold came off, the Dwarf found himself standing face to face with Albrim and jumped back a step with a surprised cry. The two spent a long moment studying one another, each thinking that the other was a very strange sight indeed.

Albrim had seen Dwarves before, if only a few. When he lived on Lord Ferule's estates they had occasionally passed through on their way to somewhere interesting. Still, he had never been this close to one. The first thing he noticed was the smell.

Not that the Dwarf smelled bad, exactly, but he certainly did smell different. Several different spices were readily apparent as were several others that blended together until they were not. Albrim could easily identify cinnamon and garlic, a lot of garlic, and a sweet smell he recognized as honey.

The Dwarf's long beard was a dark red and heavily braided with small bands of silver and copper. His clothing was mostly blue and consisted of a thick woolen tunic and pantaloons of the same fabric that were dyed tree-bark brown. A blue cap completed his clothing and was pulled well down onto his ears denying Albrim of any clue as to his hair color. The skin of his bulbous nose was stretched so thin that blood vessels were easily visible there and within his bloodshot brown eyes.

Albrim's first impression was that the Dwarf was tall for his kind but then he noticed the boots. Both were tall of heel and so made him look taller than he was, though one heel was much higher than the other, indicating the Dwarf had a short leg.

From the Dwarf's point of view, he saw a wild-haired human youth wearing little more than a cotton nightshirt, leather shoes that looked too small for him and a plain brown blanket wrapped around his shoulders. As he reckoned age, the boy must be young for a human and had unremarkable drab brown hair. His legs above the footwear bore the marks of shackles though none were there now; the thick collar about his neck prevented his escape. He smelled strongly of unwashed body but that was to be expected out here. The most noticeable attribute was the missing arm. Whatever had caused the boy to lose the arm, it had been cared for. The arm ended a little below the elbow but when fresh the wound had been neatly sewn up, leaving a heavy scar but at least the skin had been stretched back over the bone. The Dwarf had seen much worse.

"Greetings, boy," the Dwarf said, grabbing Albrim by the jaw and forcefully turning his head.

"Ah, greetings to you too," Albrim said, trying in vain to see what it was about that side of his face that the Dwarf was studying.

Having some mercy on the boy the Dwarf said, "I'm looking at your ears," he began; twisting Albrim's head back the other way and continuing his observations. "That's the easiest way to tell, by the ears."

"Tell what?"

"If someone is Cursed. Boy your age shouldn't have hair growing in there and you don't have any Elf blood in you, do you?"

"Ah, no. No Elven blood."

"Then how do you explain your ears being just the least bit pointy there at the top? You might want to tell people that you do have some Elf in you, although for myself, personally I'd rather die than say that."

Albrim was getting nervous. "I'm not Cursed, you've made a mistake."

The Dwarf grabbed his face and peered again at one ear. "Nope, no mistake. You've got the Curse and no doubt about it. I wouldn't be here, otherwise. The big fella," the Dwarf said, jerking a thumb at Mute, "he don't come to town without a good reason, and you must be it."

"Let me get to work, now," The Dwarf stated, turning from Albrim as if he no longer existed. Now that he had someone to talk to, Albrim couldn't leave him alone.

"My name is..." Albrim began but couldn't finish through the massive hand that now covered his mouth and, indeed, half his face. The Dwarf had reacted as quickly as Mute had, placing a finger in each of his ears and singing "Lalala" loudly.

"I don't want to know you, boy. I'm here for a reason and socializing with you ain't it! You want to talk; you talk, but keep the personal information out of the conversation."

Albrim had to nod his acceptance before Mute would remove his hand. From the smell he was relatively sure that the big man had recently gutted a deer.

"If that's what you want, that's fine," Albrim said. "But why?"

The Dwarf was digging around inside a large pack, removing items and stacking them into piles. "You've got the Curse, boy, and that's not something you can ever forget. There are places where you'd be killed on sight for that and you don't want anyone knowing your name or even who your family is. I've seen the families of the Cursed pulled from their beds and murdered just because some fool managed to get bitten."

Removing a book from his pack the Dwarf thought for a moment before beginning a new pile. He continued, "Not that people are being overly cruel; those that are Cursed are killers and that's a fact. Left to their own they will kill their own friends and neighbors and not remember a thing about it later. At least at first."

Albrim sat down in front of his shelter. Mute hadn't offered to remove his collar and now the boy was nervously watching the big man inspecting the chain. He would surely see the evidence of Albrim's attempted escape.

"What do you mean by 'at first'?" Albrim asked.

"Well, if a Were lives long enough, they have been known to actually become aware of themselves while in Were form. It's been said that some can even control it and don't just go wild every full moon. They can even change whenever they want and resist the urge to change too. But that takes years of practice, and during those years the Were is slaughtering every person it encounters while it's in its animal form."

Pulling a smaller bag from his pack, the Dwarf opened it and took a healthy sniff, shuddered broadly and then stood back up to throw the sack as far as he could into the forest. "Knew that wouldn't keep."

Albrim had another question ready but the Dwarf continued, "Weres on a killing spree are eventually hunted down by someone with the knowledge of how to kill them and anyone that survived their attacks to become Weres themselves. In fact there are organizations out there that do nothing but that; hunt down Weres and anyone that may have been bitten by one."

"What do they do to them when they find them?"

"Why, they kill them, boy! Haven't you been listening? The Cursed have no rights, no protections. They're put down like a sick dog before it returns to the kennel."

Albrim's spirit of depression gained more power.

Tugging something from out from under his tunic, the Dwarf began gathering things from one of the piles.

"Now, I have a few questions for you, boy. You answer me as straight as you can and then leave the rest up to me."

"Leave what up to you?" asked Albrim, more than a little scared of where this was going after the talk of killing Weres wherever they were found.

"Hush now, I'm asking and you're answering, or do I have to get old scar-neck to sit on you?"

Albrim said nothing, just nodded as his reply.

"Fine. Now, how much do your remember about the night you became Cursed?"

Albrim almost asked how the man knew it had been at night, but then realized that Weres were said to only come out at night. That made him wonder why he was able to tolerate the sun.

"Not much, really. We came out of the forest near the..."

The Dwarf held up a hand. "Less background."

Thinking a moment before continuing, Albrim nodded as he began. "Alright, the Were picked me up by one arm and then bit the other one off," he stated angrily. "Then I don't remember anything more, other than a few memories that may have been dreams, until I woke up here with Mute."

The Dwarf laughed. "Mute? That's a good name for him."

Albrim realized then that the Dwarf apparently had known Mute for some time.

"Do you know his name? I mean his real name?"

"No," replied the Dwarf. "I don't suppose that anyone does, not really. He's lived in these woods for twenty years or more, doing I don't know what. I've heard lots of stories, but you can't believe stories."

Albrim felt his heart go cold. Mute was the mysterious recluse Albrim had heard about his entire life, had even fantasized about being. He was rumored to have killed a hundred men and looking at him now Albrim could believe it. The man was powerful and very capable. Some stories called him a hermit and a self-mutilated devotee of lost or forgotten gods. Other said that he protected the settlements from Quarg attacks and Albrim believed that one, perhaps, but not the one about being self-mutilated. The scars that Mute carried were hideous; no man could do that to himself. No stories that Albrim had ever heard said that the man kept Cursed boys against their wills. Nor could he recall any that named the hermit.

Putting those thoughts away for another time, Albrim returned his attention to the actions of the Dwarf. Mute was strange but there was nothing that proved that he was the mysterious hermit of local legend. He might just be a recluse former farmer living in the forest to avoid having to work for his living or expelled for some crime he had committed. He might even have left because of his scars; not wishing to live among others and be made fun of. Albrim could certainly sympathize with that. He realized with a start that the Dwarf was still talking.

"... so you didn't notice anything unusual about the Were that bit you besides his being a werewolf and all?"

"Uh, no. Nothing I can think of," Albrim answered quickly, perhaps too quickly by the suspicious look on the Dwarf's face. Did he know that Albrim hadn't really been listening?

"Well, just so long as the Were wasn't foaming at the mouth," the Dwarf said, turning back to his chosen pile. Albrim could see that the book and a handful of scrolls dominated the heap, along with some small glass bottles of different colored liquids and a small statue of a fat Dwarf sitting on a stone.

"Wait," Albrim interrupted. "Did you say if the Were *wasn't* foaming, or was?"

"It was foaming, wasn't it?" the Dwarf demanded, then shot Mute a nasty glare. "You didn't say nothing about a 'phobee Were!"

The big man squatted down by the flat rock and shrugged. He hadn't known.

"What do you mean?" asked Albrim, a new worry rising in his already troubled heart.

"Was the Were that bit you foaming at the mouth? White foam, maybe with a little pink or red from blood but basically white?" the Dwarf demanded, shaking a finger in Albrim's face.

Albrim thought back to that awful night, wanting to be certain before he answered. "Yes, it was foaming. Like a sick mok my father killed one time."

"The mok had the 'phobee then?"

"Yes, but what does that mean to me? Do I have the 'phobee too?"

"As a matter of fact, you do have the 'phobee and since it didn't kill you, you're double Cursed!"

Now Albrim was confused.

"I don't understand. The Were had the 'phobee and gave it to me?"

"That's right, have you been suffering from a fever? The ague?"

Albrim thought about the weeks of rare and partial consciousness, of Gran sitting by his bedside cooling his brow with cold water.

"I guess I did."

"This makes things a lot tougher," the Dwarf said loudly to Mute. He seemed to be getting angry.

Mute only shrugged again and pointed towards Albrim. Apparently the Dwarf understood what he meant.

Cursing, the Dwarf began digging once again into his pack.

"Why didn't I die, then? If I have the 'phobee? No one lives who has the 'phobee."

The Dwarf snorted. "I wish that were true boy, but it's not. There are a very few people who can survive it, and they all share one common trait: they're all Cursed!"

Now Albrim was not only confused, but shocked as well.

Waving one hand angrily, the Dwarf reached beneath his shirt, pulling out a cross made of silver. Just the sight of it made Albrim's head ache and his arm throb.

"How did that mok with the 'phobee act?" the Dwarf demanded.

Albrim looked at the ground. "He was wild, vicious. Came after us as if we were mice or something. It didn't care at all that we were big enough to kill it. It attacked."

"People and animals that get the 'phobe, or hydrophobe as it is more properly known, always without question die from the disease eventually. Weres who get it do not, but they can still pass it along to others, the dwarf explained"

Grabbing Albrim beneath the chin, the Dwarf pointed at the cross hanging about his neck. "You just look at that cross and listen," the Dwarf said, chanting under his breath for a moment. Next the Dwarf closed his eyes and mumbled what sounded to Albrim like a prayer. Was he a priest?

"A Were doesn't care about passing the 'phobee along because if his victim survives they usually don't die of the 'phobee and they're Cursed besides so, who cares?" the Dwarf now stated abruptly, then pulled two small alabaster cylinders from a pouch and squeezed them within one hand. When his hand opened they were nothing but dust, which he scattered to the breeze before continuing.

"But on the bad side, not that there's a good side about being Cursed, is a little known fact that a Were with the 'phobee is less likely, and I do mean much less likely, to ever progress to the point where they can control themselves while in the Were form. Plus you'll always be a carrier and could give the 'phobee to those around you without even turning into a Were."

"So you're saying that I have no chance of controlling myself? That I'm nothing but a murderous beast?" Albrim's thoughts returned to his childhood fantasies of being like the mysterious hermit, like Mute, and living his life in the forest protecting the innocent and saving beautiful women. That life didn't seem so attractive now that he knew that he was more likely to kill the innocent and perhaps even eat the women.

Albrim suddenly felt sick and dropped to his knees.

"Then why don't you kill me?" he asked, all hope having fled from his heart.

The Dwarf laughed. "Believe me, boy, that remains a viable option."

Chapter Ten

The Duke of Firth graciously bowed his way among the well-wishers on this his wedding day. His bride, the fifth to bear the title of his Duchess, still sat atop the small dais, clasping the hands of those seeking to curry favor with this new player in the endless game of politics. A truly beautiful young lady, her eyes held a frightened look that even the talented ladies-in-waiting with all of their expensive cosmetics could not hope to conceal.

Each of the courtiers sought to ingratiate themselves with the lovely young woman in order to obtain some sort of short-term goal, as the various Duchesses of Firth rarely survived long enough to accomplish anything long-term. Her family stood protectively about; her mother weeping disconsolately while her father looked on with a haunted look in his eyes. His mind spun from plan to plan, trying to find some way to remove his daughter from this horrible situation even as he pondered how he had gotten so deeply into debt that such a thing could have happened. A minor noble in his own right, the father of the new Duchess couldn't have hoped to find a more suitable match for his daughter if one only considered his title compared to that of the Duke. However, the father had never wanted this to happen.

Finally the Duke escaped the last of the toadies and boot-lickers that were an unfortunate but necessary part of even his back-woods court and slipped through a door that all knew led to the jakes. Too much spicy food on his wedding day for His Grace. Appearances must be maintained. For a man to leave his wedding reception, there must be a good reason else people might begin to talk.

Moving quickly down the corridor the Duke accepted the thick cloak offered by a servant who obediently disappeared into a small side chamber. Flipping the cloak about him to keep the dust and spider webs at bay, the Duke paused in the midst of the hall as his lone attendant lifted a cunningly disguised trapdoor in the floor, giving his Lordship access to a flight of hidden stairs.

Hurrying now, the Duke swept down the stairs and into an identical hallway. He turned about and passed back beneath the stairs and then turned left into a room lit by a single flickering torch. The poor light did little to repress the gloom, replacing the darkness it destroyed with the smoke of its own destruction. His eyes tearing at the smell, the Duke sat himself on a filthy chair and leaned his elbows on the filthy table. The thick cloak would keep his wedding vestments clean and the smell of a burning torch wouldn't be noticed.

Across from the Duke sat another of his minions, a skeletally thin man named Dirk. Few knew of his association with the Duke of Firth and for good reason; Dirk was known in many lands as an assassin and in others as much worse. A truly unpleasant man at the best of times but very thorough in his duties.

"You have news?" demanded the Duke. He had little time to waste on pleasantries. He must return to his guests as quickly as possible.

"Yes My Lord," hissed Dirk, whose name came from his favored weapon. "There are rumors out of Aldragal concerning an outbreak. A small village on the western border."

The Duke considered the matter only briefly. "Then our scout has failed."

"Undeniably, My Lord, yes. He was under strict orders not to allow any of his victims to live."

"Who do we have available? It will have to be a conventional scout."

Dirk was prepared for this and had three names ready for consideration.

Choosing one name almost at random, since all his people were well trained and knew better than to fail at any task he set for them, the Duke arose. "See to it that she leaves immediately. I need that information."

━━

Albrim found himself sleeping on the ground over the next week as the Dwarf commandeered his root-shelter. The nights were getting colder again and finally Mute had mercy and provided a torn piece of canvas for him to use as a ground sheet. His nights were long and far from restful; his dreams were of the Curse and the Dwarf snored horribly. Mute patrolled more often at night than Albrim had ever seen him; perhaps concerned that the snores would attract unwanted attention from predators.

Six times a day the Dwarf said his prayers and pored over his books and scrolls. He burned prodigious amounts of firewood as he prepared foul-smelling concoctions one after another. Each apparently failed his standards as they were tossed out almost as soon as they were completed. Several minnows died when one was poured into the creek. On the seventh day the Dwarf shouted a strange word and danced a jig; apparently at last he had accomplished whatever it was that he had been attempting.

Albrim, of course, sulked the whole time. His depression had deepened and the Dwarf rarely, if ever, talked to him. True it was that the Dwarf had answered some of Albrim's questions that first day, but since then he had not been forthcoming about anything, even the weather. Not only did Albrim have to sleep on the ground and perform even more camp chores than ever, he still had no one to talk to.

This day the Dwarf was singing, having procured a piece of metal from his pack that looked suspiciously like silver to the uneasy Albrim. Even the sight of the metal made him a little nauseous. That was because of the Curse, the Dwarf had told him that first day during his talkative hours.

"Weres are uncommonly tough creatures to kill, but the Gods like a little death and mayhem among all creatures so Weres have their weaknesses, too."

Albrim had been eager to explain what he knew. "I know that Weres can't be hurt by regular weapons, I was told that by my..." Albrim hesitated.

Somehow he knew that he wasn't supposed to mention his Gran or anyone else from his past. "From someone I know."

"Yeah, well shut your mouth and listen," the Dwarf said distractedly as he measured some bright red berries into a bowl.

"Silver it is that harms a Were, silver and magic of course. A weapon of either will cut you quick and the silver will poison you besides. That's why you're uneasy at the sight of it. Silver is bad for you in either form but worse when you're a Were. You could hold a silver coin in your hand for days and it wouldn't do much more than make you sick, that's because the tarnish on it would somewhat shield you. But if someone poked you with a silver dagger, well then you'd have to worry about the poison. Of course, prolonged contact with purified silver would be just intolerable. You couldn't stand it."

"Do you mean that I can't be hurt by normal weapons?" Albrim asked, his ears visibly perking slightly up although only one person in a million would have noticed the movement hidden as they were beneath his hair. He wasn't too concerned about the silver, at least not consciously, as he had never seen more than a dozen silver coins and his Gran's two small silver candlesticks in his entire life. It couldn't be all that common a metal.

Not bothering to answer, the Dwarf pulled a knife from his belt and leaned over towards Albrim, making a quick slash across the back of the boy's hand.

"Ow!" yelled Albrim, holding the wounded hand to his mouth.

"Now you know that normal weapons can hurt you, so no more stupid questions."

Albrim noticed that he was licking his wound and disgustedly pulled it away. Mute walked up and dropped a clean swath of linen in his lap. The big man didn't want Albrim's wound to get dirty. As he was wrapping the bandage Albrim's thoughts returned to the night he had lost his arm.

"But I tried to use my belt knife on the Were that bit me, and I didn't even leave a mark."

The Dwarf snorted. "Of course not, boy. He was in Were form that night!" After saying that the Dwarf chuckled for some time, but Albrim wasn't aware of any joke.

"So you're saying that I am immune to normal weapons as well, but only when I've... uh... changed? Albrim couldn't bring himself to say 'when I change into a Were.'

"Yep, you've got it."

"So what if I die while I'm 'normal'?"

"Then you're dead, but that's pretty unlikely," the Dwarf said, laughing again.

"Why is it unlikely?"

The Dwarf placed the small hammer he had been using to crush mushrooms aside and looked over at Albrim. "Because the full moons are not the only reason why you change into a Were. Being wounded or close to death is another way to trigger the change, so you're unlikely to die in your human form. Of course after you die you return to your human form."

"That doesn't make sense."

"It does or it doesn't, that's the truth of it. There are stranger things about you than that."

"Like what?" Albrim asked incredulously.

"Well for example; healing. As a human you'll heal normally. That little cut I gave you will be gone completely in a week or two. However if you were to change into a Were right now and then change right back, that little cut would be gone. Completely healed, just that fast."

Albrim's head swam at the facts being thrown at him, but the Dwarf wasn't finished.

"That's not all, any wounds you take while a Were will come back with you as a human. You have your Were stomach ripped open, well, your human stomach will be in the same shape."

"So when I'm a... Were, I can't be hurt except by silver or magical weapons and any damage I take will follow me back as a human? But when I'm a human I can be hurt by anything but all my wounds will heal when I become a Were?"

"Now you're following me, boy."

An idea dawned but the dwarf recognized the light in Albrim's eyes and held up a hand to forestall his next question.

"Your arm won't grow back, son. A cut or a broken bone is a wound, not a missing arm. It's just gone."

Late on the seventh night, the Dwarf told Mute to strap Albrim to the flat rock.

"Tonight's not a full moon," Albrim protested.

"No it's not, but what I'm about to do might trigger your Curse anyway. Remember that little talk we had?" the Dwarf had answered. Certainly Albrim remembered the talk, but he couldn't for his life figure out which part the Dwarf was referring to now.

Once Albrim was safely strapped into place the Dwarf laid out some artifacts that Albrim suspected had a religious significance although he didn't know what they meant. The Dwarf must be a priest of some type but Albrim suspected more than a little bit of sorcerer could be found in his background as well. After a long hour of watching the Dwarf dance, sing, and pray, Albrim was about to fall asleep from boredom. Then the Dwarf reached into his prayer box and Albrim found himself as awake and alert as he had ever been.

What he pulled out was the piece of metal Albrim had seen earlier, but now the thing seemed alive and after him!

Albrim began to twist and strain against his bindings as the metal was brought closer. The Dwarf had shaped it into a pair of connected semi-circles, the open sides of each facing the other. To Albrim's eyes the metal writhed and squirmed as if trying to escape the grasp of the Dwarf and leap for his heart. It was the most hideous thing he had ever seen and that included the Were. On top of all else, it was silver and Albrim was well aware of what that metal could do to him.

He kicked and screamed, fighting like a desperate animal to escape the living metal that was being brought closer to him by the moment. The Dwarf's face was intense and Mute had appeared to hold Albrim's shoulders down, keeping his upper body immobile. From somewhere far away Albrim heard the howl of a wolf, a howl that was rapidly gaining in volume. He didn't care; he just had to escape this metal that hungered for his flesh, for his very soul.

Albrim passed out just after realizing it was he himself who was howling.

Albrim came to with the sun standing high in the sky. An entire day had passed. The Dwarf was the only one in the clearing with him. When he turned toward the flat rock, having heard Albrim moving, the boy saw that the Dwarf had a dark welt over one eye.

"What happened to you?" he croaked, realizing then just how dry his mouth was.

The Dwarf snatched up a water skin and stomped to the boy's side, tipping the container and pouring a quantity into Albrim's open mouth.

"You are what happened to me, you ungrateful lout! We knocked heads when you tried to bite me last night!"

Albrim grinned sheepishly. "Sorry, I wasn't myself."

"Don't I know it!" the Dwarf said angrily, but the look in his eyes said that he was at least a little mollified.

The events of the previous evening came back to Albrim then. He remembered something happening to his left arm, something painful beyond belief. Looking there now, he saw only a red mark that encircled his upper arm, perhaps three finger-widths below the point of his shoulder. Nothing was there now, but the area still tingled from the pain.

"What happened?" Albrim asked again, but this time with more emotion. "What did you do to me?"

"Only what was necessary. When old Mute gets back, I'll tell you all about it."

"Why can't you tell me now?"

Exasperated the Dwarf glared at Albrim. "Because there may just be some part of it that the big fellow doesn't want me to tell you, and I'll be hanged for a Quarg-lover before I take a chance on him getting mad at me."

To his amazement Albrim couldn't even argue with the Dwarf over that point. He had learned the hard way not to do anything the big man didn't want him to do. So, despite his desire to know, to understand what these people were doing to him without his permission or counsel, he simply lay back against the sun-warmed rock.

"Could you at least unstrap me? Let me walk around? I've still got the collar on, I can't run away."

"Different question, same answer," the Dwarf said, crawling into the shelter.

Closing his eyes against the sun's rays Albrim thought back to the night before, trying to form the various images and emotions he could recall into a true memory of all that had transpired. It was little enough, the pain blocking most of the details. He remembered struggling, and the silver being brought closer and closer to his arm. Had he been muzzled? Albrim seemed to remember something being strapped over his mouth to keep him from biting. That seemed to be a logical precaution; that was how the Curse was passed from one individual to another.

The sun had moved slightly, which was the only way Albrim had to judge the time, when Mute came back into the clearing with a smug smile on his face and three scalps hanging from one hand. They looked human, or at least humanoid. This wasn't the first time Mute had done something like that but Albrim had no way of questioning the big man as to the origins of the scalps. He hoped that they weren't human, but how could he know for sure? And would Mute tell him even if they could communicate?

Mute released Albrim before kicking the Dwarf awake. It was bad enough listening to his snoring during the night. Albrim stood and stretched, easing aches and popping joints. He did some light stretches of his legs and then jogged a few laps around the clearing, forcing Mute and the Dwarf to duck or jump over the chain attached to his collar on each lap. This angered the Dwarf, but Mute took it in stride.

Out of breath for the moment, Albrim stopped and ducked his head in the stream, then decided to strip down and wash more thoroughly. He rubbed the white sand from the bottom of the stream into his skin, invigorating himself with the chill water. As he washed he noticed the Dwarf whispering to Mute. He must have said a great deal but Mute did not respond until the very end, giving a short nod of permission or acceptance.

"Come here, boy, your friend here has agreed that I can tell you what happened last night," the Dwarf said, sitting on a log placed near the fire for that purpose.

Albrim hurriedly dressed and ran to the fire, shivering a little from the cold water.

"That's the most foolish thing I've ever seen any one do in my entire life and I'm older than both of you two put together," the Dwarf said, looking on Albrim with disdain. "You'll catch your death, splashing around in that frigid water, and for what?"

"At least I won't smell as bad as you," Albrim answered calmly. He knew the Dwarf was just stalling, trying to make him beg for the information. Mute had said that he could hear and Albrim knew, once he had decided something, the big man wouldn't let the Dwarf drag it out too long.

"What about last night?" Albrim asked.

The Dwarf started to launch into another long-winded story that likely would have had nothing to do with last night, but Mute jabbed him with a finger. In mid-sentence the Dwarf's story changed.

"What we did last night was attune you to this," the Dwarf said, pulling the piece of silver from a pouch on his belt.

Albrim began moving backwards at the sight of it but was brought up short when Mute stepped on his chain.

"Keep that away from me! You know what silver does to... to people like me!"

"I know, boy, better than you do. But you need to look at this closely and pay attention. This is your life we're talking about."

Albrim moved back, still uneasy but scared not to.

"Now what we did last night was 'attune' this little ornament to you. It is made of silver, like you already know, but there's more to this. Much more."

The Dwarf moved around the fire, holding the silver out for his inspection. Albrim's very skin crawled at the sight of it but he forced himself to look at it. When it came so close it almost touched his nose, Albrim snarled out of reflex.

"Watch it, Dwarf. I might bite you now, give you the Curse."

Laughing the Dwarf moved the silver piece even closer, causing Albrim to strain back to the length of the chain. "Boy you can't give me the curse unless you're in your Were form. Now look here."

He showed Albrim how the ornament, for that is what it was, would open and close, forming a complete circle. He explained that it was made to fit on Albrim's upper arm but the boy had already figured that out and was rubbing the red mark already there. The outside of the band was nearly devoid of ornamentation showing only a small axe head on what Albrim perceived was the 'back'. Inside, however, the band was completely covered in symbols and small engravings that seemed to move as Albrim looked at them. He didn't recognize any of them but knew that they were likely magical.

"The purpose of this band is to help prevent someone with the Curse from turning into a Were. It's a tool to help them learn how to control their changes. Works real well if you don't have the 'phobee too. Of course, you do have the 'phobee so the chance of you learning to control your changes are pretty much non-existent. So, I had to make this one a lot stronger."

"Stronger in what way?"

"Stronger as in while you're wearing it, you can't change into your Were form. As a matter of fact, you can't even touch it or take it off."

Albrim recoiled again. "You're not putting that thing on me! It'll kill me!"

"True enough if I hadn't made it in a... well let's just say a 'special way'."

"But, it's silver! It's poison to me!"

"Not any more, boy. My magic is proof against that. Silver will still kill, just not this particular piece of silver. Not that you're going to enjoy wearing it, you'll always know it's there, if you know what I mean, but it won't kill you or cause any real harm."

Albrim sat dumbfounded. It was too much for him to accept all at once.

The Dwarf kept speaking, "Seeing as how you had the 'phobee, I had to really juice this one up, and I also had to attune it to you personally or it would never have worked. But here it is, maybe the best one I've ever made. So long as you wear this, you don't have to worry about changing into a Were. Well, in most situations you don't. If you should manage it, the band will be useless to you after that, so you should avoid most stressful situations."

The enormity of what the Dwarf was saying was slow to sink into Albrim's mind. The sight of the silver was still difficult for him, and the thought of having it attached to his arm was nearly unmanning him. To have it attached and not be able to remove it was simply beyond his comprehension.

"Now I need to put his on you boy, but you have to be accepting of it. Or, at least you can't be fighting against me at the time. Either will do. Will you let me put it on your arm?"

Albrim shook his head no, all the while straining against the chain.

Mute stood, stepping over the fire and placed his hand on Albrim's shoulder. The big man looked the boy in the eye, trying to convey something. Strength of purpose? An assurance that everything would be all right? Albrim didn't know, but there was no way he could allow that band to be attached to his arm.

"No, Mute. I can't," he said, pleading with his eyes to be spared the horror that the band represented.

Mute held up one massive fist, warning Albrim of the only alternative. The boy stared long at the fist, and then moved his gaze back to the silver band. Finally he looked at Mute and nodded. It was really the only choice. Albrim returned his gaze to the object of his dread and so intent was his concentration that he didn't even see the fist coming.

Chapter Eleven

It had rained again that morning but Albrim felt sure that the spring rains were soon to end; at least he hoped so. The soil of the clearing was saturated and the stream had been out of its banks for more than a week. Summer was not far away and surely the clouds had to be running low on water by now.

Mushrooms and toadstools were sprouting up all around the clearing as he crawled out of his shelter. He would look at them later, to see if any were edible. Mute had taught him how to tell the difference by cuffing him each time he pointed at one that was poisonous. Not the best way to learn, perhaps, but he was now quite knowledgeable on the subject.

Winter this close to the mountains had been difficult and there were times that Albrim felt that he would never be warm again, particularly when the collar was on. The leg shackles were bad enough but the collar just seemed to sap the warmth from his body.

And then there was the armband.

The skin of his arm crawled where the armband touched him. Beneath it the skin had turned red and often itched and irritated Albrim to no end. It constantly ached as well, like a bruise in a sensitive place. A bruise that wouldn't be healing, ever. But the worst part of wearing the band was the distinct feeling that the band could move, usually just as Albrim was about to fall asleep or was otherwise distracted. It felt like a snake or something wet and slime-covered was crawling up his arm. Maybe not quite as bad, but very irritating, was the fact that he couldn't even touch it or rub it and had to suffer it all in silence.

At least Mute expected him to suffer it in silence. Albrim didn't always cooperate. Bathing the arm frequently helped the discomfort but that became difficult during the deep snows of the winter. Snows that kept him trapped in his root-shelter all alone for days and weeks at a time.

Not that Mute didn't drop by occasionally. Wherever he was wintering, it couldn't be very far away. He would move aside the stacked firewood that surrounded the shelter, both to provide fuel and an extra layer of insulation against the cold, and drop off food. Albrim was expected to melt snow for drinking water. It had been a long, boring winter. Once Mute brought Albrim an oversized woolen sock that he pulled up over Albrim's arm stump against his wishes. Albrim found that the sock had helped him keep warmer.

Albrim had seen no one other than Mute since the Dwarf had left after attaching the armband the previous autumn. The Dwarf had promised Albrim to see him again in the spring but he hadn't been very pleased with the Dwarf at that point and had cursed him soundly, promising to kill him come spring if he was crazed enough to come back. Laughter had been the Dwarf's only reaction to the heart-felt threat.

Still, one thing had made the hours trapped within the shelter, if not enjoyable, at least tolerable. Unlike the previous summer and fall, Albrim did have something to help pass the time.

"A little present, boy," had been the Dwarf's explanation as he left the oilskin bundle by the door of the shelter where Albrim sat sulking. The boy had merely hugged his knees closer and ignored the Dwarf, all the while planning the horrible punishments he would one day mete out in return for the armband. The bundle had sat there unopened for several days until finally Mute picked it up and tossed it into Albrim's lap.

Another easily understood communication from the big man. Open it now, Albrim. So he had, and inside the bundle he had found three small books and a pair of new scrolls tied with red ribbons.

The bottom of the three books was the largest, but still quite small compared to the three or four other books Albrim had seen during his life, being no more than a hand and a half tall and only two finger widths thick. By comparison, The Great Holy Book in the temple at Aldragal had been as thick as Albrim was tall when he saw it as a child. Lord Ferule had a few books as well, all of which were larger than these. Each of these were bound in the same tanned leather and were sewn together with thick but un-dyed linen thread. The books were reasonably new and the light-brown pages still crackled when turned.

Intrigued despite himself, Albrim carefully opened the books to find that each was written in the same neat hand. The Dwarf's? Likely a scribe hired by the Dwarf to copy other works. He noticed immediately that the three books were not copies of one another. Setting those aside he opened the two scrolls, finding that one was written in the same hand as the three volumes. The second scroll was written by a different hand, the letters were tighter and more compact. Albrim was surprised to see that the second scroll was a letter written to him. For once he was glad of the hours that Gran had forced him to spend learning to read. Most people he knew couldn't.

His excitement at the letter decreased when he realized that it was the Dwarf who had written it. Albrim was still angry at him. However he did read the letter and found that it explained what the books and the other scroll were for. Albrim was supposed to read them all throughout the winter and the Dwarf would pick them up again in the spring.

Putting them back into the oilskin, Albrim tossed the bundle aside with no intention of ever opening them. Days of being trapped inside the shelter because of the deep snow, unable to leave for any reason, had driven him to open the books and over the long winter he had all but memorized every word.

One book had been a detailed explanation of what it meant to be a Were, written by someone named Articus who apparently had suffered from the Curse himself. It explained all of the powers the Curse gave along with the side effects of the same. The second volume was a series of shorter works combined under one cover that explored the symptoms of 'phobee and what it meant to various creatures including Weres.

The third book was a journal kept by a woman named Lornwen whose father was bitten by a Were while living in a kingdom Albrim was reasonably sure no longer existed. She told of her father's problems and victories during the ten-year period that her family strove to keep his Curse a secret from their neighbors while the man himself struggled to gain control over it. The end of the book was completed by a priest named Wilus, who used the death of the family at the hands of the Were father to illustrate that Lycanthropy, another name for the Curse, Albrim learned, was an evil that could only be destroyed, not rehabilitated. The books failed to bring much solace to Albrim, only serving to depress him further.

The second scroll was the most interesting to Albrim, not that he didn't find all of the material interesting in a sick sort of way. They all dealt with things very personal to him after all. But in the scroll he found a letter from Gerder the Farrier to someone that was never named. The whole letter concerned a mysterious group of people that had dedicated their lives to hunting down and killing Weres. All of it was filled with speculation about the Were killers and the 'land of the Weres' where Gerder believed that all Weres were born.

Not likely true but that last part gave Albrim something to think about during the long nights. A group or organization dedicated to hunting people like him down and killing them didn't drift far from his remembrance either.

But the books did their job; Albrim now knew more about Weres than most people ever would. He understood that the things the Dwarf had told him were true; at least they matched the information found in the books. It didn't escape Albrim's thoughts that the Dwarf had been the one to provide them. Could it be that he was providing Albrim with false information?

Albrim didn't think so. He didn't know why Mute had helped him or why the Dwarf had been brought here to do the same. Why anyone would help him or anyone with the Curse was beyond him. Mute of course was beyond questioning being unable to speak and as near as Albrim could tell, completely illiterate. He only had the books and they had already given up all that they could. What was he to do now?

Despite his hatred of the irritating armband, Albrim had to admit it was doing its job. Since it had been placed on his arm, he had not changed into a Were even once. Not that it hadn't been close a few times. The first full moon after the armband was nearly a disaster for him, and Albrim knew it. He had seen the worry etched on Mute's face as Albrim lay screaming on the big rock. He'd even broken one of the straps. By midwinter the urges to change had eased and Mute had eventually begun leaving Albrim in his shelter during the full moons.

How he had suffered during those full moons! The need to change was there; insistent, demanding. Pain and rage beyond anything Albrim could ever remember experiencing. In the past he had passed out when the urges began but now, thanks to the armband, he was awake to suffer through the whole process and never feel the relief of actually changing.

Thankfully the urges had eased somewhat with the passing of time. Perhaps in a few years he might be able to stop dreading them.

Chapter Twelve

The Dwarf did come back and Albrim tried hard to ignore him. Being dragged from his shelter by Mute ended that effort. Immediately the books were asked for. Albrim was loathe to give up the books and scroll but took solace in the fact that he had virtually memorized them. The sting of their loss was eased when the Dwarf replaced them with two more books. Both were smaller volumes but if they were as interesting as the others Albrim couldn't wait to read them. Right then, however, the Dwarf wanted information concerning Albrim's winter and the effects of the armband on his Curse. It was long past dark when the Dwarf's questions had been answered, and re-answered, to his satisfaction.

Dawn came slowly for Albrim on the second day of the Dwarf's visit. He had a thousand questions to ask the Dwarf and again had a strong desire just to have someone to talk to. He hadn't been allowed to ask anything the first day. To ease his curiosity he did manage a quick peek at the new books.

The first was bound in green leather, which indicated to Albrim that it was old. He was surprised then to see that it was not. It was dated as having been written that very winter and used the same handwriting that Albrim suspected was the Dwarf's own. The work was an exhaustive explanation of the armband; both what it could do and what it could not do. Many pages were devoted to cautions against certain actions that might trigger the change. Albrim couldn't wait to read it. Perhaps he would find some method of removing it, or at least a way to ease the discomfort.

Opening the second book was an initial disappointment. Only the first three pages were written upon, again in the Dwarf's own handwriting, but the balance of the book was blank. Reading the first paragraph informed him that it was a journal for his use. The Dwarf had written there that it would become an invaluable resource for Albrim in the future.

"Boy, come on out," announced the Dwarf, his boots just visible to Albrim in the predawn light. The Dwarf had brought a tent to sleep in this time; allowing Albrim to remain in his root shelter.

Albrim crawled out somewhat nervously, not certain what was going to happen but also hopeful. Was his future to be discussed today? Was he ever going to be allowed to leave this tiny clearing?

Seeing that Albrim was on his way, the Dwarf retreated to the fire pit and sat on the stump, waving the boy over to sit at his side. Mute watched Albrim closely, perhaps concerned that the boy would follow through on his threats and try to harm the Dwarf. Maybe try to strangle him with his collar chain. He didn't attempt anything, just sat where he was told to.

"Boy, I know you have a lot of questions, and I'm here for the next few days to answer them. After that I'm leaving, and don't you ever try to find me, understand?"

Albrim agreed that he did.

"Fine," the Dwarf smiled. "I suppose you've already looked at the new books?"

"Yes, I did," Albrim replied. "I don't see why a journal is important, but I'm willing to try it for a while."

Nodding the Dwarf continued, "One day the journal will be an important resource for you as you look back at your thoughts and mistakes; that's one thing I can guarantee. You may have figured out that you're not the first of the Cursed that I've helped, though in truth it hasn't been many."

Albrim didn't say anything. He wasn't entirely sure that the Dwarf really had helped him. Mute had done more in his mind; keeping him chained up during the full moons until he learned to control his changes. If he could learn to control them.

"The other book is self-explanatory but one thing you must keep in mind is to never, ever let either book fall into anyone else's hands. You can read them, but no one else. I'm serious about this, boy, if the wrong people get hold of those books you are a dead man and there's always the chance that they'll be traced back to me."

"I will be careful with them. You have my word."

Barking a laugh the Dwarf replied, "The word of a Were! But then, that's all you have to give, so it'll have to be enough."

Albrim was surprised by the harsh reply but thought that he understood. The Dwarf would be put to death, at the least, if it was found that he was aiding a Were.

"Now I have something else for you here. I'm not sure if you'll be interested in this or not. Your big friend over there seems to think that you will, but I'm not entirely convinced," the Dwarf said, waving at Mute.

Mute nearly smiled, his eyes lighting up with good humor like Albrim had never seen in the man. Excited despite himself Albrim leaned forward, hanging on the Dwarf's every word.

"Mute tells me, or rather he pantomimed for me, that he has been sparring a little with you."

Albrim had no idea what 'pantomimed' meant. "We've sparred some, using tree branches and the like."

"That's good boy, you've got a hard life ahead of you and defending yourself is a good skill to have."

Albrim sighed. "Not much chance of my defending myself with only one arm."

"Feeling sorry for yourself will get you killed, boy. You don't have the luxury of that. You have to make do with what you have."

"What I don't have is an arm to hold a shield, or a bow. I was a great shot before, what can I do to defend myself now?" he snarled, shaking his stub for emphasis.

"You can learn to use a one-handed blade, that's what! When someone comes to kill you, boy, they aren't going to make allowances because you don't have two hands. They also aren't going to care if you beg for mercy. You will defend yourself or you will die, and maybe both will happen. It's all up to you."

Glaring at the Dwarf didn't make Albrim feel any better, but it was all he could do. He would get no sympathy from either of his companions. What did they know about trying to live their lives with only one arm? His remaining hand was his off hand and even the simplest of tasks remained nearly impossible.

"I can't give you your hand back, but there is something I can do," the Dwarf said, pulling up his backpack and untying the flap. The tone of his voice was more conciliatory.

"Mute didn't ask me for this but he has agreed to pay for it, just as he has all my expenses up to now. It's quite a feat of engineering, if I do say so myself. Not that I made it all, but I was involved in it every step of the way," he laughed, finding what he wanted within the backpack but hesitating before pulling it out.

Albrim barely registered the part about Mute paying for the Dwarf's services. That couldn't be true; where would a man who lived alone in the forest come up with any type of money? Unless the stories that labeled the big man as a thief and murderer were true. That would explain any accumulated treasures. But why would Mute spend years of his life living in such a lonely place killing and robbing travelers and then spend it on Albrim? None of it made sense, so he found it easy to dismiss it for the moment. He was more interested in whatever the Dwarf had in his pack.

"You had mentioned before about being an archer, a fact I asked you not to share with me but since you did, I decided to use it advantageously. If you'll recall I took a lot of measurements of your arms and your stump when I was here last year. They were in preparation for building... this!"

The Dwarf pulled something from his pack and held it up with a flourish. He was obviously proud of it, whatever it was, but Albrim felt somewhat let down after an initial burst of excitement. It certainly didn't look like much.

Laughing at Albrim's obvious confusion, the Dwarf tossed the thing into Albrim's lap. Picking it up Albrim inspected it; certain that he had no idea what it was. He noticed that it was heavy.

Made from slender rods of steel and several straps of leather, the contraption had a recess built into one end where four rods were spaced equal distances apart around a network of smaller rods. The other end was made of more of the smaller rods, a thick spring, a bent hook, and what looked to be a long spoon protruded near the opening of the recess. Albrim knew what spoons were; they were things that nobles used to eat soups as they were too genteel to just drink from the bowls. Was that what this was? Some type of elaborate spoon?

Again the Dwarf laughed, leaning over and taking his gift back from Albrim. Turning it about he slid the recessed portion over Albrim's arm stub and used the straps to secure it into position. The steel was cold against his arm and he knew that the leather would quickly cause him to chafe. A solid steel plate fit up against the end of his stump and leather straps between the upper rods and lower rods allowed him to bend his elbow. Other than that he wasn't sure what to think. He had a spoon strapped to his elbow. How was that supposed to make his life better?

"Hold it out towards me, boy," the Dwarf said, still chuckling at Albrim's confusion. "I'll tell you what it does eventually, but for now just humor me."

Albrim did as he was told, pointing the hook towards the Dwarf.

"Now hold up your other arm next to this one."

His mind spinning as he tried to envision what was supposed to be happening; Albrim held his good arm up next to the contraption. He noticed that his hand was somewhat longer than the mechanism when it was strapped on.

"The length is right, now bend your elbow."

Albrim complied, bending both just to be sure which the Dwarf meant. The spoon portion stabbed into his side. The Dwarf clucked at this and took the contraption off, turned it slightly, and then reattached it. Satisfied for the moment, he had Albrim bend his elbows again. This time the spoon didn't stab him.

"Good, now we're in business!" the Dwarf exclaimed. Albrim didn't know what he as so excited about.

"Now watch this," the Dwarf said, grabbing the contraption and lowering it to a rock near the edge of the fire pit. The edge of the spoon was placed against the corner of the rock and the Dwarf pushed Albrim's arm down. With an audible 'click' the spoon moved outward until it was pointing straight out from the hook and the rest of the apparatus. When this happened the top portion of the hook moved forward. When the pressure was released, both the spoon and the hook remained in their new locations.

The Dwarf was obviously pleased. "So far, so good," he laughed.

Albrim was even more confused than ever.

"Now bring this part," the Dwarf pointed at the spoon, "Up next to your face."

Albrim did so, turning slightly as he lifted his elbow and brought the spoon up near his face.

"Now lean over and put your chin against it," the Dwarf said, helping Albrim to get his chin exactly where he wanted it against the spoon. When he was finished the spoon rested just beneath Albrim's chin as if cupping it. The smooth metal was cold.

"Good, good," the Dwarf said, his eyes bright with excitement. "Now! I want you to use your chin to push the spoon downward! Just open your mouth."

Albrim opened his mouth but nothing happened.

"No, boy, you can't move your whole head!" the Dwarf said, growing angry. "You have to hold your head still and just use your chin to push that part down! Use the muscles of your jaw."

It took Albrim several tries. It was awkward to use his jaw muscles in such a way; it just felt natural to move his upper jaw to avoid the pressure of the spoon against his chin. Finally he did it correctly and the 'click' sound happened again. This time it was much louder.

The Dwarf hooted in excitement, then leaned across the fire to shake Mute's hand. Albrim wasn't sure what exactly had happened but as he inspected the apparatus strapped to his stub he noticed that the hook had returned to its original position.

"Do it again, boy. See if you can do it without any help," the Dwarf said, clapping Albrim on the back.

"I don't understand. What did I just do?"

"Just do it again and I'll explain everything afterwards."

More confused than ever, Albrim complied. First he pushed the spoon back against the edge of the rock; this turned out to be more difficult to do alone than he had thought, and then he used his chin to manipulate the spoon downward. This time he saw the hook at the end of his 'arm' snap open.

Again the Dwarf laughed, leaning over to slap Albrim on the back.

"Now you're in business, boy!"

"I don't know what you mean. What business am I in?"

The Dwarf patted the contraption lovingly. "It may not be pretty, but that little beauty is going to be a big help in your life."

Albrim was getting upset. "I don't understand what you mean! I push on this spoon and that hook opens. What does that mean?"

The Dwarf again clapped Albrim on the shoulder. "For one, it means that you can grab onto stuff with your bad arm, and even pick it up if you can find something around to push the spoon down with. You could hold a shield in it, for example, or at least a buckler. That's pretty good, but that's not the half of it," he said, beaming.

Albrim was pleased that he might be able to hold a buckler. That could be of some use. But what else could this odd contraption do?

The Dwarf spoke to Mute but Albrim didn't hear the exact words. Mute handed over his longbow and Albrim began to get the idea.

The Dwarf was beaming as he handed the bow to Albrim. "Boy, it'll take a lot of work, a lot of practice, but if you work hard enough with that little beauty strapped to your arm, you'll be an archer again!"

Summer came on with a vengeance; seemingly intent on burning away all the spring's rains. It was blistering hot, even in the Kenabruk mountains, and Albrim knew that Mute was concerned about wildfires. Mute had told him so by pointing at their cook fire and pantomiming it spreading to the nearby trees. Each day the big man climbed the largest tree on the edge of the clearing and sat in a platform he had built among the branches near the very top. From there he would watch the horizon for signs of smoke. This confused Albrim until he questioned Mute about it. Wildfires were a natural part of life in the forest and cleared away undergrowth and even some older trees to allow new growth to take root. Surely they would be able to leave ahead of the fire if necessary.

Not that Mute could answer but the big man had a way of making his thoughts known when he cared to. After more than a year Albrim was becoming better at communicating with him, when Mute wanted to communicate. If Mute chose to be reserved on a subject, Albrim had no chance of getting any information out of him.

He approached Mute one evening after their meal.

"Why are you so concerned about wildfires?"

Mute looked at him for a long moment. So long in fact that Albrim thought that for a moment that he wasn't going to get an answer. Finally the big man came over to the boy and squatted down beside him, sitting on his heels in that peculiar manner he had. Taking a stick from the kindling pile, he began to draw in the sand of the fire pit near to the dying fire.

Mute's strokes were quick and without any wasted motions. He had a good hand at the task and Albrim soon was able to make out a nicely detailed drawing of the profile of a humanoid. It had small eyes and a piggish snout and even had small tusks protruding from the corners of its mouth.

Albrim looked up to catch Mute's eyes. "Quarg?" he asked.

Mute nodded, standing up and walking over to the underground storage area. He removed the waterproof tarp that both helped conceal the entrance as well as keep the supplies inside dry. He flipped open the hidden door, a feat Albrim knew that he couldn't do even if he had both hands, and dropped into the hole. Mute quickly returned, crawling up out of the hole and hurrying back to Albrim with something large held in one hand. Something large and very hairy.

At first Albrim thought that Mute had retrieved a fur of some sort; possibly a mok by the color. When Mute dropped them by Albrim's feet the boy realized that they were the scalps Mute sometimes brought back to the clearing. Separating one from the pile he draped it across the profile of the Quarg he had drawn.

Again the man had made his point clear without talking. "You think that the Quargs will set fire to the forest because you take their scalps and they know that you live here?" he asked.

Mute nodded, absently using the stick to draw another Quarg next to the first. This one was looking straight ahead and had a scar along one cheek. Mute added another scalp to that drawing.

"You've taken a lot of Quarg scalps?"

Mute nodded again, holding his hands out wide.

"You've taken many, many scalps."

Mute almost smiled. Albrim had long ago decided that smiling was difficult for the big man due to the scars on his neck, some of which reached up past his jawbone. Albrim had seen him bathe once or twice; the scars looked worse to him each time he saw them.

Albrim smiled in return. "You don't like Quargs?" he asked, hoping that was the case. It might be that Mute killed anyone that dared enter his forest.

Mute nodded emphatically, pointing at his neck and then the drawings.

The light of understanding dawned again. "Quargs did that to you?" Albrim asked, pointing to Mute's neck and receiving another nod in return.

Mute picked up his stick and drew another figure. This one was smaller than the Quargs and again in profile. Albrim had no difficulty identifying a wolf.

"A Were?"

No, Mute indicated. Not a Were, just a wolf.

"A wolf that was trained by the Quargs?"

Back to nodding. Albrim had heard that Quargs trained wolves.

"And you've taken so many Quarg scalps that they now hunt you?"

This earned Albrim another nod along with a satisfied partial smile.

Albrim smiled too despite his reservations. He wished he dared ask Mute if Quargs were his only source of scalps. Some of the legends concerning Mute were apparently true; he did work to keep the Quarg tribes from raiding the lowlands. At least he tried. Albrim wondered how many of the legends were true.

"So the Quargs hunt you, and since they can't find you they set fires in the forest to drive you out of hiding?"

Mute looked away. Not denying it, but obviously saddened by the destruction caused on his behalf.

Rarely did the big man leave the clearing over the next few weeks. He stayed close by, sparring with Albrim as the younger man practiced with his new 'arm' and the leather buckler Mute had made for him. Fighting left-handed remained awkward but Albrim felt that he was improving despite the casual ease with which Mute 'killed' him in their mock battles. However it was being able to fire a bow again that was doing wonders for Albrim's self-esteem.

At least it did eventually. At first all Albrim did was snap the feathers from arrows and watch them fall within paces of his own feet when he shot. The contraption made by the Dwarf was crude and awkward but Albrim persevered. Eventually he discovered the secret of firing the bow without deflecting the arrow after figuring out how to hold the arrow onto the string and hold the bow long enough to pull the bowstring back. That took a bizarre balancing act of putting the arrowhead into place with his hand and drawing the bowstring while holding the bow stave with his palm. Not easy, but doable. Then Albrim learned how to release the bowstring without it stinging his face or ear. It took more than two months before he was able to strike a target. Mute stayed busy just making new arrows for Albrim's target practice needs.

One problem with the contraption surfaced immediately. Albrim needed something very strong to re-cock the spoon-trigger. He could do it with his left hand but only barely. If he was holding his bow it was impossible. Each time he fired the bow it took him far too long to kneel down to the nearest rock and force the spoon into position. That is, if a suitable rock was nearby. He explained the problem to Mute and within a few days the big man had carved a small squarish piece of limestone so that it had a gap passing through it just large enough for Albrim's leather belt. With the limestone on his belt Albrim could prepare his arm to fire the bow by forcing the spoon down onto the block of stone. This would work great until the leather of the belt gave out. Albrim quickly developed some nice bruises from the belt as well, but he didn't mind.

Two weeks after Mute drew the figures in the sand, Albrim was writing in his journal with a piece of charcoal while his companion sat in his tree stand. Albrim was having a difficult time making the words legible with his offhand, but some progress was being made. It was around noon when a pinecone struck the ground near Albrim's foot.

Jumping to his feet in surprise, Albrim looked around and then realized where Mute was. Looking up into the tree he saw the big man looking back at him and pointing to the west. He pantomimed drawing his bow and then held up the fingers of both hands. Finally he tugged at his hair and made a slashing motion across his forehead. Albrim wasn't sure but he thought Mute was telling him that a group of Quargs were approaching from the west and that he was to ready his bow.

Heart pounding and pulse throbbing in his temples Albrim dashed to the shelter where he dropped the journal and picked up his bow and quiver. He only had a few arrows and all had been used repeatedly. He hoped that they would fly true. Once he had his weapons in hand he ran to the creek and dropped down into the water. It was the only shelter he could use to fire from without exposing himself.

In the tree above Mute rolled his eyes at the noise the boy was making. Between the rattling of his neck chain and the splash of his feet in the stream, he was making enough noise to alert a dozen stupid Quargs. Mute was reasonably sure these particular Quargs were too far away to have heard and he didn't really blame the boy. Still, in the back of his mind the big man was already determining how to explain to the boy what he had done wrong when the time came for punishment.

Albrim sat in the ankle deep stream, peeking above the sloping bank with an arrow already notched on the longbow. Trying to keep the weapon out of the water, he was holding it horizontally with his hook already in place on the string and the spoon cocked. He nervously scanned the forest to the west, which lay both uphill and across the stream from the encampment.

After enough time had passed that the icy water swirling around his ankles had actually begun to feel uncomfortable despite the heat of the day, Mute silently descended from his tree and waved Albrim into the camp. The Quargs were gone.

Not sure if he should be happy or dejected, Albrim climbed from the stream and returned to the very edge of the cook fire. Once there he took his silent scolding from Mute and then a cuff for not having put out the fire. Albrim could tell that Mute's heart wasn't in the rebuke. The big man kept watching the forest, as edgy as Albrim had ever seen him. He wasn't happy about Quargs coming this close to the camp.

Coming to a decision Mute went to his hidden supply hole and began tossing things out. Extra water skins and rations were first, along with a greasy old backpack that smelled absolutely horrible. Next came a moth-eaten blanket and other basic supplies. Finally Mute emerged with an oilskin wrapped parcel which he laid carefully at Albrim's feet. Waving a hand to tell the younger man to open the bundle, Mute busied himself at packing his chosen supplies into the smelly backpack. Once finished, he brought a new quiver filled with arrows to Albrim, who sat stunned at the wonderful gifts found within the parcel he had opened.

Gran had packed this, Albrim knew it without asking. Everything had her careful attention to detail. He found new clothes and two pairs of soft leather boots, all made to fit the Albrim he had grown into rather than the one that had left Cobble. There were bowstrings and arrowheads, both made by his father as well as water skins, a new hemp rope and other minor supplies including his own flint and steel. He'd always wanted his own flint and steel, but Borel had maintained that the price of the steel was too dear for a boy to carelessly lose. Albrim had always known that he could have picked up a small piece of discarded steel at Yogarn's smithy but obeyed his father's wishes nonetheless.

Each item Albrim pulled from the pack brought new tears; his Gran had done everything that she could for him. It had been Gran that saw him to Mute and Gran who likely had given the man enough money to see to Albrim's needs. It had been Gran who gave him the chance, small though it may be, to conquer his Curse and find some type of normal life. She had made sure that he wouldn't be hunted down and killed because of some accidental wound by a Were while also making sure that he wouldn't harm anyone else or spread the Curse further. It had all been Gran; she hadn't abandoned him.

Strangest of all was a scrap of paper folded inside a single sheet of parchment that he found in an inside pocket of his new coat. The page was covered in Gran's scrawl and was obviously a letter written to him. Drawn on the scrap of paper was a circle with a strange symbol. A tree, Albrim recognized, as well as some strange letters or symbols. A chain had been drawn into the top of the medallion, for that was what Albrim decided that it was, but he had no idea what it was for or what the symbol meant. Perhaps the letter would tell him.

The softest cuff he had ever received from Mute, though it still knocked him on his back, brought him back to the present. Shedding his rags, he donned the soft leather breeches and cotton tunic, grateful to be wearing real clothes for the first time in so long. Untanned furs had been his winter apparel and thin cotton nightshirts his summer. In moments he found himself dressed with a new knife belted at his waist and Mute's second best bow in hand. The drawing and the letter he folded neatly and replaced it in the inner pocket before repacking the coat for travel. The letter had waited a year; it could wait a little longer.

Albrim felt fit and ready to conquer the world. He was pleasantly surprised when Mute removed the chain from his collar. He had thought perhaps that he was to be left behind to defend the clearing.

Mute warned him with hand signals to stay close and keep quiet; they were leaving the clearing. It would be the first time in more than a year that Albrim had been allowed to leave save the short runs around the area. He was excited to be leaving, but somewhat frightened as well. Quargs were vicious brutes and would kill them if they were found. He was glad that he wasn't going to be left here alone and relieved that they were not going to sit around waiting. They were going Quarg hunting.

Chapter Thirteen

Adjusting the cushion beneath his bottom, the Duke of Firth waited patiently for Dirk to arrive. The man had been very busy lately, doing the Duke's will, and so an occasional bout of tardiness could be forgiven. Besides, the Duke needed the time to reflect on certain recent matters of state that had arisen.

There was trouble in the northern edge of his independent duchy, with several outbreaks of lawlessness. He was likely going to have to put down the insurrections through use of his troops and that meant he himself would have to lead them to prevent any defections of his forces. Such a bother. Weeks spent in the mud which he much would rather spend enjoying his wife's charming attributes; such as the new estates and trading concerns he had obtained through their marriage. Such were the difficulties of being born a Duke. Worse was the fact that he would have to pull some troops away from his other interests; just when things were beginning to fall into place. He mentally shrugged. The troops could use the combat experience; it would come in handy soon.

Dirk swept in, bowing low and apologizing for the lateness of his arrival.

"My sincere apologies, Your Grace, I was delayed by a young couple picnicking near the entrance to the tunnels," Dirk explained. "I had to await their departure before I dared to open the entrance."

The Duke laughed. "The young will ever be a nuisance. I shall send a patrol into the area beginning tomorrow, to keep such rubbish from my grounds. Be wary, and see to it you are not among those they find there."

Dirk smiled. "Of course, Your Grace, they shall never know that I am about."

Believing that was easy for the Duke. Few could find Dirk when he did not wish to be found.

"You have news for me?" The Duke asked.

"Indeed, Your Grace, I most certainly do. Handramahr the Merchant has died; it is believed by natural causes. He was found in his bed ten days ago as cold as a stone."

"That is indeed wonderful news," the Duke said, laughing aloud. "Do see to it that our friend in this issue is well rewarded for his... delicacy in the matter."

Dirk smiled in return. Having a murder look like a natural death was almost always preferable. Fewer questions were asked.

"Please continue," the Duke ordered with a wave of his hand. He never allowed himself more than a moment to gloat over a success. He believed that it distracted one from the next opportunity.

"Yes, Your Grace," Dirk said, ever dutiful to his Lord. "I have a number of other items on my agenda today, but this next one I have a bad feeling about."

"Do go on. Bring it to the surface and allow the light of day to cleanse it," said the Duke, quoting an old proverb.

Dirk did so, pulling a single sheet of folded parchment from a pocket. "Our agent in western Aldragal has not been heard from in some months. This was the last missive we received from her. She has now missed two consecutive contacts."

The Duke accepted the letter and opened it, scanning it quickly and returning it to his minion. "Then she is likely dead."

"Not entirely certain, My Lord," Dirk responded, "but it is unlikely that she would fail to check in, otherwise."

Taking a moment to contemplate, the Duke continued to pace around the tiny room. Dirk waited patiently, shuffling several sheets of parchment on the table in preparation for the continuation of his report.

After several laps around the table, the Duke began, "According to this last report, our agent believed that a woman named Gran hid her grandson after the Were attack in her village. The agent believed the boy did not die as reported. We've seen that before in Were attacks. Foolish peasants never want to believe that their own family members will turn on them," the Duke laughed.

"Indeed, Your Grace."

Resuming his pacing, the Duke placed one hand over his mouth, occasionally closing his eyes as he considered his options, making several more circuits of the room before making his decision.

"Who do we have available from among the Brakahl?"

Dirk shuffled his parchments to the desired page even though he knew there was but one available name on it.

"Currently we have but one uncommitted member of the Brakahl," Dirk explained, sliding the single sheet across the table to the Duke.

The Duke of Firth glanced at it but once. "Fine, keep this agent close. If the other agent misses a third contact, dispatch this agent at once with whatever resources you deem necessary. I want to know what happened to our first two agents and the whereabouts of any new Weres in that area. If we wait much longer, it may not be possible for us to gain any significant advantages from Aldragal."

"Yes, Your Grace," replied Dirk, making a note to himself on yet another parchment. "Next we have a report from our contact in Llandwynn..."

Chapter Fourteen

The lead Quarg ran bent at the waist, his snout-like nose as close to the ground as he could get it. Every dozen steps or so he would stop, lower his nose the rest of the way and inhale the available spoor. They were close.

Looking back, the Quarg gave the sign for caution, then held up two fingers. The leader of the war party signaled back; the message had been received.

Like silent ghosts, the Quargs moved through the brush, using all their woodcraft to avoid the snapping of twigs or the rustling of leaves. When the wind blew, they moved. When the breeze paused, so did they. Their lead scout was good at his job and he had said that their quarry was close. This time they would not miss out on the kill.

Too many years had the *Keon-din* haunted their forests and killed their warriors. A whole generation of Quargs had grown up in fear of the big human that attacked their war parties and disappeared back into the forest without a trace. Today they were prepared; never again would this most hated of foes escape them. Two forest fires flanked their efforts and a long line of lesser warriors slowly climbed the foot of the mountain, beating the brush and driving their ancient enemy into the hands of these their greatest warriors. In all, the Quargs had a thousand warriors in the forest this day. That today the Keon-din did not hunt alone mattered little. This would be the day that the Quargs would have their revenge.

Shog held back from the main advance of his hunters. As chief of the *Nok-birk,* or Long Tusk clan, it was his honor to lead the six Quargs that represented the best warriors his tribe had. Being more intelligent than most of his people, he also recognized that his bulk and superior armor would work against his scout's efforts at moving silently. He was content to lead his powerful young warriors along the chosen trail and await the fires and brush beaters to drive the prey to them. Then, he would add the title Kor-Keon-din to his name; Killer of the Forest Demon.

Not that Shog wanted to face the Keon-din himself. He hoped to bring him down with the arrows of his scouts or the spears of his elite warriors, but Shog was no coward and would face his enemy if necessary. Once his other warriors had sufficiently worn that enemy down, of course.

Shog gave the signal for his warriors to move along the trail, halting them again a dozen paces along. Motioning for them to take a knee, Shog moved up to the lead scout for a whispered conferral.

"Two sets of tracks, Shog," the scout said, indicating the dust of the trail at their feet. "One big, must be Keon-din. Other small, maybe baby Keon-din."

Shog silently growled at the scout's stupidity. Most of the Quargs of his tribe maintained that the Keon-din was some species of giant and not a human. Shog knew differently or at least suspected it very strongly. Only humans and elves would choose to live alone in the deep forest and spend years deterring Quarg raids against the ever approaching human settlements in the lowlands. And the sheer size of the footprints on the path below proved that the Keon-din was no elf. The smaller feet probably belonged to a female.

"Where are they?" Shog asked, barely breathing the words. The smoke of the fires was getting thick now and Shog didn't want to breathe too deeply and begin coughing.

The scout looked around, trying never to look at any one spot while allowing his gaze to drift over all. This was an intelligent move on his part for three reasons. One was because the eye more easily picked up movement or discrepancies using the peripheral vision. Not that the scout understood this, but he knew it to be true through practical use. The second reason was that to pause his gaze overlong on a particular spot might indicate to someone hiding there that they had been spotted, which might make them move or even attack. The final reason was related to the second; the scout didn't want the Keon-din to decide that putting an arrow into the scout might help him remain hidden. The woodsman's skill with a bow was legendary among the Quarg.

"Below us on the slope is a deadfall, actually several. One of them is the most likely place for the Keon-din to hide. He may be able to slip past us if we fail to search them carefully and if attacked, he will have cover. It is the best place for him to be. The noose tightens quickly."

Shog was pleased. He couldn't have hoped for better. He and his warriors would have the high ground in their assault. Even if the Keon-din had cover, allowing him to kill more of Shog's warriors, it would also pin the man down so that he had less room to maneuver. Shog could spare a few warriors; his legend as the Kor- Keon-din would quickly replace them as new followers left their own tribes to join his.

"Are you sure they are there?" Shog demanded in a half-whisper, fingering the steel knife at his belt.

The scout shivered in fear. "Certain, my Chieftain. Where else could it be? The beaters approach us from below, your scouts come down from above and the fire drives even the game to this spot," he explained, pointing to a deer that was bounding close by them, more afraid of the fire than the Quargs.

Shog sniffed. "Keon-din is no deer. He has no fear of the fire or of us. If we trap him, he will choose his ground to fight us. We will bleed when we take him and that I can accept, however if you allow him to bleed us more than necessary because of your stupidity, I will see to it that you regret it."

Shog had no true need to threaten his own warriors. The scout knew what Shog was capable of.

Smoke had begun to cluster in the lowest spots of the hillside even as the bulk of it filled the air above. Shog heard one of his scouts coughing off to this left; they would soon lose the element of surprise, if they had not already. Visibility had not yet been affected but that would be next. He needed to make his move soon or he would lose the Keon-din. But then again, perhaps the fire would do his job for him if the Gods of the Quargs smiled upon him.

Shog smiled broadly. The Gods of the Quargs did not smile upon those that avoided combat when it remained the best way to resolve the issue.

He whispered his commands to the scout and sent him on his way to tighten the noose around the area and to stop the approach of the beaters whose noise was growing louder by the moment. Somewhere on the slope below, the Keon-din had taken shelter; Shog could see no other way for the man to have gone. He was surrounded, and the fires were coming this way. Shog's scouts would not allow anyone to slip through their lines; they were walking practically arm in arm to prevent just that, and anyone foolish enough to climb the trees would quickly reveal himself by reacting to the choking smoke that filled the air above.

Resting on one knee, Shog allowed his elite warriors a few moments respite. The scouts needed time to do their job; to find the hiding Keon-din without alerting him to their presence. Once they located the prey, Shog would be alerted and his plans would be put into action. He could afford to wait and allow his warriors to rest. Let Keon-din use up his strength running and hiding. Shog would be rested and ready for the coming battle.

Time passed and the smoke grew thicker. It was still not so thick that their vision was affected beyond the watering eyes that irritated the Quargs without harming them. Breathing freely remained possible so long as the warriors kept their breaths shallow and Shog saw to it that they did so, forcing them to stay low to the ground and ordering them all to drink from their water skins after Shog personally sniffed each one to ensure that all were filled with water and not the fermented urine that the Quargs loved.

The scout was among them before they saw him, touching his chief on the arm. Shog nearly gutted the man before he realized who it was. The scout placed his hand over his own mouth, indicating that Shog should not speak. They were that close.

More hand signals followed. They allowed the Quargs to pass simple commands, like those needed for raids and hunts, without speaking. The Keon-din was within twenty paces, just down the slope in the nearest deadfall. Movement and a flash of color had been seen, indicating the position. Not likely that the Keon-din would have given himself away in such a manner, the scout signaled, but perhaps the one with him had. The Keon-din must be there as well; there was simply nowhere left.

Shog ordered all the warriors to converge as quickly as possible on the indicated deadfall. Archers were ordered to line the slopes to either side to ensure that there was no escape. Shog and his elite warriors would lead the charge.

When all were in position, Shog bunched his elite warriors in a knot and gave the signal to attack. Two hundred arrows littered the area where the Keon-din was hiding, covering Shog's attack and hopefully killing the enemy before he even arrived. With a howl of triumph, Shog and his elite warriors swarmed over the deadfall, bloodlust in their eyes and their weapons probing and thrusting every perceived threat. Logs and branches were 'killed' and a bright blue scrap of cloth was nearly destroyed with arrows and Shog's own blade.

The deadfall was empty.

Roaring his rage, Shog ordered the lead scout brought before him and then lay about him with his fists, punishing those unfortunate enough to be closest to him as he waited. The nearby area was stripped of all possible cover, and even the leaves of last year's autumn were turned in the Quarg's efforts at finding their prey. By the time the lead scout was dragged, sniveling and crying, to Shog's feet, it was clear even to the dullest among them that the Keon-din had avoided them again.

It was nearly dark before the scout was allowed to die. Shog ordered his tent, a rare and awe-inspiring item for a Quarg chief to own, to be set up on a nearby level patch of ground. The fires were beginning to die out and his scouts assured him that this was as safe a place to avoid the final blazes as anywhere. The wind was shifting and rain was expected that night. Unsure what else to do, Shog left the corpse of the scout before it was even cold and stalked into his tent. He hadn't even enjoyed making the scout suffer and needed time alone to think.

Chapter Fifteen

Mute rolled the hollow log over and cautiously stood up. The moist dampness of the inner log clung to his hair and beard and he knew from experience that the musty smell would travel with him for days to come. By rolling the log over and then pulling it back into place, he had easily avoided the scout line as they passed by him, thankful that a more experienced scout had not been around. Above him, the night was dark with neither moon in the sky. The trees here were thick and the odor of smoke lay heavily over the area. A stiff breeze shook the upper branches of the trees, hopefully disguising any minor sounds he might make.

Moving over to another portion of what had once been the same tree that his log had come from; Mute moved it aside to reveal the sleeping Albrim.

A gentle kick woke the boy and Mute motioned for him to rise. Three days of running and hiding would exhaust anyone, but Mute still found himself mildly annoyed that the boy had fallen asleep. If he had snored, they would both have been discovered. Some of the Quargs had paused near them. One had even sat on the log that had concealed Mute.

"Sorry," Albrim said. He was disoriented from his brief nap, and sure of nothing more than that Mute looked upset with him.

Mute led off, moving back towards the line of the nearest fire. Had the blaze come nearer to the logs, the two of them would have died from the smoke or from their logs catching aflame. Mute had taken a gamble, but at that point, he had had little choice. The scout leading the Quargs was very good at his job, forcing him to be more than a little daring in his tactics.

They had avoided the Quarg's best efforts to find them, and had now slipped through their lines. A thousand Quargs had been devoted to the project, and Mute had beaten them all. Now to exact a measure of payment for three days of running.

Mute set a fast pace, using the well-trodden trails the Quargs had used. He had little to worry about leaving tracks now. Even if something was left atop the incoming tracks, they would be assumed to be Quarg runners returning to the mountains on some errand. Particularly since nothing else lay in this direction save the Quarg villages. There was no reason why the Keon-din would be traveling deeper into Quarg territory, save for vengeance. That would be foolhardy.

At least that was what Mute wanted them to think. He had no intention of being caught now and the opportunity of several Quarg villages left virtually unguarded was something he couldn't pass up.

The nearest Quarg village was one that Mute knew well. Too well. Whenever his thoughts returned to his first visit there, his hand invariably returned to his neck. It was his favorite target. It was also the home village of the Long Tusk's current chief.

They ran through the night and then slept most of the morning away inside a thick bramble patch by crawling through the openings in the thicket left by rabbits. Albrim found this very difficult to do without leaving bits of skin and clothing behind. Mute slid through virtually untouched, despite his bulk.

Around noon, they left their shelter and moved west again, traveling well below the line of the ridges so as not to be easily seen. Twice they hid while Quarg runners passed them, once moving the same direction as they were and once moving back the other way.

Mid-afternoon found them at the base of a cliff wall that showed every sign of being a waterfall in the spring. At this time of year it was nothing more than a rock covered with moss, or at least it appeared so until Mute showed Albrim his secret. The thick ivy growing at the base was of a type that remained green year-round, even this high up in elevation. When Mute reached into the ivy Albrim thought he was looking for something he had dropped. The young man was amazed when Mute lifted up a section of the ivy as if opening a door.

Years before Mute had found the cave and devised the frame of branches that the ivy eventually grew to cover. When he carefully cut away the tendrils growing on three sides of the frame, he had a door that would remain green through the roots of the fourth side. It was the perfect concealment for the narrow passage behind it.

Even turning sideways, Mute had to remove his pack and most other equipment to be able to squeeze down into the narrow crack in the base of the cliff. Albrim passed through more easily, but still found the walls a bit tight. The pathway continued downward at a steep angle for at least twice Mute's height before they reached the floor of the cave. There awaited a large pile of detritus washed in with the rain from years before the doorway's addition. It stank of ancient rot and mildew. At Mute's nod, Albrim closed the door behind himself, plunging the cave into a dim half-light that consisted only of the sunshine that filtered through the ivy.

As Albrim watched, Mute did a quick inspection of their surroundings. Apparently satisfied with whatever he found, or didn't find perhaps, the big man led the way deeper into the cave. Just as the dim light of the entrance began to fade, Mute paused and reached up onto a high outcropping of sandstone that clung near the roof to one side. From there he pulled down a twisted torch of leechvine, a thick woody vine that grew on healthy trees and eventually killed them. Kneeling down Mute used his flint and the blade of his knife to strike a spark and soon the thick tar-like substance on the end of the torch was burning, putting off a thick smoke and only just enough light to see their feet.

Albrim had been in a few caves as a younger man; Lord Ferule's estate at Aldragal had two of them. They were not deep or infested with any sort of dangerous creatures, but they had seemed the epitome of adventure to he and his friends. If Albrim really thought about it, he would have to admit that those caves had been remarkably clean, with level floors and even stairs cut into the walls to assist in climbing. They were very civilized caves. This cave was nothing like those.

At no point did the passageway they traveled open up much wider than Mute's shoulders. The floor was not just uneven, it was rough with outcroppings of rock and there were enough fingers of stone pointing in from the sides to slow their progress to a crawl just to avoid dashing a head or a knee against them. Mute clearly knew where he was going, but Albrim was starting to wish for daylight and the freedom of movement leaving the cave would bring. At one point they passed a small hole in the wall the size of Albrim's fist. Through the hole, a steady breeze was blowing and Albrim could distinctly hear the sound of running water.

Time was beginning to blur to Albrim when they reached what seemed to be a dead end. Mute held up his torch and indicated that they would have to climb. Albrim was dreading that, picturing a climb of a hundred feet or more and nothing but smooth water-slick stones for handholds: particularly when he only had one hand and a hook. He need not have worried; the climb was no more than fifteen feet before the chimney ended on a smooth and level landing just large enough for the two of them to sit knee to knee. Mute had climbed behind him, giving him support when he needed it and so made the landing just after Albrim. The bigger man had to stoop to avoid the low ceiling, even while sitting. The only exit was small and angled upwards.

Giving Albrim only enough time to catch his breath, Mute again led the way, crawling now up the steep slope. Just as Albrim's knees began to seriously protest at the abuse, the passageway ended. Mute disappeared suddenly from Albrim's view. When the young man reached the end of the tunnel, he found that he was able to stand, and found himself waist deep in a hole in the midst of a much larger chamber. Mute was waiting.

The entire room was shaped like a bowl with a slight slope that led to a hole in the middle of the floor. The walls in this part of the cave were limestone, as was the ceiling above, but the floor was sandstone and had been shaped by flowing water. Albrim thought that he could detect a slight breeze coming from somewhere, but no exits were visible.

Mute cautioned him to silence and then unrolled his blankets. Albrim followed suit and then the two men shared jerky and water. Albrim wanted to ask if they should set a guard but Mute was asleep before he could. Apparently, the big man was not worried about being discovered here.

When they awoke, Albrim was initially disoriented and a muscle in his back was complaining loudly at his choice of bedding. Mute had lit a new torch and sat patiently awaiting Albrim's awakening, which meant that he was staring at the younger man as he kicked him softly in the shin. After another bite of jerky, they moved to the back of the chamber and squeezed into another narrow passageway. At least they could walk upright here and for that Albrim was thankful.

A steady breeze was blowing down the passageway from the front. Albrim tried to sniff the breeze as Mute had taught him, to perhaps pick up some clue as to what lay ahead. Unfortunately all he could smell was Mute and his torch. Eventually he began to hear the sound of running water.

Mute stopped in place where the walls temporarily faded back, leaving them just enough room to squeeze past one another. The bigger man motioned for Albrim to stay behind with the torch and then moved forward alone. Mute never quite left Albrim's sight while he performed some task that caused him to grunt with effort and then returned quickly, taking the torch and motioning his young companion to move forward cautiously and then look up.

Picking his steps carefully, Albrim followed the instructions; easing his way up to the point where he had seen Mute moments before. There he found himself at a blank wall of fitted stones with one missing. Gazing up through this opening, he saw the stars of the night sky. Around the edge of the top of the hole were more fitted stones like the one that Mute had removed from this wall. The breeze was blowing through the hole and he heard the running water much more clearly now.

Returning to Mute he whispered, "Where are we, exactly?"

Mute smiled slightly, pulled a Quarg scalp from his pocket and placed it atop his own. Then he pantomimed a roof over his head. He then pulled out his water skin, poured a little out and then pretended to refill his water skin. It took Albrim only a moment to figure out what he was being told.

"We're in a Quarg village? No, we're in the well of a Quarg village?" he asked.

Mute nodded, putting the water skin and scalp away. Squeezing past Albrim, he moved up to the wall of cut stones and began removing them, starting with the one he had placed on the floor of the cavern earlier. Handing them back to Albrim, who was barely able to carry each without dropping it, Mute motioned for him to stack them in the wide spot in the tunnel. In a short time, enough blocks had been moved to allow them access to the well shaft.

Again, it was Mute that squeezed through the opening first. From yet another hidden rock shelf, he pulled out a set of what appeared to be wooden stakes attached one to another with straps of leather. When he shook this out, it snapped into place as it was designed to do; leaving him holding a short ladder with two steel hooks on one end. Albrim was amazed at the device and glad to see it as well. He knew that he couldn't have climbed up the water-slick surface of the well shaft one-handed. The stones were much smoother here than the chimney they had climbed earlier. With one hand, Mute slipped the ladder over the lip of the well above and quickly disappeared from Albrim's sight.

Moving into the position just vacated by Mute, Albrim found himself standing on a narrow lip of stone. Actually, he realized that it was a cut stone just like those he and Mute had removed. Mute had left the torch behind with the stacked blocks, and upwards, about Albrim's own height, he saw the big man's boot disappearing over the edge of the well.

Grasping the bottom rung of the ladder, which hung down to about his chest, Albrim hesitated before putting his weight on it. It didn't look strong enough to support him, but he knew that wasn't true. It had held Mute easily enough and none of the rungs looked bent or broken. Trusting in the construction, he placed his open hook on the second rung and stepped off into space.

Naturally, the ladder held. Climbing was not easy for Albrim, but he managed it, struggling to the top of the ladder and peeking over to see where they were.

He might have been in any one of a small handful of villages he had visited in his short life. The buildings were more rundown, perhaps, but were made of the same materials the peasants on Lord Ferule's estates used. Some were made of blocks of sod and seemed to blend into the sides of the steep slopes on either side of the single dirt street. Albrim could see goats standing on one of the slopes, eating the grass that helped make up a building's roof. Others were made of fieldstone and timbers, but the logs looked uncut, as if pushed into place because they looked to be the right size rather than being cut to fit precisely. None of the buildings within sight was taller than a single level and some seemed to be made of nothing but poorly tanned hides.

Mute was nowhere in sight, so Albrim remained where he was for the moment. The cut stones of the well came up only one layer above the ground and sat in the absolute middle of the road, which left him with little or no available cover. Both moons were up, but the light of each was indirect as each was behind a different mountain peak, leaving the darkness somewhat lessened but not dramatically so. Still, Albrim felt sure that if anyone was looking at the well when he climbed out, he could be seen from any point in the village.

Just enough time passed as Albrim clung there to the ladder that he had begun to doubt his decision to wait. Perhaps Mute had expected him to follow. Should he try to find him now? He was just about convinced that he needed to leave the well when Mute came back out of the darkness and motioned Albrim to climb back down.

Hurrying as fast his hook would allow, Albrim dropped back to the narrow ledge and squeezed back into the tunnel. Mute followed closely behind, smirking at whatever had happened above. There were no shouts of pursuit and no arrows pursued the big man down the well. Whatever it was that Mute had done; he had gotten clean away with it.

The two worked feverishly to replace the cut stones into the wall of the well, Mute's shoulders shaking in laughter the whole time. Albrim was torn between anger at being drug along with Mute and curiosity about what the man had accomplished in the village above. He had never seen Mute laugh before, and the sight was both frightening and humorous. What could make the big woodsman laugh?

With the blocks replaced and Mute's folding ladder replaced in its hiding place, the two retraced their steps down the chimney and along the lower tunnel. Somewhere along the way, Mute called a halt and the two squatted side by side to rest. Feeling that it was probably safe to speak at this the approximate halfway point between the two exits, Albrim questioned Mute about what he had done in the Quarg village.

The big man began laughing again, his scarred fast twisting horribly as he tried to make the sounds. Nothing came forth but his shoulders continued to shake, and despite his uneasiness, Albrim found himself laughing too.

"What did you do?" he demanded.

Mute used his fingers to draw something on the bare stone, hoping that Albrim would be able to pick up on his meaning by watching the strokes. When the young man remained confused, Mute pointed to Albrim's pack, waiting patiently while it was opened and then pulling out Albrim's journal and a piece of charcoal he had saved for writing.

The sketch was also largely inconclusive to Albrim. After some time of drawing and hand signals, he decided that whatever Mute had done in the village had involved the local idols or totems that the Quargs worshiped. Apparently, desecration of Quarg centers of worship was not beyond Mute's sensibilities. There was also some indication of a surprise for the Quarg shamans when they sacrificed some sort of animal; Albrim thought that it might be a goat, on the following day. All that he knew for sure was that the shamans would not be happy. Whatever had happened, Mute was certainly pleased with his efforts. Albrim would just have to be content as well, if a tad frustrated.

"When do I get a chance against the Quargs?" Albrim demanded.

Mute cocked his finger once in the air and then placed his torch near to the ground on one side, then rotated it up and over to a similar position on his other side. Albrim had been with the big man long enough to understand so simple a signal. He would have his opportunity against the Quargs in the morning.

Chapter Sixteen

Shog and his elite warriors sat in a glum semi-circle as various shamans and tribal leaders argued one with another over assessing the blame for the failed hunt. One shaman had a thin cut across his face from a knife blade as testimony to one such disagreement. Not only had the Keon-din avoided their best traps and three separately started fires, the man had disappeared completely, leaving no tracks or other indications that he had even been in the area. A small but vocal minority believed that the Keon-din had died in one of the fires and his body burned beyond recognition. Most believed that the Keon-din was truly a demon and had walked through the fires unscathed.

Shog inwardly seethed at the incompetence of his minions. Not once did he acknowledge that the plans that had been so unsuccessful had all been of his design. In his heart, all the blame belonged on those who had failed to properly carry out his orders. One scout had already paid for his incompetence. The Keon-din had made him look the fool by preying upon his idiot followers.

Every one of them stank of fresh blood, unwashed bodies, and the smoke of forest fires. So strong was the reek that even the Quargs noticed it and they were a people who had an aversion to bathing. Scouts were reporting difficulties in finding adequate game in the immediate areas around the Quarg encampment and Shog knew that he had to change tactics. He also knew that he had to distance himself from any further failures. His new allies would be coming soon, and he didn't want them to know of the incompetence of Shog's minions.

Using a stick to draw his new strategy on the ground, after first using his fists to gain the attention of his minions, Shog outlined a plan by which the Quargs would reestablish a skirmish line across one particular section of the forest. That area had long been suspected to contain the home of the Keon-din, based on years of encounters with the man. It was in this area that he most often attacked them, as if he was more intent upon defending that area or perhaps lived there. In any event, it offered the most logical place for them to begin their hunt again. Not that Shog intended to be with his warriors this time.

Noon found Shog and his elite warriors traveling back to their home village of Breg-shun, literally translated as 'village rich in goats,' the ancestral home of the Long Tusk clan since Shog had taken control six years before. Quargs did not dwell on ancestry in any significant way.

A screen of scouts ranged around the column, and behind the elite warriors trailed a line of Shamans and minor tribal leaders following Shog's lead and distancing themselves from the debacle that the hunt for the Keon-din had become. Most of them were not warriors; at least not in the sense that Shog and his men were. They were of no real use to the effort and would have contributed little to the hunt. In Shog's opinion, most of them contributed little to anything, but they were a necessary part of his rule. They did the menial tasks of governance he didn't care to do himself.

The hoot of an owl alerted Shog of an incoming Quarg. He ordered his entourage to halt as they waited for the arrival. To his surprise, the runner came in from the west along the very trail they were following. This meant news from Breg-shun.

Stumbling with exhaustion, the young Quarg made it to Shog's feet and dropped to his knees, sucking great gasps of air into his tortured lungs. Shog had been a runner as a young Quarg and so waited patiently for the warrior to regain his breath. An experienced runner, the fellow took no more than a half-dozen breaths before his heart rate slowed enough to allow him to talk plainly. He did not want to bumble his message before the great chief himself!

"Chief, I bring word from Breg-shun. Shaman Torgkic sends his affections and prayers for your well-being and begs to report that the glorious ancestral seat of your legendary power has been attacked! The great shrine of Slobab-rajtol has been desecrated! The holy goat of Slobab-snutrub has been slain!"

At these words, the various shamans among those gathered around began howling in grief, one even chewing at the bark of the sacred walnut tree in a fit of self-chastisement. Shog wished that he had his whip. He knew it had been a mistake to leave it behind.

"We searched the village for whoever the culprits were but they had vanished. Some believe it may have been a Quarg dissatisfied with your rule, a few believe that it was Slobab himself, showing his disfavor of our tribe," the young man hesitated.

"When did this happen?" the Chief asked.

"Last night, my Chief, between mid of night and early prayers."

"Anything more?" Shog demanded, aware that the religious-minded among his people would be more than a little upset over these occurrences. This could be a major problem for him.

"Yes, my Chief. In the mud near the water trough of the holy goat Slobab-snutrub we found a single track, perhaps left by one of the invaders," the runner produced a string from a belt pouch. "It was this long, my Chief, and this wide," he added, producing a second, smaller string. The runner laid the two strings onto the ground and then placed his own foot next to them for size reference, just as he had been commanded to do when given this mission. The strings dwarfed the runner's foot in both length and width.

The chief had to speak up to be heard over the yammering voices of the shamans. Each was demanding or pleading for either justice or retribution depending on their religious stance towards such things. He ignored them as best he could

"Rest, runner, I shall need you soon," Shog said, turning away.

Raising his hands, Shog eventually managed to make himself heard.

"I will meet with my council. The Chief Shamans of each order shall attend. Go now and prepare a place for me."

Few in the crowd dispersed; most simply talked or shouted louder in an effort to be heard before the Chief managed to retreat from earshot. The Quarg elite warriors placed themselves as a barrier between Shog and the shamans to give him a chance to escape their pleas. He needed time to think before a decision had to be made.

In record time, Shog's tent was constructed in the midst of the trail. The council consisted of only two Quargs: Shog's brother and a one-eyed old uncle that was stooped and gray with years and among the wisest men Shog had ever known. With them came four shamans, the leaders of the four orders and each quite elderly. These four entered the tent trying to speak over one another and did not cease until Shog ordered his brother to beat them into silence. Few actual blows were required.

Once Shog had their attention, he began the council.

"What do these desecrations mean to my rule?"

Shog's brother spoke first. He was the largest and most powerful of those gathered, other than Shog, and so took the opportunity to voice his opinion before all others.

"Worship is for sheep, it means nothing!"

Shog's uncle flipped his eye patch up and scratched deeply inside the empty socket. "The common Quarg is a religious Quarg. Desecration is something that will reflect badly on you, Shog. The people will take it as a sign from Slobab, no matter what."

"It is a sign from Slobab!" shouted a shaman. "He does not approve of your rule!"

"It is a sign from Slobab," agreed another shaman before abruptly disagreeing. "You must punish the transgressor and you will be the blessed of Slobab."

The eldest of the shamans jumped atop a broken stump that the tent had been pitched over. "Slobab wants only that we leave our villages and take to the paths of blood! We must soak the lowlanders in the flow of their own hearts!"

Having been ordered to attend, the runner arrived and knelt to one side, awaiting his chief's command.

"Runner!" Shog spoke loudly to drown out the arguing shamans. "Tell me of this footprint that was found."

"My chief," the runner said, bowing his head as was proper. "The print was found beside the holy water trough in the place where water leaks from a weak seal. The print was huge, as you saw from the string, and very deep."

Shog absently fingered one tusk, deep in thought. "And this was the only place around the trough where there was any mud? And the only place in the village where any strange tracks were found?"

"Yes, my Chief."

"Then the track was left deliberately," Shog announced, shutting the various shamans up with his words.

"Very good, Shog. I agree," cackled Shog's uncle. "The size of the footprint indicates a human or larger. That the person was able to move about the village without leaving any sign save for in the one patch of available mud sounds very deliberate to me." The uncle turned to the runner. "What sort of print was it? Bare foot?"

"The runner looked the uncle in the eye. He need not abase himself before this old has-been. "No, Grimage. The track was of a shod boot."

Turning back to Shog, Grimage said, "I agree with what you are thinking, Shog. It was a sign from the Keon-din. You tried to kill him and he is letting you know that he can not only avoid you in the forest, but reach directly into your home village and desecrate your gods without effort."

"Slobab will destroy the Keon-din!" screeched a shaman.

Shog only partially agreed with his uncle. He believed that the desecration was not done in a fit of braggadocio; it was the act of someone who was frightened. They had come close to catching the Keon-din in the forest and so the man had taken his revenge out on the Quargs in a way that would embarrass them without putting himself at risk. It was just the sort of spiteful attack he himself would indulge in if the situation were reversed. But, that was where the Keon-din had made his mistake.

His decision made, Shog acted. "Call in the scouts and strike the tent, Uncle. Bring the shamans along to the village as swiftly as you can. Parg and I," Shod jerked a finger at his brother, "will take the elite warriors and half the scouts with us on a straight run back home. Send a runner to the army and order them to remain in their skirmish lines but to return to Breg-shun immediately"

"We must punish the transgressor!" howled a shaman as his eyes rolled in religious fervor.

Smiling evilly, Shog responded, "We shall, shaman. Because of this mistake made by the Keon-din, we once again know where he is! I shall go with all speed to the village to organize all who are there and pursue the Keon-din. I shall either catch him and kill him myself or drive him into our army as they speed towards us. The fool is as good as caught."

Chapter Seventeen

Mute was a master at concealment, Albrim had to give him that. Using the natural fallen logs, leaves, and brush, he had constructed a blind so close to the main trail leading to Breg-shun that if Albrim had extended his bow with his good arm, he probably could have touched the packed dirt. All of this Mute had accomplished in the pitch black, just before the dawn. Yet Albrim was certain that no one traveling along that path would ever see them. Proof of that belief was the young Quarg who had passed them just as the sun was rising. The young warrior had stopped to make water only a few feet away and never once suspected that the greatest enemy of his people lay in hiding so very close.

Albrim had wanted to take the Quarg right then, in revenge for the narrow brushes with death they had suffered in recent days. Mute, however, would hear nothing of it. When Albrim later questioned him, after the runner had passed on down the trail, the big man had simply wagged a finger at him. "Not now" was the best translation Albrim could devise. They needed to wait.

"Wait for what?" Albrim wondered. They were obviously concealed to perform some type of ambush. Why not remove that lone Quarg while they could? They could easily have hidden the body before their real prey arrived, couldn't they?

Albrim had plenty of time to think as he lay in hiding, which also gave him time to sulk. He was tired of being unsure about what was going on. Mute shared little with him, less even than their communications barrier should have caused. Quargs had been slaughtering humans for years and with all that he and Mute had been going through the last few days, Albrim wanted to be a part of the return strike. All of his training with the militia, plus years of firing a bow for Borel, added to the last year spent absorbing bruises from Mute had prepared him for more than lying on damp leaves in a pile of brush while lone Quargs watered the nearby plants.

He was a man! A member of the Cobble militia! He'd fought a Were, even if he did have to be saved by his grandmother. At sixteen, he was an adult by the laws of Aldragal and yet Mute watched over him like a mother hen. For pity's sake, he carried the Curse in his veins! Didn't that at least qualify him to fight a few Quargs?

They lay in their shelter for some time, seeing no more movements by Quargs or anything else for that matter. Albrim was convinced that Mute had fallen asleep, so long did the big man go without moving. Just as he was about to give up, Mute's head snapped up, and with a quick grip on Albrim's arm, warning him to stay down, the big man leapt from the blind and disappeared silently into the brush.

Now Albrim could hear something. Someone was coming down the trail moving towards the village. Moving right towards him. Through the brush he caught a glimpse of something brown. Then came a flash of yellow as one or more individuals came into his sight moving from his extreme left. They were moving more quickly than a walk and someone was shouting something Albrim did not understand. Another language? Probably, but they were too far away for him to be sure.

An opening in the brush finally allowed him to see who it was that was approaching. It only took a single glance for Albrim to recognize the lead individual as a Quarg. They were traveling in a tight knot save for one who traveled some distance ahead. There seemed to be six of them. The one in the very front was carrying a short bow in both hands and was panting heavily as he shuffled his feet. Those clustered in the rear were holding spears and wore some type of leather armor. It was the largest among them that was shouting, apparently urging the others to continue to run despite their obvious exhaustion.

He'd seen Quargs before; a few were captured when they raided a caravan and had been given over to Lord Ferule for justice. Quargs were stupid, brutish humanoids and were widely exterminated in all but the most remote of areas. These were as ugly as the prisoners had been with their piggish features and ragged clothing. The main difference was that those Albrim had seen before had already been defeated and knew they would soon be dead. These were far from beaten and likely full of fight despite being tired from their run.

Now that they were closer, he could tell the language he was hearing was most definitely not his own. Nervously Albrim cocked the spoon of his metallic arm and notched an arrow to his bow. Surely this was the reason they were here. Mute had told him to wait, but wait for what? Not for the first time, Albrim despaired over the communication gap between him and the big man. Would there be a signal? A thrown pebble? Perhaps Mute would appear behind the Quargs and wave. How would Albrim know for sure if the signal wasn't something obvious? He needn't have worried. When the signal came, it was very obvious.

From out of the forest came the whistle of an arrow in flight. Before Albrim's eyes, the leading Quarg, the one with the bow, suddenly sprouted an arrow from the side of his head. Immediately the scout collapsed; his nerveless fingers dropping the bow before him.

The battle was on.

Chapter Eighteen

Shog urged his warriors along, but it became apparent that all would not be able to stay with him on the run. The shamans fell behind almost immediately. Most of their lives were spent praying and butchering sacrifices, so they had little heart for so grueling a run. His scouts, smaller Quargs with less strength, gradually fell behind as well save for one hearty fellow whom Shog bullied into running ahead as a precaution against ambushes. Not that he was worried about an ambush this close to his home village.

Once it became clear that most of the other Quargs were simply unable to maintain the pace, Shog let them fall behind but kept his elite warriors moving through intimidation and threats. Even they had begun to lag. Now only four of his elite remained with him and the lone scout. Somewhere not too far behind, his pathetic brother and perhaps one or two others still followed. Occasionally, Shog caught sight of them in the distance. Perhaps he would call a brief halt soon, and then order them all back to running just as his brother reached the rest stop. It might be worth it just to again establish dominance over the fool.

But Shog did not want to stop, not even for a short rest. The Keon-din was in the area and this effort remained Shog's best hope of killing the man once and for all. First, they had to return to the village of Breg-shun and organize the warriors there to use as the anvil while the remainder of his army swept in as the hammer. For the first time, the Keon-din had made a mistake, and Shog intended to make him pay.

Another hour and they would be in the village, perhaps longer as the exhausted Quargs would have to rest soon. Perhaps he should continue alone? No, he decided. That would be foolhardy. Better to take the risk of the Keon-din escaping than risk himself to a forest predator or a surprise attack by another Quarg tribe. His own life was far too precious to risk needlessly. His brother's was of no real value, perhaps he would order him to run on ahead.

His scout was slowing again. The little Quarg was almost done. If he fell, Shog would have to stop. There was no way he was going to keep moving without someone out covering his path. Snarling another threat at the scout, Shog was gratified to see the little wretch push himself one more time, his shuffling footsteps increasing in speed ever so slightly.

And then, the scout fell to the ground.

"You lazy *Crokmah!*" Shog roared at the scout, belatedly realizing that his elite warriors had all paused in their run. It was then he noticed the arrow protruding from the scout's skull.

"Ambush!" he screamed, clawing at the sword sheathed at his side. Another arrow struck the Quarg to his immediate right, the big warrior screaming as the missile plunged completely through his neck. Shog watched in horror as the warrior fell, the bloody head of the arrow thrusting a hand span out from his neck. No bow had that much power! Turning to his right he saw a brief flash of movement in the forest. Someone was there, behind the underbrush. He was kneeling, no, now he was rising to his feet. It became clear to Shog then. The large form he was seeing was that of the Keon-din!

"There," Shog screamed, grabbing another of his elite warriors and pointing him towards the now visible Keon-din. The big human had stepped from his shelter and was calmly drawing another arrow from his quiver. The bow in his hand was massive, nearly as tall as the big man himself. He looked as if he were practicing with his bow, not as if three powerful Quarg warriors were even then rushing towards him. Each of the warriors were screaming some sort of battle cry, the sound of which had turned the blood of enemies to water in the past but to all appearances the Keon-din seemed completely unaffected. The charging Quargs might just have been so many screaming children for all the reaction he gave.

As he watched his remaining elite warriors in their mad charge at the Keon-din, Shog felt his blood run cold. This was his first true glimpse of the big human. He was larger, stronger, and more powerful than any man or Quarg that Shog had ever seen. No one could stand so calmly when outnumbered three to one, even with an arrow ready to fire. Shog realized that he could not fight this man while he stood hale and strong. Not one-to-one. He needed to give himself an edge.

If his three elite warriors could not kill the Keon-din through their advantage in numbers, then Shog knew that he, too, was dead. Hoping that his warriors could at least wound the man, Shog turned and ran up the path towards the dead scout, tossing the small body aside with one hand as he snatched up the fallen bow. He pulled a handful of arrows from the quiver as well. He was not the best shot in the world, but the range was not that great either. His brother and the warriors with him would be here soon. One well-placed shaft and the Keon-din would dead or helpless. That thought brought a smile to Shog's face.

Mute sighted along his bow, watching in satisfaction as the three charging Quargs all hesitated as the point of the arrow wavered between each. Finally, he chose his target and drove the arrowhead into the lead Quarg. The warrior tried to sidestep, causing Mute's aim to be slightly off, striking the shoulder rather than the chest. Dropping his bow, Mute reached to pick up the sword he had left leaning against a tree.

The first Quarg to arrive used Mute's reach as a free attack and brought his sword in a full swing from well to his right horizontally through to his left. Had the blow landed, Mute would have been either cut in half, or at best, eviscerated. His sword barely clasped in one hand, Mute leaped back, just barely avoiding the swinging blade. Landing lightly, he immediately had to twist to his left to avoid the spear thrust of the second Quarg, who had moved slightly from his companion to avoid the wild swing. Mute slapped the point of the spear out wide with his left hand as he tried to reverse his sword without dropping it.

Neither Quarg waited for Mute to set himself. They were veteran warriors who knew better than to give an enemy an even chance. Keeping up their assault, the spearman continued to thrust at Mute's midsection as the swordsman ceased his wild swings and followed after the human, looking for a misstep before taking the opportunity to bring his blunt edged weapon down onto Mute's head. For his part, Mute kept backpedaling, thankful that he had prepared the area in advance and removed the worst obstacles. He couldn't afford to fall down now.

Jab after jab, the spearman kept up the attack, giving Mute no opportunity to counter attack. The swordsman worried Mute more; the way he kept back out of reach but held the sword ready behind his head for a quick step up and a downward slash onto Mute's head. If it wasn't for the spearman, the swordsman would never be able to stand so open and ready for the attack. He'd have to put some thought into defense as well. However, the thrusting spear kept Mute both off-balance and with no hope of offense.

The shadow of the branches on the ground told Mute that he was about to run out of room. Just past the tree he was using as a reference, the land slid steeply down into a shallow depression. Even three steps more and he would run out of ground. He would have to make a move soon.

Mute faked a step to the side and away from the swordsman, which is what he would think that the Quargs would be expecting. The thrusting spear adjusted that direction slightly as the swordsman stepped forward intent on making up the distance he would lose if Mute had indeed gone that way. Too quickly for them to recover, Mute used the flat of his left hand to slap away the spear and in the same motion stepped towards the swordsman, even as he dropped his own sword. Now he was too close for the swordsman to make his attack and wide open for anything Mute decided to do. It is certain that the swordsman did not expect the attack that came.

With all of the strength and weight he could put behind it, Mute drove the heel of his right hand up into the Quarg's nose, bursting it amidst a shower of blood. Squealing like the pig he resembled, the swordsman dropped his weapon and staggered back.

The spearman hesitated at his companion's distress before readjusting his grip on the spear for another thrust. Mute didn't allow him the time, grabbing the haft of the weapon just below the point, preventing it from being turned towards him. When the Quarg stepped back and used his momentum to jerk the spear away from Mute's one-handed grip, the spearman thought for a moment that he still might win the fight. He had forgotten about the human's other hand. During the struggle for control of the spear, Mute had drawn his butcher knife.

Mute followed the spearman's turns and drove the knife home in the Quarg's gut. For a moment, their eyes were only inches apart as the Quarg's eyes filled with pain and fear while Mute's were empty, devoid of any emotion. One set of eyes soon became cloudy with impending death.

As the spearman fell, Mute relieved him of his spear and then turned to find the swordsman only then trying to rise. Mute pinned him to the ground with the spear, leaving him squealing even louder than before. The Quarg curled up around the spear and kicked spastically. He was finished.

Looking back the way the Quargs had come from; Mute found that the Quarg with the arrow in his shoulder was on his feet and trying weakly to draw a dagger from his belt. The warrior looked pale and was in obvious pain but there was no quit in him. He was staggering towards Mute with murder in his eyes. Picking up his sword, Mute moved to meet him. Both knew who was going to win.

On the trail, Shog had the first arrow notched and hurried back to the point that gave him the best view of the battle. He saw that two of his elite warriors were already down and the third was staggering as if close to death himself. The Keon-din looked unhurt and was stalking the remaining warrior. The finish there would be swift, Shog could see. The remaining Quarg seemed unable to lift one arm and clutched nothing but a dagger in the other. There would be no avoiding the human's blow. When it came, it would be the last one of the skirmish and Shog would be alone.

At least he knew that he would not be facing an uninjured Keon-din. Drawing the feathers of the arrow back to his cheek, he sighted along the shaft and waited until the injured Quarg below stepped to one side, or fell from the blow that killed him. That would give Shog the clear line of sight that he needed to finish the fight. It would only be a moment now.

Mute was not a cruel man and did not wish the Quarg to suffer. Had the warrior tried to flee, Mute would have likely let him go. That he wished to fight rather than run was something the big man could respect, so he intended to finish it quickly. Holding his sword with both hands, he prepared for a slash at his enemy's neck as he moved closer, looking for his opening.

And then it came. A single step and a powerful swing and the fight was done, the Quarg's neck crushed from the blow of the sword. The warrior was dead almost upon impact and fell limply to the ground. Mute looked back towards the trail just in time to see the triumphant look on Shog's face as he released his arrow.

Chapter Ninteen

Shog had the Keon-din dead to rights! There was no way he could avoid the arrow; the man was standing out in the open with no cover. Even if he managed to avoid one arrow, or if Shog missed, the human would never avoid two of them. Even a wounded Keon-din would easily fall prey to an experienced warrior such as Shog.

Taking careful aim, he released the arrow. How surprised the Keon-din looked! His eyes were wide, his mouth was slightly open! He was looking death in the eye and found himself unmanned by the experience! All of these things passed through Shog's mind in the same instant that Albrim's arrow did.

The big Quarg toppled to the ground without a sound, a snarl of victory forever etched on his face and an arrow buried in one temple. He never saw the dirt and pine needles his sightless eyes came to rest against.

To Albrim, the Quarg's body seemed to fall slowly to the ground, taking forever to finally strike the earth. He was shocked at the sight and nearly forgot to pull another arrow from his quiver. He did so only because of his father's years of training.

"You fire, then you draw another arrow, son," he had said, explaining that a second shot on prey was rare but you had to be prepared if it occurred. Particularly when hunting boar or some sort of carnivore like a wolf. Such a creature was doubly dangerous when wounded or in pain, and may not be traveling alone. So it was purely reflex that caused Albrim to pull out another arrow and re-arm his hook. Thankfully, this meant that he was not completely unarmed when another Quarg crested the rise in the trail.

First one Quarg, and then two more slid into Albrim's line of sight. By the looks on their faces, each must have been as startled as Albrim. The Quargs were gasping for air from their run just as the first group had been. The three shouted and clawed at their weapons as Albrim lifted his bow and fired.

Perhaps from inexperience, perhaps from a touch of fear, but whatever the cause, Albrim released his bowstring too quickly, knowing as he did so that he had missed. His arrow passed wide to the right leaving all three of the Quargs unhurt. Forgetting their exhaustion, they lowered their weapons, two carrying spears and the other an ax with a curved blade, and charged the boy they saw before them.

Too slow! Albrim knew that he was going to be too slow reloading his weapon. Fear choked him but his training still won through, as he deliberately drew an arrow with his left hand and he cocked his hook against the stone on his belt. Closer came the Quargs; up came Albrim's bow. The arrow came into line as the Quargs spear points were almost within reach. He didn't need to aim.

All three Quargs dived to either side as he fired, stark fear clearly outlined on their faces but one was not quick enough to prevent the arrow from driving into his side. Albrim had chosen one of the spearmen, fearing the longer reach of those weapons more than the hideous wounds that could be caused at close range by the ax. The Quarg with the ax was the first to roll back to his feet and he immediately rushed at Albrim, snarling as he brought his weapon around to cleave the skull of this puny little human.

By then, Mute arrived, taking the ax wielder's arm off at the elbow with a powerful overhand swing and using a shoulder to drive the Quarg to the ground. He followed through by circling his blade up to his left and throwing a backhand slash at the last healthy Quarg, causing him to stumble back and give Albrim enough time to pull his dagger. He didn't have time to take his buckler free from its place on his side, but did drop his bow to the ground.

Mute, surprisingly, left the healthy Quarg alone as he turned back and drove his sword into the Quarg with the arrow in his side. Mute's rush had left him in the middle of all three Quargs, so he was trying to clear out a safe direction to turn his back to. Shrieking in pain, the Quarg had barely regained his feet and now tried to run from the newly arrived Keon-din. He only made it a few steps before collapsing, trailing a looping line of his own intestines along the way. A quick glace at the Quarg whose arm he had removed proved that he was down and unlikely to be getting up soon, which allowed Mute to turn once again to check on Albrim and the last remaining uninjured Quarg.

Seeing that the Quarg he faced was still off balance from the bump by Mute, Albrim took three quick steps to get inside the Quarg's spear. Once there he slashed at the Quarg's face, keeping him off balance, regretting that the spearhead was on the same side as his weapon hand, which prevented him from grasping it and attacking at the same time. After a second near miss, the spearman had the clear realization that he was the only Quarg still standing, and the warrior dropped his weapon and ran. Albrim was too surprised to pursue, and missed his wild slash at the Quarg's back. Bursting through a thick thorn bush, the warrior fled into the forest.

Mute didn't bother to chase the last Quarg; he knew that it was time for them to leave the area, and fast. More Quargs could be on the way, and they had more than accomplished their mission here. He had recognized the first Quarg Albrim had killed as wearing the markings of a clan chief and the armor and weapons carried by most of the others were much better than those carried by the average Quarg. These had been the best warriors in their village. He regretted not have enough time to at least strip the bodies of their armor. He would have preferred to have buried the armor in the forest to keep the next generation of Quargs from having it. As it was, he didn't have time, but did stop to pick up the small curved-bladed ax of the now one-armed Quarg as well as the sword of the chieftain. Both were finely crafted and would likely bring a good price.

The two humans gathered their equipment and after a quick check on the one-armed Quarg, who had already bled to death, they ran to the north along a route scouted earlier by Mute for just this sort of quick escape. The big man set a blistering pace, running at the fastest speed that he thought that Albrim could maintain with his shorter legs. All the months of running with Mute suddenly seemed to Albrim to have been time well spent. Eventually they left the thick forest undergrowth and turned onto a game trail that led along the ridges in the approximate direction that they wanted to go. By the time the next Quarg came along the trail and found the bodies, the Keon-din and his companion were long gone.

Mute ran until he knew that Albrim was getting tired, and then he called a brief rest. As soon as their breathing slowed, he led them off again. In this manner, he hoped to get as far from the sight of the ambush as possible, yet retain some strength to fight if they should have the need. At this point, Mute felt that distance was more important than stealth but after they had rested the third time without sign of pursuit, he decided that it was now safe to change his mind.

Altering their direction, he led Albrim up the steep slopes towards the mountains to their west. He took great pains to hide their trail, and twice doubled back to watch for pursuit. None was in the offering. Well after dark, the two humans took to a stream and changed directions again, moving eastward in a crouch to remain below the level of the banks and thus hopefully not be outlined against the brighter sky by a luckily-placed Quarg. Once they had covered some distance, Mute led Albrim up a smaller creek that descended from one of the foothills they were traveling between. Halfway up the steep slope, the water ceased to run in the creek. Likely the stream was fed by mid-slope by a spring and occasional rainstorms had carved the upper streambed. When this occurred, Mute abruptly turned off the creek bed, climbed a few feet upslope, and then descended down into a shallow depression.

Reaching the bottom of the depression, Mute signaled for Albrim to be silent. They sat there in the thick damp leaves for some time, listening for any sounds of pursuit. When Mute was satisfied that they were safe for the moment, he reached into the leaves with one hand and lifted up some sort of barrier. When it was out of the way, he motioned to Albrim to enter the pitch black hole the hidden door had concealed.

Rolling so that he could lower his feet into the darkness first, Albrim was thankful that the hole was only about half his height in depth, but with a pile of loose stones mounded up there that gave him poor footing. He knocked over the stones before finding a solid place to settle his weight. Dropping the rest of the way into the hole, he felt around and found three solid walls with one direction that was open. Easing back into this alcove to give Mute room to climb into the hole, Albrim sat down to wait.

It was a long time before Mute finished concealing the entrance behind him. He was careful to smooth the leaves out, ensuring that none of the wet ones from the bottom had been kicked over onto the dry leaves on the surface. Not easy to do in the dark. Once he was satisfied, Mute eased the door down and felt his way into the alcove, only to find Albrim fast asleep.

Chapter Twenty

Albrim awoke to a feeling of disorientation. Mute was asleep beside him, but he wasn't completely sure where they were. There was little light in their bedchamber, only what filtered through the layers of leaves above the wooden planks of the ceiling. The boards were not close together and looked more like a fence than a door. All four walls were smooth limestone, each sweaty and damp with cool moisture. Only the alcove they sat in prevented the room from being a near-perfect circle. After studying his surroundings, Albrim decided that they were in a shallow sink hole. He knew the area was full of them.

As he moved about, Mute awoke as well and without even acknowledging Albrim, began to dig into his pack for a piece of jerky. Sharing a few strips of the dried meat - by the taste Albrim believed it was mountain goat but knew that it could just as easily be venison - they sipped water from their skins and rested.

For the first time, Albrim had the chance to think about what he had done. In killing the Quarg, he had taken a life for the first time. At least the life of anything more intelligent than a deer or a mok. It had not felt like he had thought it would. One moment, the Quarg had been alive, and the very next instant, he lay dead upon the ground. Not that he regretted it; the Quarg had been about to kill Mute after all, but he knew that the sight would be with him forever.

Albrim was somewhat surprised at being troubled by killing the Quarg. As a race, the Quargs were not innocent creatures. Rarely did a year go by that the humanoids, which publicly worshiped both false and evil gods, did not descend from their mountain homes to kill and rape. Tales said that the Quargs had been actively hunted and destroyed in some parts of the world to end their ceaseless attacks on civilization.

Albrim had known people who were killed in Quarg attacks, specifically a traveling merchant who regularly stopped by the home of his old friend Borel. The man had taken to the young Albrim, and often brought him small gifts. Then one day he did not arrive as usual and Borel had to break the news to his son. Such thoughts helped ease the guilt but suddenly the smallness of their hole was beginning to bother him, as was the heavy quiet.

"Where do we go now?" Albrim asked, breaking the silence.

Mute looked at him a moment in a manner that told Albrim that the big man was contemplating whether to answer, and how to do so if he did. That answer might involve hand signals, a drawing in the dirt, or a punch depending on Mute's decision.

It was the drawing but with no dirt; Mute again had to borrow Albrim's journal and charcoal. The sketch was crude but more than adequate to reveal their destination as the clearing where Albrim had lived for the last year and more. He found himself somewhat disappointed by that revelation.

"We are done with the Quargs?"

Mute agreed that they were, and then drew a profile of the Quarg that Albrim had killed along with a couple of others. The big man chuckled silently as he added Albrim's arrow jutting out from the first Quarg's temple. Mute then used hand signals to indicate that the Quarg was someone special and eventually relayed that he had been the tribal chieftain.

Albrim finally understood. "So you're saying that since we killed the chief of the tribe that the Quargs will be leaving us alone."

Mute waved his hand, tilting it back and forth.

"They will leave us alone for a while at least?" Albrim guessed.

Mute nodded, and pointed again to the picture of the Quarg Albrim had killed, then spread his hands in a gesture that Albrim had learned meant either 'new day' or 'tomorrow'. In this instance he correctly guessed what Mute meant.

"We won't be seeing the Quargs again until they elect a new chief?"

Mute shrugged and then waved his hand again. That was the most likely scenario.

"When will we be going back?"

One finger pointing straight down.

"Tonight? Then we're going to rest here all day?"

A nod for yes and then Mute pointed at the other Quargs in his drawing. Next, he used two fingers of each hand to 'walk' around.

"Just in case the Quargs are still looking for us? I understand."

It occurred to Albrim that he and Mute were slowly learning how to communicate with one another. Mute used certain hand signals in the same way every time, and simply being around the man so much was giving Albrim insights into the man's thoughts. Perhaps he couldn't read or write, but Mute was an intelligent man and more than capable of overcoming his speaking handicap, if Albrim was willing to learn. Mute certainly had the patience, but then he hardly had any choice if he wished to be understood at all. Albrim surmised that that may be one of the reasons that Mute chose to live alone. That and the horrendous scars on his neck. At that moment, Albrim truly felt as if he understood Mute and felt close to him for the first time.

Perhaps it was this sudden feeling of closeness that caused Albrim to bring up an old question that he had never gotten a reply to.

"Why have you been taking care of me?"

Mute looked at the ground for a long time. So long was he ignored that Albrim began to believe that the big man wasn't going to answer him. Then he was surprised by a sudden hand signal that he didn't understand. Mute pointed once to his own arm, and then rolled over, placing his back to Albrim in a gesture which said clearly, "Leave me alone now." Rather than push the issue, Albrim lay back with his pack as a pillow and thought about the motion.

Mute had pointed at his own arm, not Albrim's. Did that mean he was saying he felt sorry for Albrim losing an arm? Sympathy for someone who had also lost something like Mute had lost his voice? Perhaps he was saying that he wanted Albrim to help him, be his 'good right arm'. Perhaps he envisioned Albrim taking his place as the so-called guardian of the forest. It could just be that he wanted someone to help fight the Quargs, who were obviously better organized this year than they had been in recent years. Maybe there had been others like him over the years.

The two men dozed throughout the day, which wasn't always easy. As the sun rose higher, the humidity in the sinkhole rose as well, leaving them both drenched in sweat by midday. Both of their water skins were dry long before nightfall. Albrim had taken to holding a pebble in his mouth to encourage it to water. Mute remained reticent to communicate so Albrim spent much of his time reading and writing in his journal. Finally, the light in the sinkhole dimmed and Mute signaled that it was time that they prepared to leave.

Lifting up the gate, Mute slid from the hole first to scout the area before full dark. Albrim marveled at the big man's ability to slide out through the layers of fallen leaves with virtually no sound. He waited impatiently for Mute to return as his emotions warred within his heart.

Albrim did not want to return to Mute's camp. His daily life was filled with periodic episodes of depression over his life as it was, but the thought of being chained back to his root shelter again made the depression worse. One of the moons would be full again soon, and likely Mute wanted to be back in the clearing, just in case Albrim had a relapse. Even knowing that going back there only made good sense, Albrim's spirits still sank by the moment as he thought about it.

The worst part of his whole situation was that he trusted Mute and thought that the man was looking out for him as best he knew how. Albrim didn't believe that he needed a nursemaid, but obviously Mute did, which only fueled his depression further. What if the big man was right? Thinking of turning into a mindless Were and killing innocent people scared Albrim worse than almost anything did, but that was what the armband was for, wasn't it? That Mute was still concerned bothered Albrim badly.

Full moons remained difficult times for him. Mute had stopped chaining him down to the flat rock in the clearing, but he still left him chained by the neck during the nights and usually slept outside the camp. Albrim rarely slept well on those nights, feeling unbelievably restless and irritable. When he did manage to sleep, his dreams were terrible, awful nightmares of death and bloodshed. The question was; did Albrim trust himself? Mute certainly did not. At least, not when it came to the Curse.

Finally, Mute returned for Albrim and they left the sinkhole behind after removing all signs of their presence. Mute pointed out several landmarks to his young companion, urging him to remember them so he could find the hidden place himself one day if necessary. Albrim did so, promising himself that he would later add the details to his journal. That way, he would not have to trust only in his memory.

Navigating by the occasional star visible through the forest canopy, Mute and Albrim walked the night through, stopping only twice; once to refill their water skins and later to rest after both moons dropped below the horizon. During this period, they sat back-to-back in the middle of a game trail they had been following, waiting for their eyes to adjust to the deepening gloom.

When Mute was ready they moved on, Albrim resting one hand on the other's pack to keep from losing him in the darkness. In this manner, they kept moving, albeit slowly, until the sun finally made an appearance.

They spent a few hours in the ruins of a small house that looked to have been partially burned a year or more in the past. Albrim wondered if it had been the work of the Were. There they took turns sleeping and standing watch, leaving around noon to continue their journey. They reached a deep stream about dark and paused for a quick meal after they had crossed. Finally, Mute felt safe enough for them to run along the next clear trail until again the moons both went down and then they camped. Albrim knew that if tonight had been one of those nights where the moons took turns lighting the night sky that they would likely have ran all night. As it was, they slept only a few hours, again taking turns standing watch, and left again at dawn. The next night was spent back in Mute's clearing, Albrim once again sleeping in his root shelter. He had been appalled and saddened when Mute insisted he be chained again to the collar.

For three days, Albrim sulked in his shelter without catching a single glimpse of Mute. The night of the next full moon came and went, badly for Albrim, as he fought against the terrible pain shooting through his head and his good arm. His missing right arm tingled and ached in a different way, with visions of the Were biting it off passing again and again before his eyes. The next morning, Albrim saw Mute sitting against a tree along the edge of the clearing. He looked to have been there all night.

For two more nights, Jacet sat fat and full, but alone, in the sky. Each night passed with slightly less discomfort for Albrim, but he dreaded them all just the same. The following night both moons were full and he spent the night sweating through a living nightmare where the taste of blood was ever on his lips and the moons called to him. In the morning, he found that he had bitten through his lip.

Each night after that the discomfort lessened, and after the full phases of both moons had passed, Mute released Albrim from the chain and allowed him free movement about the camp for the first time. Albrim reveled in his freedom but had no doubt that Mute was always nearby, even when Albrim didn't see the big man.

As for Mute, he spent the days hunting and scouting for any sign of the Quargs, and his nights standing watch over Albrim's nightly terrors. He watched the young man very closely for any signs of changing, the cautions of the Dwarf ever-present in his mind even as he stayed beyond the young man's reach. Mute wasn't entirely sure that the armband was truly able to repress Albrim's ability to spread the Curse during his full moon inspired fits.

The morning after the last full moon, Albrim awoke reasonably well refreshed, having only had a few nightmares and very little pain the night before. His skin was irritated where it touched the armband and that beneath nearly rubbed raw. Albrim still could not touch the armband, not even to soothe liniment on the inflamed skin. To his surprise, Mute did it for him, dribbling the liquid over the armband so it would flow between the metal and Albrim's skin. Then Mute rubbed the liniment in above and below the armband, giving Albrim some much-needed relief.

Another month dragged by, with only brief breaks in the monotony of life in the forest. Albrim was allowed to expand his horizons slightly and wander short distances from the clearing alone. However, he had a strict time limit to return by and on the one instance that he was late he met Mute coming to get him. Each day they ran, fought their mock battles and practiced with the bow. Albrim was improving in all three areas, but still despaired of ever regaining his former level of marksmanship.

By the time the full moons returned, Albrim had again sunk deeply into depression, dreading the awful nights ahead that would be made worse by the fact that the full moons were coming back to back this time, with the second moon taking over the very night after the first one faded. Needless to say, Albrim was not surprised when Mute reattached the chain to his neck collar.

Albrim did indeed suffer, but not so badly as before. Mute sat with him each night, forcing him to concentrate on other things besides the pain of the Curse; making him run around the clearing for hours and carry piles of stones from one place to another and then back again. He drew the prints of animals in the dirt and made Albrim identify them even through the haze of his pain. When Albrim didn't cooperate, Mute would douse him with buckets of water, still icy cold from the stream. Somehow this cut through the pain and allowed him to regain some measure of himself. However, Mute would not allow Albrim to come within reach of him during these nights. Just a precaution, Albrim understood, but it still made him angry.

By the time the full moons passed, Albrim was exhausted from the constant battles. There was no doubt in his mind now that the attacks of the Curse were lessening in their severity, but he still grew sick when thinking about the next one. He was beginning to think again that he might be better off dead than living like this; dreading every full moon and living in the deep forest to keep from killing the innocent. What kind of life was this?

After the full moons had passed, Mute took Albrim hunting. They went looking specifically for bears or the small forest buffalo. Mute also taught Albrim how to trap for mok and beaver and twice they ambushed war parties of Quargs out looking for trouble. One had been from the same tribe as the chieftain Albrim had killed earlier in the summer, while the other group had worn different markings. In one ambush, Albrim had killed another Quarg but in the second, both his bowshots had missed their marks. Both times the Quargs had been driven off without a hand-to-hand battle, for which Albrim was thankful. He was not yet confident in his ability to defend himself and with his depression, he wasn't sure that he wanted to, and that scared him.

Harvesting the bearskin had been a new experience for Albrim, as his father never hunted such a large beast. Using the fur of the one Albrim had taken, Mute showed him how to preserve the hide and make it into a coat. He used a buffalo hide to make one for himself, then leggings that strapped over their regular clothing to keep those warmer as well. Mok and beaver furs they used to make scarves and hats for them both, preparing them for the coming winter.

Mute disappeared one day without chaining Albrim up, and did not return until a few weeks before the beginning of autumn. When he saw Albrim had remained in the camp, he nearly smiled. Apparently, Albrim had been tested. However, the man was not in a good mood and immediately upon entering the clearing, motioned Albrim to join him by the fire pit.

Once they were seated to Mute's satisfaction, the big man dug into his pack and removed a wad of folded parchments and unceremoniously dumped them in Albrim's lap. Albrim was concerned by the look of anger on Mute's face, hoping it wasn't directed at him, and unfolded the pages one by one. They were all torn at the upper corners where Mute had ripped them from the nail that had attached them to a tree or sign.

The first page was an Official Decree; at least that was what it said in large letters across the top. Albrim had seen many of these posted on the wall in the Bucket of Ale back in Cobble. They contained reports of new laws or mandates from Lord Ferule and, less often, the King himself. Sometimes they were announcements of an increase in taxes, or a warning concerning bandits or rampaging monsters. Sometimes, they were announcements of an offered reward for a criminal and sometimes contained a hand-drawn picture of the person. Several of the papers in the stack were of the latter type.

Glancing back through the pages more carefully, Albrim found the first one to be an announced reward for a criminal that he immediately recognized. It contained a crudely drawn image of a wild looking creature that was more ape than bear and stood easily ten feet tall if the proportions of the drawing were to be believed. Albrim recognized it because he had seen copies of it many times in his lifetime. They were of the wild demon that lived in the deep forest. They were of Mute.

Risking a sidelong glance at Mute, Albrim wondered if this was what his friend was angry about. Surely he had seen his own wanted poster before. They had been around for years and looked nothing like Mute. The second and third pages of the bundled documents revealed nothing of real interest to Albrim, but he read each one carefully, explaining them out loud to Mute, as he had done once or twice in the past. One announced a new tax increase by Lord Ferule and the second was a Royal Decree from the King telling of a treaty with some bandit-warlord-minor-noble from a bordering kingdom. Nothing so far that should have upset Mute.

The next few pages were more wanted posters but of no one that Albrim knew. Then he reached the bottom page, and nearly laughed aloud. It was a wanted poster and the drawing was a pure caricature if ever Albrim had seen one. The person was perhaps human, but could have been a Dwarf with a face full of wrinkles and a single tooth showing inside a mouth that had been drawn open as if the person were yelling. The eyes were scowling and one fist was shown to be clenching a branch, or perhaps a magic wand, next to the person's face. The caption read 'WANTED FOR MURDER' and named a ten silver piece reward for the capture of this dangerous woman.

"Woman?" thought Albrim. The drawing had been so crude as to make it difficult for him to distinguish that. He glanced at Mute to see the man red-faced and staring at the page as if ready to rip it to shreds the instant Albrim dropped it. What could be making him so angry? Albrim studied it again, reading carefully the description of the woman twice before the truth struck him.

The woman in the picture was Gran!

Chapter Twenty-One

Gran was wanted for murder! His Gran! The woman that had cared for him every day of his life since his mother had died! Gran!

Albrim was still stunned. Weeks had passed since he first saw the wanted poster with the open-mouthed caricature, and he simply refused to believe it. Weeks spent busily moving from place to place to avoid death, but whenever he had the time, the memory rushed back into the forefront of his thoughts. There had to be some mistake.

Mute had taken it worse than Albrim, giving him the first clue that he and Gran might actually know one another. Had Mute grown up on one of the estates Gran had lived on? She had been the primary midwife wherever she had lived for decades, so it wasn't beyond reason to think that she might have delivered Mute as well. The more Albrim thought about it, the more it made sense to him. Why else would he have been brought to Mute? The big man was someone that Gran had known.

Albrim took another cautious step, careful to place his feet only where Mute had placed his. His boots had been removed and stowed away in his pack. Today as most days, the two of them were wearingonly a strip of soft leather on their feet. Thin the footwear was, but not as thin as what Albrim had worn growing up. Mute had shown Albrim the advantage of wearing them: not only did you keep a little bit of protection between your feet and the briars and thorns so common in the forest, but the leather was so thin that you could feel the presence of sticks under your feet and so avoid putting your full weight on them. Not advertising your presence by snapping a twig was a big advantage in a forest full of enemies.

Full was the word, all right. The Quargs had come out in force. Not only the village of Breg-shun and their allies, but also the Keer-tun and the Lak-snaz as well. Nothing like this had ever happened before, or so Albrim gathered from Mute. Quargs rarely cooperated this well together, and they did not even represent the biggest danger to the two humans. That honor belonged to the wolves.

From Mute, Albrim had learned that some Quarg tribes, specifically the Lak-snaz, trained and domesticated wolves for both hunting and warring purposes. Not that Albrim hadn't heard that story before, but from Mute it just seemed more realistic, or fatalistic. Those wolves were the same animals that the men of Cobble and surrounding towns occasionally hunted to keep their numbers down, and rarely did those beasts find the courage to face down a man. The Quargs had these wolves in abundance. Mute was more than prepared to deal with them and had even demonstrated a number of times that he could fool them into losing his trail. The real danger were the larger wolves that Albrim remembered all too well from his encounter with the Were. Wherever they had fled to after the death of the Were at Cobble, they had returned.

Those massive brutes seemed to be everywhere. Mute would no longer allow them to sleep in any of his hidden shelters on the ground, insisting that they climb trees for concealment and even then, they only slept an hour or so at a time. Albrim learned that his friend had a number of these treetop hideaways prepared, just as he had those in caves and sinkholes. In some places, where the trees were tall and strong enough, there were even crude ladders and walkways that connected one tree to another so they could travel short distances without leaving their scent on the ground.

What was driving the Quargs to cooperate one with another rather than fighting among themselves as they usually did? Had a powerful chieftain united the clans? Mute indicated that he didn't think so. He seemed to believe that he would have heard something if that were the case. Albrim couldn't imagine where or how Mute would have heard anything from anyone. He rarely left Albrim's side and, as far as he knew, never left the forest.

All of that perplexed Albrim, but the real question was: where did the wolves come from? There were simply too many to belong to one tribe and the giant wolves were new to this area. On that, Albrim agreed with Mute. Borel had confessed to Albrim that he had never seen one of the brutes before that last fatal wolfing, and he had been an experienced hunter. The wolves could be the sign of another Were.

Those thoughts truly scared Albrim. Why, he wasn't sure; he could no longer get the Curse and dead was dead whether it was by Were bite or Quarg spear. Despite his repeated bouts with depression, Albrim knew that he didn't want to die, and being torn to shreds by a wolf or Were was not how he wanted to go if he did. Not like his father had died.

Mute held up a hand clenched into a fist, telling Albrim to freeze in place. Barely daring to breath, the younger man watched as the older one listened intently into the silence of the forest. The only sound either heard was the wind in the treetops, a distant roar that somehow didn't qualify as sound and only added to the silence. Nothing was moving, or calling. No birds were singing. Those were all bad signs.

Doing as he had been taught, Albrim took a slow, quiet breath through his nostrils and sampled the breeze for anything out of the ordinary. He scented honey, which meant either a beehive or a late crop of honeysuckle, more likely the hive. Albrim also detected the scent of wood smoke, but it was old. Yesterday's fire, likely. The Quargs were everywhere, so finding a recently used camp was not surprising.

Mute dropped to one knee, dropping his fist in the agreed upon signal for Albrim to drop as well. Doing so, Albrim made the faintest of sounds as his knee encountered last year's crop of fallen leaves. It was no more than a whisper of sound but he knew that Mute would warn him about it later. Once they had concealed themselves, Albrim heard the distant but distinct sound of voices.

Kneeling as they were, both men saw the distant movement at the same time, more a flash of dark brown against a lighter brown than anything else, through the thick brush in front of them. Soon enough the hunters hove into sight: a dozen Quargs trailing a like number of wolves. Walking along as if it were in command of the group was one of the big wolves.

Not for the first time, Albrim wondered where the large wolves had come from. He considered giving them a different name to help distinguish them from the smaller wolves. Something that big deserved their own name. Somehow 'wolf' just didn't describe them adequately. They had to have come from somewhere and wherever that was there had to be people there, maybe not humans but people, and it seemed natural to Albrim that they would have a name that distinguished them from the average wolf. If he thought of it, he'd ask Mute when they had the chance.

Watching their enemies closely, Albrim was relieved to see that the band was moving across their view from left to right and were far enough away that the outer most wolves were unlikely to stumble across them here in their hiding spot. Assuming, of course, that the men weren't scented, but that was unlikely as the wind was wrong. To fight that band would be the end of Albrim and Mute. There were simply too many enemies in the group for them to fight alone.

Using a tactic he had used before, Mute waited until the enemy had passed from sight and then led Albrim directly to the closest point where the war band had passed. Mute would find such wandering bands and then travel up or down their trail to disguise their own tracks among those of the enemy. This time they turned away from the Quargs and hurried along what turned out to be a well-traveled trail. Following this sort of tactic worked well with tracks, but was nearly useless if the Quargs had wolves along. Hiding their scent was possible, but not that easy. Mute had other tricks hidden in his devious mind for that.

They ran for a time, and then stopped as the tracks passed near another of the elaborate bramble hedges that grew sporadically through the forest. There Mute pulled open his pack and removed a small glass bottle from one of the rawhide loops attached around the inside. When the cork came out, a strong odor emerged that reminded Albrim of a mok during mating season. Without hesitation, Mute shook out a few drops onto both of his feet and then Albrim's. Another favorite tactic of his; disguising their scent with a natural and more pungent one. Yesterday he had used fox urine and the day before that it had been buffalo musk. Albrim couldn't decide which one had stunk worse but thought that this one might be the winner.

Next Mute did something even Albrim hadn't expected. Once their scent was disguised he grabbed a grape vine hanging from a springy willow and pulled hard, actually bending the young tree down a good bit. Then he stopped pulling and motioned for Albrim to hold on to the vine. When Mute allowed the tree to spring back upwards, Albrim clung desperately with his single arm and was lifted by the vine a foot or so off the ground. Lifting his legs, Albrim easily swung over the brambles and dropped to the top of a convenient stump. Smiling he tossed the vine back to Mute who followed suit then tossed the vine back to its previous spot.

Not for the first time, Albrim marveled at his friend's forest savvy. The man seemed to know everything there was to know about the forest and constantly made the pursuing Quargs look foolish. He believed that if it weren't for the occasional hit and run attacks Mute insisted on visiting upon the Quargs, the man might easily avoid his enemies forever. Albrim wondered if this was how Mute spent every summer.

That night was again spent high atop a forest giant. The platform Mute had constructed there was merely the living branches of the tree pulled slightly together and tied by using vines that naturally grew there. Just below the platform was a massive nest that Albrim recognized as having been built by giant squirrels. Nothing seemed to be living there at the moment, for which he was grateful, but the ball of broken branches and harvested vines helped conceal the platform from the ground below. Once before they had slept here and a passing Quarg patrol had shot an arrow into the nest, either in an attempt to strike a squirrel or to check it as a possible shelter for the humans they searched for. Either way, no one was harmed, and the arrow could still be seen jammed inside the nest.

So high were they in the tree that Mute even allowed Albrim to speak so long as he kept his voice to a whisper. This was a relief after the long day of silence.

"Where are we going?" Albrim demanded as soon as was allowed. They were due for another raid.

Mute responded by tapping a finger against one ear and then pointing to his temple. They were going to gather some type of information. The point to the ear had meant 'listen,' while the one to the temple had meant 'learn'. They were going somewhere to learn something, but further explanations by Mute proved fruitless. Where they were going remained a mystery to Albrim.

They spoke for a while of what they had seen and accomplished in recent days. Or rather, Albrim spoke and Mute signed. Slowly they were developing a language they could both understand using hand motions and body language. Really important words, such as those used preparing an ambush for Quargs, had come easily to them. Mute was confident enough in Albrim's understanding that he allowed the younger man to participate more and more each day. Not that he had anywhere to hide him even if he had wanted to. The Quargs were everywhere in the forest, it seemed, and had even staged a raid on one of the human settlements. Albrim suspected that the attacked settlement had been Spicer, but wasn't sure. When he asked Mute for the town's name, the big man only shrugged.

"Mute, why do we keep coming back this way?" Albrim asked, suddenly changing the subject. They were in familiar territory now; in fact, they were very close to the clearing where Albrim had spent so many months chained to his root shelter.

Mute signaled that he didn't understand the question.

"Well, we come back by the clearing at least once every few weeks. The Quargs have already found it, so we know it's not safe to go back there. I was wondering why we keep returning? Does the place mean so much to you?"

Mute waved that thought away. One place meant nothing more to him than did another. Then he pointed to his arm in that odd signal Albrim had yet to truly decipher. When he saw the confusion on Albrim's face, Mute tried a different tact, pretending to start a fire and then lifting the flames up towards the sky.

"Fire, campfire. A hearth? The clearing is your home?" Albrim guessed but seeing the look on Mute's face, he knew that wasn't right. "No, wait! The fire going up, that would be easily seen. You're going to do something to the Quargs, something that'll be recognized as..."

Albrim's voice trailed away. It was obvious that he was off track by the disgusted look that Mute gave him. Again, the big man went through his motions, building a fire and then lifting it to the heavens but this time he scooted a short distance away, not that he could go far on the tiny platform, and shaded his eyes while looking up. He then pointed toward the stars as if recognizing something he had seen.

Something about the clearing was a signal, or would be a signal. Perhaps Mute was to leave a signal and was waiting for the Quargs to leave and give him the chance. No, Albrim decided against blurting that idea out. It just didn't seem right. Finally, it fell into place, or at least it seemed to in Albrim's mind.

"You're here watching for a signal, or a sign?" he asked. Mute responded with a wavering hand. Not quite right, but getting closer. "You're waiting for something? Someone?"

Mute nodded, that was it. They kept coming back to the camp because someone was supposed to meet them there.

"Who is it?"

Mute again pointed at his arm.

"The Dwarf?" Albrim guessed, really having no other ideas. "He made my new arm, is it him that we're waiting for?" That made sense to Albrim. The Dwarf had come by twice and was the only 'guest' Mute had ever allowed in the clearing, other than Albrim himself. Well, a few Quargs had been there, but they hadn't been invited.

This time Mute shook his head. No, it wasn't the Dwarf. Now that Albrim thought about it, the Dwarf had been blindfolded and led to the clearing by Mute. It was unlikely he could return on his own.

"Someone else, then... Someone besides the Dwarf, someone that knows to find you here," Albrim said, more thinking aloud than talking to Mute. He looked up in surprise to find Mute agreeing enthusiastically.

"Who is it, Mute?" he asked, exasperated. Sometimes it seemed that they could communicate so well and then other times it was as if they spoke different languages.

Again, Mute pointed to his arm, and then threw up his hands in disgust when Albrim obviously didn't understand. He waved off Albrim's apologies. It was no one's fault. They would one day manage to share this. It would just take time.

By dawn they were well away from that tree and perched in another that overlooked the clearing from a distance. Albrim wondered how many times Mute had observed him from this very platform. The underground storage space had been found, and all of Mute's belongings had been stolen or trampled into the mud. Some Quarg had tried to burn the root shelter but dismally failed at the task, leaving only a charred area of grass before the entrance.

Twenty Quargs and a mule they had stolen somewhere had worked for a week to turn over the flat rock Albrim had spent so many nights chained to, perhaps thinking there was some type of treasure hidden beneath it. Even the stream had been befouled as much as the Quargs could manage, tossing in heaps of garbage, filth, and dead branches from the forest. Two Quargs had been killed by traps that Mute had left, and later, the Quargs had cannibalized them before tossing what was left into the water.

Leaving Albrim in the tree, Mute left twice to scout around the clearing over the course of the morning and afternoon. No sign was seen of anyone approaching the clearing, nor were there any indications that anyone had entered the area since the last time the Quargs had been there. While he was out, Mute took the opportunity to reset a few of his traps and move a couple to previously safe approaches to the clearing. Once darkness fell, they moved on by use of a series of ropes that Mute had used to connect several trees. One was to stand on and the other was higher, to provide a grip for your hands as you walked along the bottom. Back on the ground, Mute held his hand to his ear; it was time to gather the information now.

Dodging patrols all night, because the Quargs seemed particularly active, Mute and Albrim moved due west into the mountains. Three days later, they turned south and moved along the higher peaks dodging things more vicious than Quargs by far. Albrim saw creatures and monsters on that trip that he'd only heard about before; including the massive mountain bear and even a pair of griffons. Albrim was fascinated with the new sights, but Mute wouldn't allow him any time for observations. He seemed to be in a hurry to get somewhere.

A week to the day since leaving the clearing, the pair were hiding in a hollow tree with Mute standing on Albrim's shoulders, bringing the bigger man to just the right height to see out of a hole in the trunk that allowed a view of a Quarg camp on the shore of a small lake below them. At this distance, it was doubtful that Mute could hear anything but he seemed only interested in observing for now. Albrim hoped that he didn't take long, as he felt sure that his shoulders would soon break.

The camp below was busy, and while not a permanent habitation, it had obviously been in place for several weeks. The dung heaps alone proved that. Temporary kenels on the far side of the camp contained easily a hundred wolves while a dozen more had the freedom of the camp. Another dozen of the larger wolves stalked about as well, forcing the smaller wolves and even the Quargs to give way before them. In fact, the larger wolves almost seemed to be in command, so confidently did they move about, but Mute knew better than that. The wolves, no matter their size, were animals and nothing more. However, it was whomever the wolves worked for who was truly in command. All he needed to do was figure out who that was. It certainly wasn't the Quargs, who cowered away from the big wolves or avoided them altogether. Someone else owned the loyalty of those wolves.

Mute took as much time viewing the camp as he dared before signaling to Albrim that he was ready to come down. Squatting carefully, Albrim lowered the man to the point where Mute could step off onto a protrusion inside the trunk before the younger man scrambled out of the tree so that Mute could follow him.

"I guess you must have memorized the whole place," Albrim sulked, rubbing his sore shoulders. "Next time I stand on your shoulders!"

Mute smiled and flicked something imaginary off his shoulders.

Albrim smiled back. Mute had just made a joke about Albrim's weight being inconsequential to him.

"Where to now?" Albrim asked, figuring that they were off on another mystery destination. Mute did that a lot, moving from place to place for reasons Albrim didn't always understand.

This brought a negative response. Pulling out long strips of jerky, Mute pointed to the ground at their feet.

Sitting down there at the base of the hollow tree, Mute used simple signals to inform Albrim that they would be entering the Quarg camp that night.

Chapter Twenty-Two

No moons were out, so being seen was unlikely. Both Mute and Albrim were well coated in a disgusting blend of natural scents that left them with watering eyes but also made them nearly unnoticeable to the wolves. The scents had been carefully chosen from plants and creatures that wolves do not prey upon, so long as they weren't hungry. The Quargs made sure that they kept their wolves, particularly the larger ones, well fed. Lone warriors tended to disappear if they did not. Albrim believed that they stank so badly the Quargs and the wolves would both pass out from the odor and so make the excursion into the enemy camp completely without risk. Even Mute smiled at that opinion. Albrim didn't understand that even a few feet from the two the scents melded together so well that it was unlikely anyone would notice them; their scents would simply fade into the background odors of the forest.

Avoiding the outer line of enemy pickets was easy; they were already inside the camp. All day the pair had lain hidden, Albrim in the hollow tree and Mute up in the branches of a living one not too far away. Slipping down the hillside into the center of the camp had been a little difficult, at least for Albrim, as they had a great deal of distance to cover without being seen or heard. Fortunately, the Quargs were lazy creatures and had already harvested all of the loose dead wood and brush in the area for firewood and so the way was surprisingly clear of such obstacles. It was only a matter of time before their hollow tree was harvested.

Two long lines of shallow latrines already overfilled with waste lay along their chosen path. Few Quargs would risk the area after dark; no one wanted to fall into one, and the smell kept even the wolves away. Moving between the ditches gave them a direct path to the center of the camp, removing the issue of slipping past sleeping Quargs. Those not on duty, and some that were, lay wrapped in blankets at scattered points all over the area. Mute felt that it would be next to impossible to travel any other route without eventually stepping on someone.

Once they reached the relatively level ground, Mute took Albrim by the shoulder and led them in a stooped-over run. The only lights were the dim coals of a few late campfires and a single tall torch that burned before the large canvas tent that was their destination.

The stink of the jakes combined with their own artificial odor to leave Albrim a bit lightheaded but he kept his balance and somehow avoided falling into one of the ditches. Once they approached the main tent, the light of the torch on the other side was blocked by the bulk of the tent itself, and the darkness was nearly absolute. It was only Mute's hand on Albrim's chest that prevented his running directly into the tent. Kneeling down where Mute told him to, by placing a heavy hand on his shoulder and applying pressure, Albrim tried hard to find some clean air to breathe.

Mute felt along the base of the tent until he found the seam he expected. The tent was not a self-enclosed shelter, meaning that the floor was not attached to the walls the way that the walls were attached to the roof. This made it easy for him to slip inside the tent; he wouldn't have to cut the canvas and leave an obvious message to the Quargs when they found it in the morning. Now all he needed to do was remove a single tent peg and they could simply crawl inside.

Finding the nearest peg by feel, Mute carefully pulled it free and set it aside. Lifting the edge of the tent wall a few finger-widths he lay on his side to peer beneath. He didn't want to enter in plain view of a dozen Quargs.

It was bright inside the tent with more than one lantern and a few torches contributing to the effort. The torches were dangerous inside such a shelter, as the canvas could easily catch fire. However, if you intended to have someone awake inside the tent at all times to warn those who were sleeping, most of the danger could be avoided. Quarg chieftains were rarely popular and apt to have a number of guards on duty, so it wasn't really an issue. Still, Mute wondered why so much light was needed.

The more he thought about it, the more that Mute believed that the light couldn't be for the Quargs. The ancestors of the evil humanoids had originally lived beneath the earth. Their above-ground brethren had lost some of that ability, though they still had the advantage over humans. This much light indicated that there was someone inside whose night vision was less than that of the Quargs. Mute had a good idea who that might be, but needed to be sure.

Peeking below the edge of the tent was the most dangerous part of the trip to his mind. All Mute saw initially was a thick carpet of uncured furs, so he was forced to lift the tent wall further. There he saw that his view was blocked by something made of polished wood.

A chest? Possibly, or perhaps it was an armor stand or even a simple box taken during a raid on a caravan. Returning the canvas to the ground, Mute edged over to his left and removed a second stake. Laying back upon the ground he repeated his move and was grateful to find himself looking at an empty sleeping area, filled with furs and blankets and an interior canvas door that blocked his view to the main part of the tent. This also prevented anyone there from seeing him crawling under the wall. After gaining Albrim's attention, the two slid silently through the opening.

Voices in the tent were loud, filled with shouted curses and laughter, punctuated with occasional squeals of female laughter. They must be interrupting a party. Before taking further risks, Mute searched the room they were in, making sure no one was asleep among the pile of furs. Next, he approached the chest that had blocked his first look into the tent and, after a check for any traps, eased the lid open. A quick search revealed nothing of interest or value until he reached the bottom. There he found an ivory tube as long as his forearm with a broken seal.

Removing the scroll case he tossed it to Albrim, indicating that the young man should read it. The light in this room was less than in the main area, but enough leaked through around the doorway to make reading possible. Sitting on the pile of furs, Albrim removed the parchment and began to read.

Mute crawled to the doorway and peered through one of the gaps in the ill-fitting canvas. The outer room was painfully bright after the darkness of the night and he had to allow his eyes time to adjust. At least two-dozen figures were scattered about the room sitting on furs of one type or another. Some were tossing bones, wagering weapons and a few small value coins. Others were singing a rowdy song in Quarg, a language Mute understood very well. One was involved with a pair of hideous female Quargs in one corner. It was the others that caught his attention.

Six figures sat in a circle around the central fire pit, sharing a bottle that might contain wine but could just as easily be homemade *Gidgack* in a reused bottle. Gidgack was a Quarg favorite and was made from a mixture of fermented wheat and goat urine. Mute noticed that three of those sitting at the fire were not drinking but passed the bottle without raising it to their lips. Those three were not Quargs.

Humans, Mute could tell, even with their backs to him. One sat slightly in profile, but the heavy furs he wore concealed him as did the thick head of hair and bushy beard. A second man wore only leather breeches and a thin shirt of cotton, making the excessive body hair that covered his back easily visible. The third man was almost concealed by the second man, save for when he occasionally shifted his seat. The one arm Mute could see was also hairy.

Each of the humans were large men, strong and powerful looking. They spoke Quarg well and the conversation flowed easily between them and the three Quarg chieftains. All three of the local clans were represented here, with the Lak-snaz and the Keer-tun recognizable by their clan markings. The third Quarg was a young warrior that Mute had never seen before. Apparently Shog's clan had not wasted time mourning his death before someone had replaced him. Such was the way of the Quargs.

Mute used a skill learned through decades spent alone in the wilderness. There were times that blocking out all background sounds was important. Being able to focus all your concentration on one particular sound could save your life. Doing so now, Mute excluded the noise from the revelers and concentrated only on the words being spoken by the six warriors around the fire. It wasn't perfect, and he didn't catch every word, but much of it was clear.

"We cannot waste any more time on your Keon-din, Tras. It is time that you honored your part of the bargain," announced the closest of the three humans.

The Quarg from the Lak-snaz nearly dropped the bottle of Gidgack in surprise. "Our deal was that you would use your people to help us kill the Keon-din once and for all. You cannot desert us now; the man cannot be left behind if our warriors are away."

Responding to this was the man that Mute could not see. "We agreed that we would help you, and we have. We must strike soon to accomplish our goals or we'll have to wait another year. This Keon-din is but one man. He will be caught eventually, and until then, what can he do? Kill a few goats? Desecrate another shrine? Nothing!."

"One man cannot cause any lasting harm to your village," the first man quickly added. "He will eventually make a mistake, and one of your warriors will spit him on a spear, or one of your wolves will feast upon his eyes."

The youngest Quarg snarled his agreement, grabbing up the bottle and draining it.

"I am in agreement with Tras," interrupted the chief of the Keer-tun. "We must be close to killing the Keon-din. Our scouts and yours agree that we have him trapped in the *Yub-zuk*. We must finish him!"

Mute smiled at the words. The Yub-zuk was the round bowl-shaped valley far to the north and east. Only a few days from the new human villages. He had led the Quargs that direction weeks ago, leaving false sign that he was in the valley and leaving some traps behind. That they still believed he was in that area was gratifying.

"Yes, and before that we had him trapped in the *Blek-tor*, and before that the *Pok-tok*," spoke up the second man. "Not once have your scouts even caught sight of him, or his offspring."

They thought that Albrim was his child? Mute couldn't wait to relay that along to the younger man.

"And neither have your wolves," snarled Tras. "For all their abilities and their size, we combined have not found the Keon-din. That alone should convince you that the man must die! You cannot leave such an enemy to roam freely in the rear of your army!"

Army? Mute did not like the sound of that. Army of what? There were no organized kingdoms or other governments in the mountains. Was the invasion meant to destroy Aldragal? Perhaps it was intended for Skallist to the south? Were Elves the target? More questions than answers at this point, but Mute was intrigued by the answers that he did have.

"He is one man," stated the third human. "If he survives the winter, I will hunt him down myself."

"As will I," stated the second man.

"If you wish to worry about a single person, then you should join us in our search. There is one out there somewhere more dangerous than all the rangers in the kingdom. One person who can destroy us all," added the first.

"This is ridiculous, to speak of halting our search for the Keon-din," argued Tras. "We have him trapped in the valley now, all we need to do is finish the search and he will be dead and beyond harming us. Then we can follow through with your plans."

"When? A year from now? Even a month's delay would push our plans back a year. Catching your Keon-din is not important," scoffed the first human.

The chieftain of the Lak-snaz rose up to his knees. "We do not need a month! Two weeks at most to search the valley, less if you send more of your wolves there to help! We cannot let him just walk away when we are so close! To do so would be to void your side of the bargain!"

"Wait," stated the third human when his fellows began to stand. "Confer with me," he said, motioning the other humans to step away from the fire with him.

Mute strained to hear the conversation of the men but could not over the loud grumbles of the three Quargs. Only the young chieftain agreed with the humans and he was arguing on their behalf. At least he finally got a good look at the third human and found him to be as hairy as the others. Each sported long matted beards, looking more like tall dwarves than humans. He did not recognize any of them.

Finished with their side-conference, the three humans returned to the fire. The first man spoke for them.

"We will dispatch more wolves to this valley. It will take them four days to arrive. From the moment they do get there, we will allow you their use for one week, not a moment more. At that point you will abandon the search for the Keon-din if you have not already killed him. You will move your forces into position at that time."

The chieftains of the Lak-snaz and the Keer-tun huddled together, pointedly ignoring their junior counterpart from the Nok-birk, or Long Tusk clan. It was obvious to them that he was already in the human's camp on this issue.

"We agree," they said, neither looking particularly pleased with the idea, but believing that it was the best compromise they could negotiate.

"Fine," stated the third human, leaning forward so that Mute could see the wide smile on his bearded face.

"Let's drink on it!" added the second man, leaning back in order to reach a leather pack behind him and pulling out a pair of wine bottles. "This time we'll drink of the grape, rather than the goat!"

The human's laughter was louder than that of the Quargs. Apparently, the humanoids were as happy to drink wine as the humans had been to drink Gidgack.

Feeling that he had pushed his luck far enough, Mute rolled back from the door and relieved Albrim of his scroll, returning it to the bottom of the chest and carefully replacing everything that he had removed. Next they did a quick survey of the room and tidied up anything that they might have disturbed, such as the furs Albrim had sat upon, and then left the way that they had came.

As Mute led the way back through the latrines he pondered the humans he had seen within the tent. They were not foolish city-bred ruffians. They also were not local people. Mute kept a careful watch on the peaceful dwellers of the forest. These men were from outside, likely from the other side of the mountains. They were also without apparent scruples, or they wouldn't be agreeing to treaties of war with Quargs.

Reaching the base of the hill, the two men moved upwards. Albrim thought only of what he had read and the excitement he expected Mute to show when it was revealed. Mute thought only of the humans and their unorthodox appearance. He didn't know them, nor did he recognize anything that would indicate their place of origin from their clothing or other accoutrements. The only thing he saw that looked at all familiar about the men was their excessive body hair, and that was something that he was seeing more and more apparent each day on Albrim. Like his young friend, these men were Weres.

Chapter Twenty-Three

"So what do we do?" demanded Albrim, so nervous he would have been pacing if they hadn't been so high up in the tree. Or on such a small platform.

Mute tried to calm his friend. The news of the three Weres had been too much for him. Albrim was frightened and Mute understood why. The last time he had encountered a Were Albrim had lost everything important to him.

Holding both hands before him with palms down, Mute lowered them slowly towards the platform. Albrim knew he was being told to calm down.

Trying to relax Albrim sat and watched Mute closely as the big man went through a long series of hand motions. By the time he was finished Albrim had a lot of questions but thought that he basically understood what Mute had in mind.

"The Weres and the Quargs are going to attack the settlements again?" he asked.

Mute nodded that they were.

"But why? What could Weres possible want with a punch of peasant villages?"

This time he shrugged. He had some ideas but nothing for certain.

"There is someone the Weres want dead, someone that they believe is dangerous to them. Just one person?"

Leaning forward to convey earnestness, Mute nodded while pointing to Albrim's pack. He wanted to draw something.

Albrim turned over his journal and charcoal while searching for his next question.

"Who could be a danger to them? No one from Cobble, certainly. Most of them died in the last attack anyway. Could it be someone from one of the other villages? Do you think that was the purpose of the last attacks too? Just to kill one specific person?"

Mute shrugged again. The Weres in the tent had seemed to think so.

"But who of any importance lived in the settlements?"

Neither man had an answer although Albrim did mention some names. Each town had a Reeve nominally in charge in the absence of Lord Ferule like Yogarn in Cobble, but those men or women were nothing more than freemen or even peasants elevated by the Lord. Albrim was certain that none of them had ever been out of Aldragal, or at least he would be surprised to learn that they had. No one of any power had ever even visited save for Lord Ferule and his son Sir Garen. But would either of them represent real danger to a group of Weres?

Mute held his hands in the air, signing that there was no way to know. Next he opened Albrim's journal and turned a page, informing Albrim that they needed to move on to the next step and not waste time on something they couldn't answer.

Indicating that Albrim should now talk of what he had read in the scroll, Mute began sketching something in the journal, holding the book up so that Albrim wouldn't see until he was done.

Albrim couldn't wait to share what he knew so he was quick to comply. For once he knew something that Mute did not.

"The scroll I read was a letter giving orders to someone named 'Haverstrike,' whoever he is. He was given command of the garrisons from three locations. I can only remember one; it was called 'Fang Keep'. The others were similar names, like 'Claw Castle' or something."

Mute briefly looked up from his sketches and searched his memory for the place names Albrim had mentioned. Coming up with nothing he shook his head and motioned for his friend to continue as he returned to his drawing.

"Well, whatever creatures these garrisons were made up of, they had wolves in them. This Haverstrike was to send the 'packs' of two of the garrisons here to aid the Quargs in their hunt for the Keon-din," Albrim glanced up briefly and smiled, "with the rest of the packs going to a place called 'Point Bluff'.

Mute looked more interested now. He knew a place called Point Bluff.

"Haverstrike is commanded to deal with the Keon-din problem as quickly as possible and then move all available forces into position for the autumn attack."

Albrim frowned. "I don't remember the scroll saying anything about where they were attacking but it did mention that they wanted to 'sweep' the area and kill all of the inhabitants."

Mute reversed the journal to reveal his drawings of the three Weres he had seen in the Quarg command tent. Every detail he could remember had been added but they were little enough. Only the first Were was at all complete and the second was little more than a back. At least the third had a partial profile. Signing to Albrim that he wanted the younger man to study the drawings he told him that they were Weres. Mute then asked if Albrim recognized any of the men.

Obediently concentrating on the journal Albrim saw men that were more hair than skin with thick beards and long curly hair growing even on their shoulders. Surely Mute had exaggerated that. From what Albrim could see they were all strangers. He didn't have hair growing on his shoulders, did he? Suddenly his back itched.

"No, Mute. Sorry, I don't recognize any of them."

Mute accepted the journal back and looked them over again, hoping to remember some minor detail he had overlooked that he could now add. Anything might trigger a memory if Albrim had any of the men to recall.

Albrim picked up his tale where he left off.

"So the scroll went on to say that once the attack began the army was to kill every one and capture their fields and herds intact to see them through the winter."

Albrim stared at Mute and said, "That doesn't sound like a raid, does it?"

Mute shook his head and then made a fist which he placed hard against the platform. The invaders intended to stay.

"Haverstrike was supposed to secure the area and then use the winter to build defensive positions and above all he was supposed to be sure that the 'Bearer of Salvation' was destroyed. Do you have any idea who that might be?"

Mute did not, so he shrugged as he again showed his drawings to Albrim. He had managed a few more details.

"Sorry, Mute. I've never seen any of those men."

Since the men would have had to travel through Cobble within the last couple of years for Albrim to have seen them, Mute wasn't exactly surprised.

"By what the letter said the person writing it was very confident of successfully conquering the villages, except for this 'Bearer' person. The letter was very explicit concerning the details of the tortures that Haverstrike would suffer if he failed to eliminate him."

Holding his arms out with palms up, Mute indicated his thoughts.

"I don't know who the Bearer is," Albrim replied. "But he must a great deal of power if a bunch of Weres are frightened of them."

Mute shook his head slowly, agreeing that it was a confounding mystery.

"The letter also referred to the Bearer as a Carrier, does that many anything to you?"

Pointing at Albrim Mute pantomimed howling at the moon.

"Well I guess I am a carrier in a way. I do carry the Curse. Do you think they mean me?"

Mute considered it for a moment but then shook his head in the negative.

Albrim agreed. "I think you're right. The letter talked of the failure to kill the Bearer the last time and that wasn't me then. I didn't get the Curse until that attack failed.

They sat in silence for a few moments. There wasn't anything to say. Whatever mystery they were involved in, at the moment they did not have any real clues as to where it led.

"You know what, Mute? We need to find this Bearer, whoever he is."

Using one finger to circle his ear, Mute made his reaction to those words clear.

"Shut up," Albrim said good-naturedly. "Maybe it was obvious to you but it just now occurred to me!"

Mute responded with his half-grin and a playful punch to Albrim's good arm.

Not being able to dodge the punch without falling off the platform Albrim took it then voiced his next question.

"If we need to know who this Bearer is, but we don't know who it is, then who do we know that might know?" he asked, then stopped and looked at his feet, wondering if he had said that plainly enough for Mute to catch his meaning. "You know?" he added weakly.

Holding up his arm, Mute nodded emphatically and pointed at his forearm, again using the sign that Albrim didn't understand. Wasn't that the answer to Albrim's question of why Mute had taken care of him? And again when he asked Mute why they kept returning to his clearing?

"You know I don't know what that means."

A look of exasperation on his face, Mute leaned closer and again pointed at his arm. When Albrim continued to look confused the big man took a different tact and pointed to his own neck. That didn't help Albrim at all. Perhaps he could understand Mute helping him because he had lost an arm, giving them a common bond with the damage done to Mute's throat, but was that a reason to return to the clearing? How did that give them any insight into who exactly the Bearer was?

Copying a sign of Mute's, Albrim only shrugged.

Making the sign of the Were, which they had agreed was two fingers pointing upwards like a wolf's ears while barring your teeth, Mute then drew a thumb across his throat.

"We're going to kill the Weres?" Albrim asked, a jolt of fear running through him, followed quickly by a second when Mute nodded once.

"With what? I don't have any silvered weapons. Do you?"

Mute signed that he did not but seemed to believe that the issue didn't matter.

"It matters, Mute! I read about it in one of the books the Dwarf brought to me. You can't hurt a Were without a magical or silver weapon! You just can't hurt them!"

Pretending to think about what Albrim said, Mute stroked his chin with one hand and then surprised the younger man by drawing his blade and drawing it lightly across the back of Albrim's hand.

Yelping in surprise at the pain, Albrim brought his new wound to his mouth out of reflex. "Why did you do that?" he demanded.

Carefully cleaning his blade before sliding back into his sheath, Mute made the sign of the Were once again, then pointed to Albrim's chest and then the wounded hand.

"Yes, I'm a Were! Yes you cut me! But have you forgotten that I wear this," Albrim said, waving at the silver armband he couldn't touch. "I can't become a Were, I have to stay... human..." he finished as his voice trailed away and his friend's plan became obvious.

"You intend to kill them while they are human? And not give them the chance to Change? Is that possible?" Albrim asked sheepishly. He should have thought of this on his own.

As an answer Mute simply pointed at Albrim's hand, which again was as plain an answer as if it had been spoken. It had worked on Albrim, so it would work on the Weres.

Again borrowing Albrim's journal, which was filling up quickly between his own notes and Mute's drawings, the forester drew out the plans for a trap that was both simple and complex. It would require little in the way of effort, using only natural elements found in the forest and the proper bait. The bait being, of course, the two of them.

Once darkness fell the two were on their way again. Mute seemed to have a destination in mind and led Albrim to the face of a sheer cliff that overlooked a deep valley. The trees that grew there were massive old things with branches as thick as Albrim was tall and predatory vines as thick as his good arm that choked the trees and stole away the nutrients and water the shallower roots of the vines could not provide for themselves. These trees grew right to the edge of the cliff and even hung over in some cases. Mute signed that this was the perfect location and immediately set about making his preparations.

First he scouted along the edge and found two specific locations. At the first he lowered himself over the edge and entered a small cave Albrim would have sworn was not there from the rim. When the big man re-emerged to scale the cliff, if he was frightened of the great height it was not apparent, he had several coils of hemp rope wrapped around his waist. After three trips he had several hundred feet of the rope carefully coiled and ready for use. Albrim was suitably impressed by the presence of yet another of Mute's carefully hidden stashes of supplies.

At the second location Mute chose a tall tree and scaled it, dropping one end of a rope down to Albrim who he then pulled up beside him. There they spent the last hour of the night wedged in the forks of the tree. When morning broke Mute made a careful survey of the area to ensure that no Quargs or wolves were nearby and then the two men built their trap.

A wide and well-traveled game trail ran up to the cliff edge and then followed along the top towards the north. Mute signed to Albrim that the trail had been created by griffons that used the stiff winds of the cliff's edge to take flight. This made Albrim nervous because Mute's plan called for him to remain there alone for perhaps a few days. How would he handle a pack, or was it herd, of griffons if they decided to pass through? Mute waved away his protests. He was confident that wouldn't happen but was unable to explain why to Albrim.

Climbing like he had been born among the treetops, Mute harvested long straight branches from well to the tops of the trees. Each pole was perhaps twice Mute's height and both strong and springy. Meanwhile he had Albrim cutting some of the rope into precise lengths which were then supplemented with vines and attached to the poles to make a long fence-like structure that was left lying on the ground across the trail. Shallow holes were dug near the base of each pole and the far side of each was reinforced with a stone. Mute used his skills to conceal the whole structure where it lay. Even knowing it was there Albrim had trouble spotting it.

With those preparations complete, Mute moved on to the most dangerous part of the trap. Ropes and thick vines were twined together to make a strong line that was attached to a massive rock that set on the edge of the cliff top. They then dug beneath it on the outer edge and replaced the removed earth with a series of logs that propped it up to tilt it dangerously close to falling over the edge. The rope was ran over a thick branch larger than some trees and then split with one portion leading down to pass around a lower, smaller branch before being attached to each of the tops of the poles lying on the ground in turn. The thicker portion of the rope led to another tree farther down the trail. There a log was hoisted into the tree and set to swing on a pivot along the line of the trail itself when the rock fell.

The rock was rigged to fall when a lever was broken that would allow the balancing logs to roll away down the cliff face and its own weight would cause the rock to follow. Finally a last long vine was harvested and tied off so that it hung near the very edge of the cliff. One last careful pass to ensure everything was hidden and the trap was complete.

Mute built a quick platform in a tree to one side of the trap. There Albrim would have a clear bowshot at the area around the lever without being seen or heard. All he would to do was cut a rope that hung by the platform and a counter weight would break the lever and spring the trap. After stocking the platform with food and water and coating the younger man with a healthy coat of mok urine, more than was absolutely necessary but Albrim didn't know that, Mute left on his errand to lure the Weres into the trap.

They didn't speak of the dangers but both understood how risky Mute's plan was. He had to find the Weres and separate them from as many of their allies as possible while leading them to this very spot. Albrim had nothing to do but wait on the platform for however many days necessary for his friend to return and then trigger the trap.

If Mute ever returned.

Chapter Twenty-Four

Mute managed to return to the main Quarg camp in only two days, finding most of the warriors as well as the big tent gone just as he had suspected. Per the agreement made between the Weres and the Quargs the night he had listened to their plans, most of the wolves and Quargs would have left in pursuit of him. Mute still found that funny.

But not all had left. A quick scout indicated that the bigger wolves had gone and so likely had the Weres. He didn't bother to try to track them from the camp. There had simply been too much activity there, too many feet making tracks. Besides, he knew where they were going. Most would be going to where he was supposedly trapped. The others would be on their way to Point Bluff to join the main army, as the scroll read by Albrim had indicated.

Traveling straight towards Point Bluff put Mute ahead of any Weres traveling that direction as they followed the gaming trails known by the Quargs. Those trails made travel easier, but they rarely ran straight and followed the gentlest slopes even when that took travelers out of their way. Another two days of travel allowed Mute to circle far enough ahead that all he needed to do was wait.

That very night he saw a point of light in the forest. Being as cautious as he could Mute scouted the camp most of the night, only daring to approach it just before dawn from downwind. There he spied upon the camp of the Weres.

Mute saw all three of the Weres from the meeting at the tent along with a dozen of the massive wolves and several times that number of smaller ones. Too many for his plan. He had to even the odds somewhat.

Finding a stream Mute scrubbed away the various scents he had been wearing and then left a serious of false and switchback trails all along the Were's probable line of march. Once he had enough false trails laid, that took him another three days, he refreshed his 'natural' scents and circled around behind the formation. It didn't take him long to realize that his plan was working.

Wolves and Weres had split into smaller and smaller groups as they followed his trail. They must have thought him wounded or insane to be so obvious but the Weres were arrogant and the wolves just animals. A drop of fresh blood would drive the latter into a frenzied pursuit of their prey while Mute used his resources to move safely in another direction. Twice he placed arrows in the flanks of stray wolves, encouraging them to stay in packs. Finally Mute had his target chosen and everything prepared to make his move.

Three of the larger wolves and a single smaller wolf traveled with a lone Were in the direction Mute wanted. Scrubbing in another stream he left a trail as plain as any city dweller could have straight across the country and up into the foothills. Sensing that the prey was giving up on the tricks and was now running for some perceived safety, the Were and his wolves increased their pace and pursued. The Were couldn't wait to throw his killing of the Keon-din into the faces of the Quargs and the wolves simply needed to feed. They had been on the hunt for days and their Were master had not allowed them to take the time necessary to run down prey. If they didn't stumble across a rabbit or mok while following along Mute's trail, they didn't eat.

Once he had a comfortable lead on his pursuers, Mute slowed his pace and closed directly upon the trap he had prepared with Albrim. By the time Mute reached the forest above the cliffs, the wolves were only minutes behind him. Just enough time to signal Albrim to be prepared. Mute wasn't worried that Albrim wasn't at his post in the tree. After all, the young man couldn't descend the tree with only one hand unless he fell out. Mute just wanted to make sure that Albrim was ready in order to limit the number of things that might go wrong.

Up in his tree Albrim had been dozing. Bored out of his mind, nearly out of food and long past the point where his water supplies ran out, he was considered leaping out of the tree and taking his chances on surviving the fall. Chewing heavily salted jerky without water had become impossible and if it hadn't rained once briefly he believed that he would already have gone mad with thirst. When the bird call he and Mute had agreed upon came from the forest it caused his heart to race and he leaped to his feet, causing his small platform to sway slightly.

Was this a natural bird or Mute? Albrim had been surprised that his friend could make some bird calls when he couldn't speak a word, but Mute had shown him how to make the sounds by using his hands to concentrate his blown breath into whistles and warbles. It was only good for a handful of animals but it was enough; Albrim had been alerted to Mute's approach.

The baying of wolves sounded through the forest. They were close, Albrim knew. Very close. Watching the trail down which he knew his friend would be coming Albrim waited for the movement he would see through the branches before colors or distinct figures became visible.

Breathing deeply and heart pounding wildly Albrim waited, his hands sweaty and the thick rope-vine he was preparing to cut was soon slick with it as well. Too many things could go wrong now. He might cut the rope too soon, or too late, leaving Mute to be killed by wolves or a victim of his own trap. It was possible that the Were or Weres with the wolves might escape the trap altogether and then he and Mute would have to deal with them personally. Not a happy thought. Nervous and frightened, Albrim tried to calm himself, certain that his heavy breathing must be audible to the wolves. "Come on, Mute! Show yourself!" Albrim whispered, scanning the direction they had agreed that Mute would approach from. If the big man didn't show up soon, Albrim was going to crack! Despite his pleas time continued to drag along and still there was no sight of Mute or the wolves.

And the howling was getting close. So close in fact that each time the wolves voiced their cry it felt as if someone were dropping snow down

Albrim's shirt, tickling its way down his spine. The beasts had to be within sight! They were just too loud! Peering into the trees, straining to catch some glimmer of movement, Albrim nearly stepped off the edge of his platform. He had just regained his footing when he saw Mute hobbling down the trail.

"Hobbling?" Albrim thought, then looked again. His friend was limping, injured! The wolves were right behind him, also coming within Albrim's sight. Mute looked over his shoulder, the fear in his face plain to see even from this height. Nearly panicking Albrim tried to think of something to do. Anything to help Mute. The trap would be useless if the wolves got Mute before he reached it and it would take time for Albrim to string his bow. What could he do?

Albrim almost dropped his knife but the lessons taught him by Mute remained in his thoughts. Mute had told him to stay here no matter what. He had also said to wait for the wolves and the Weres to be in precise position before he released the trap. Mute had said nothing about his being safe when this happened. Swallowing his fear Albrim watched the scene unfold below as his friend stumbled ahead at his best pace, trying desperately to reach the edge of the cliff. Behind him came the wolves, no longer howling now. They had their prey within sight.

Closer came the wolves. Albrim could now see that there were four of the beasts, and three of those were the larger breed. Where were the Weres? Watching in fascinated horror he saw Mute pick up a little bit of speed as he crossed the place where the poles were hidden beneath last year's leaves. Was his limp less prominent now?

Mute answered Albrim's unasked question by suddenly bursting into his top sprinting speed, leaving behind the fake limp even as the wolves closed within striking distance. Snapping at his very heels the wolves pursued him as a pack, two fanning out to the sides to prevent their prey from changing directions while the strongest, the pack leader, followed behind their target ready to strike the first blow. The smallest wolf trailed the others by only a few feet, too intimidated by the bigger wolves to run with them but encouraged by its nature to remain with the pack. All were starving and ready to feed. They were not going to allow Mute to escape.

Which was, of course, what Mute wanted. He didn't turn to the right or left, but ran straight ahead towards the edge of the cliff itself. His timing was impeccable, it had to be. Only the width of two fingers separated his heel from the lead wolf's muzzle and the four-legged beast was closing fast. Just as it prepared to take that first bite, severing the prey's tendons and bringing it down, Mute grabbed onto the vine hanging there for the purpose and swung out over the cliff.

As its prey passed out over the deep drop the surprised lead wolf initially followed the human with its eyes and didn't see the death that awaited it. Twisting and turning the wolf tried to halt its forward momentum, scrabbling at the smooth rock with its claws, but it was too late. The cliff edge was there beneath its feet and before it had time to truly know what was happening it was falling. Those behind it fared better, seeing the fate of their leader they managed to halt themselves, sitting down and planting their feet to stop.

From his perch in the tree Albrim found the whole scene somewhat hilarious. The lead wolf disappeared over the edge and the others twisting and squirming their bodies about to avoid the same fate was comical after a fashion. However he had another task now and that was to trip the trap itself. Dragging his knife across the rope he parted it without effort, he had had days to hone it after all, and then stepped back to avoid the moving whip that the rope ends had become.

With a groan the rock tipped as its supports fell away and then pitched over the edge of the cliff. The ropes snapped the hidden poles forward so that their bases hit the holes and came up against the rock supports placed there. This resistance caused the ropes to pull the poles upright, forming a semicircular fence. Then the slack of the rope was gone and the fence was jerked forward towards the wolves at the same speed as the massive rock plummeted down the cliff face. Two of the wolves were swept over the edge with barely time to whimper. The smallest wolf tried to jump the fence but the barrier was moving too fast. All his jump accomplished was to allow him to land further from the base of the cliff than the bigger wolves.

Mute swung out as far as his vine would allow and watched as the fence and the wolves were swept over the edge before his momentum forced him to swing back to solid ground. One of the most beautiful sights of his life was that of the Were standing back along the trail, open mouthed at what had just happened to his wolves and having no clue that he was next on the list. Mute knew when the Were finally saw the log that was swinging towards his chest. A flash of fear and recognition passed through the man's eyes just before the log itself did.

The dull thud of the impact drove the Were off his feet and hurtled him back along the trail. The log finished its swing and returned the way it had come like a gigantic pendulum. It repeated its track three times before the ropes broke and the log fell to the trail. Once the log bounced to a standstill, Mute leaped over it and ran to the Were's side. If the Were had been taken completely by surprise, he was dead with a crushed chest. If he had managed to trigger the Change in time, there was a chance that he might still live.

Mute needn't have worried. The log had missed the Were's chest, but in this case a direct blow to the head had been good enough. A good portion of it was gone, peeled away by the rough grain of the wood. Ever cautious Mute removed the remainder of the Were's head, he recognized the man from the Quarg camp, with his knife before dragging the remains to the cliff edge and tossing them after the wolves. Before letting it fall he removed a peculiar medallion from the creature's neck and stuffed it in a pocket. From above he could hear Albrim's whoops of joy at the perfection of the trap and their successful killing of the Were. Only Mute knew how lucky they had been. He had expected something to go wrong; it always seemed to.

Just then the forest all about them was filled with the howls of wolves. Many wolves.

Chapter Twenty-Five

Mute scampered up the tree like a squirrel, the end of the last bit of rope clenched in his teeth. Once he reached the platform he rigged a quick seat on the line that hung there and Albrim sat upon the hemp so that he could be lowered from the tree. Mute was proud to see no panic in the young man's face, only determination and the lingering vestiges of joy at their successful trap. By the time Mute had reached the platform Albrim had gathered his few possessions into his backpack and strung his bow. He had also cocked his metallic arm.

Dropping Albrim as fast as he dared, Mute was scampering back down the tree as quickly as the younger man's feet struck the forest floor. The wolves were closer now and their howls echoed from all directions. There had been two traps set this day; Mute's had gone off perfectly and now someone else was triggering theirs. Now Mute had to find a way to avoid the jaws of this trap where the Were he had killed could not. At least Mute didn't believe he had to worry about being struck by a falling log.

Once both were on the ground Mute led the way to the south at a full run. As always he had prepared a route of escape; something he did when anytime he spent time in one place. This one began with a gaming trail that Mute had cleared to give them clear running room but now wasn't sure that they weren't running right into the teeth of the coming wolves. By the howls there seemed to be a lot of them and coming in from all sides as well. Surely they had found the trail and were following it too.

Well off to their right the bushes exploded in a wave of running wolves, thankfully heading towards the area the men had just left. Mute figured that they had pushed their luck as much as they dared along this trail so he turned back to grab Albrim by the sleeve and led him of the trail towards the cliff. They circled another of the massive trees and dropped to one knee, sucking air and watching for more wolves. Almost immediately a pair of the creatures ran past along the trail. Had Mute and Albrim remained on the path even a few more steps they would have encountered the beasts.

Behind them, towards the cliff edge, another group of wolves trailed by a pair of Quargs worked through the underbrush. They were moving rapidly but not running all out as the others had been. These were not the quick kill force but were tasked with preventing anyone from slipping through by stealth. So far it was working well; Mute had no idea which way to go now. Trying to make use of the time he removed his bow from his back and strung it, hoping to avoid a fight but not willing to die without defending himself if one came upon him.

Knowing that they didn't dare wait there, Mute hesitated long enough for another pair of wolves to pass by them on the trail, their noses high off of the ground. They were traveling, not searching, or they might have picked up the human's scent. Once they were past, Mute circled back around the tree and regained the trail. Motioning for Albrim to stay low they again ran along the trail until they saw other groups of Quargs moving cautiously through the woods to either side. Dropping behind a thick hedge of thorns they waited for the Quargs to pass before regaining their feet to flee again.

It was time they got off the trail for good now, Mute decided. Perhaps they were behind the Quarg skirmishers. Just ahead his escape route left the trail anyway, so all they had to do was follow that. It seemed that good fortune was shining upon them now.

They remained bent over and crossed the trail intending to leave it and head again towards the cliff edge. That was when they saw the wolf.

Standing in the middle of the trail the beast was perhaps the largest such animal that either had ever seen. Its fur was gray in places and scars crisscrossed its hide as testimony to the many battles it had survived. Thick muscles bulged and long sharp fangs were barred as spittle dripped onto the packed dirt of the trail. The silent wolf was standing not three body-lengths away.

Bursting into motion the wolf went from standing still to full speed in a single motion. Mute knew that he didn't have time to draw a longer weapon or get of a shot with the bow in his hand. He felt the breeze past his cheek long before his mind could register the swift flight of the arrow that came by his shoulder. To him it seemed that Albrim's arrow just magically appeared in the wolf's chest.

Yelping the great beast stumbled and collapsed, driving the arrow further into its own body. Drawing an arrow from his quiver Mute quickly loaded his bow and drove the missile into the wolf's neck just as the beast regained its feet. Snarling the beast came forward anyway, a great bubble of blood bursting from its mouth as it ran stiff-legged towards the two humans.

Pulling a second arrow Mute placed it in the wolf's chest next to Albrim's, slowing the wolf but by no means stopping it. Stepping back he reloaded the bow again, watching as the animal staggered towards him, no more than an arm's length away and dying on its feet but unwilling to simply lay down. Taking careful aim Mute placed his third arrow through the wolf's head, right between the eyes just as he heard the 'click' of Albrim's metallic arm being cocked.

Eyes closed the wolf finally stopped its jerky movements and simply stood in the trail, its legs trembling and sides heaving. Albrim pointed his bow at the animal intending to finish it but Mute motioned him to lower the weapon. The beast was as good as dead and he would allow it to fight the darkness as it would. This was the sort of adversary that Mute could respect. It would not want to be put out of its misery but would prefer to fight every inch as it was dragged down into the void. Moving carefully around the wolf, the two sprinted into the forest towards the cliff.

Howls went up immediately as they left the trail and the moving of leaves and brush told Mute that at least three different groups of wolves or Quargs were coming for them. They were outnumbered, there was no way they could stand and fight. Their only course of action was to flee and hope that their escape route was not blocked. A Quarg arrow thumped into a tree near his head. It was time for speed.

Keeping their heads low Mute and Albrim ran. They did not avoid bushes or go around fallen logs but barreled through the first and jumped over the second, struggling through the deeply piled leaves as the shouts of Quargs joined with the snarls of the wolves as they closed in from all sides. Recognizing a tree he had been watching for, Mute altered directions slightly and within moments they found themselves on the cliff edge once again.

Another arrow flew just over their heads, then a second ricocheted off a tree and with its momentum lost and its point blunted, bounced off of Albrim's pack. The humans continued to run along the cliff top towards the south.

The ground where they ran was smooth stone and so was mostly clear of brush save an occasional hearty bush or blade of grass that managed to struggle for life in a crack or crevice. This left no cover for the two running men. Quargs began to emerge from the forest behind and before them and lined up their bows for what amounted to an easy shot despite the moving targets. Wolves of all sizes also entered the clear area and shot towards their prey at full speed. A dozen arrows were fired, then two dozen as twice that many wolves drew near. Shouts of victory arose from the throats of the Quargs. Years of torment and death would be repaid this day; today the Keon-din would suffer for his crimes against the Quarg. Their revenge would finally be complete.

About the Author

Trevis Powell was born in rural Howevalley Kentucky and resides there with his wife and four children. After spending his school-age years more interested in sports than grades, he followed a six-year stint in the U.S. Army Reserves with various manual-labor intensive jobs. Eventually he went back to college, earning a degree in electronics.

After his marriage he settled down in his hometown and his creative desire, something he had dealt with since he was a teenager, finally became too strong to ignore and he began to write. Reading, and later gaming, had become outlets for his creative side and he noticed that his adventure designs and gaming worlds were always far more detailed than necessary to play a simple game. Over time these became even more elaborate, and he finally had to admit that he needed more. Falling back on his natural story-telling ability he began to experiment with writing.

Two years later Trevis found his first publisher in Elmore Productions. Over the next five years he saw his name in print in a variety of outlets, including short stories, magazines, and gaming material. Again he found that he wanted more; feeling the need to develop the stories and characters he invented in greater detail. Now focusing on novels, Trevis is proud to be among the first authors in the new Blackwyrm Fiction line.